ALL WE KEEP HIDDEN

ALSO BY KRISTEN MARTIN

Beyond the Stars and Shadows

THE INTERNATIONAL BESTSELLING SERIES
Shadow Crown

Renegade Cruex

Jaded Spring

Crescent Fire

Arcane Haven

Midnight Reign

THE INTERNATIONAL BESTSELLING SERIES
The Alpha Drive

The Order of Omega

Restitution

ALL WE KEEP

HIDDEN

KRISTEN MARTIN

BLACK FALCON PRESS

ALL WE KEEP HIDDEN

Copyright © 2025 by Kristen Martin

For information contact:
Black Falcon Press, LLC
https://www.blackfalconpress.com

Library of Congress Control Number: 2025919368

ISBN: 978-1-7361585-9-3 (paperback)

Cover Illustration by Damonza © 2025
Map Illustration by Inkarnate © 2025

10 9 8 7 6 5 4 3 2 1

Author's Note—Content Warning

Hello, reader! Before diving into this story, I did want to mention that this book contains mature subject matter and is intended for adult readers. Please be aware that the story includes strong profanity and coarse language, explicit sexual content (where all depicted encounters are consensual), deconstructed biblical references, heinous crimes (i.e. filicide), and graphic descriptions of violence, including references to both modern and medieval methods of torture. While I've done my best to handle these topics with care, they could still be potentially triggering. These elements are integral to the narrative and the world in which it unfolds. Reader discretion is strongly advised.

Happy reading!

To the witches, sages, and mystics—
never ever doubt or fear your power.
The world needs you just as you are.

PRONUNCIATION GUIDE

NAMES

Maren: Mare-in

Cordeau: Cor-dough

Caragh: Kuh-rah

Riona: Ree-own-uh

Bhavna: Bhav-nuh

Halcyon: Hal-see-on

Nerine: Nur-een

Imogen: Em-oh-gin

Lilith: Lil-luth

Morrighan: Morr-i-gen

Lisette: Lie-set

Conall: Con-ull

PLACES

Sephiran: Seff-uh-ran

Mohra: Moy-ruh

Chasm: Ka-zum

OTHER

Sable: Say-bull

Noire: No-are

Ovetyr: Ohv-tier

Sigard: Sigh-guard

Aether: Ee-thur

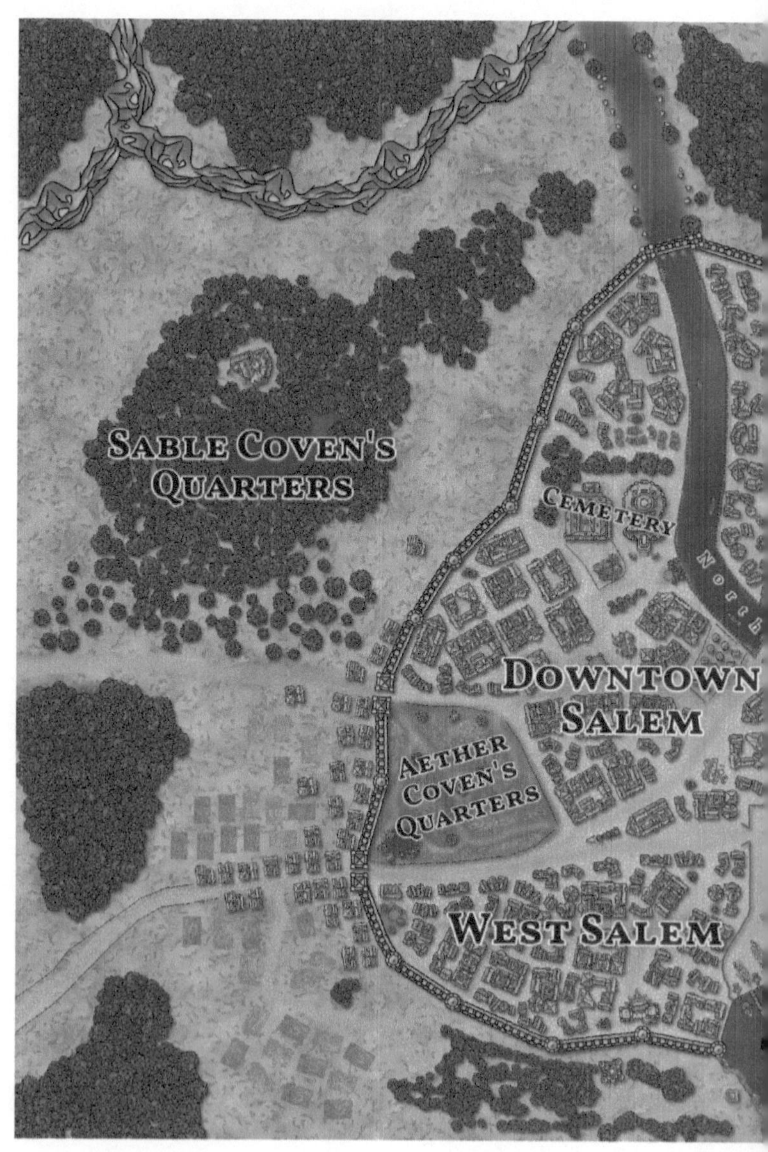

Sable Coven's Quarters
Cemetery
Downtown Salem
Aether Coven's Quarters
West Salem

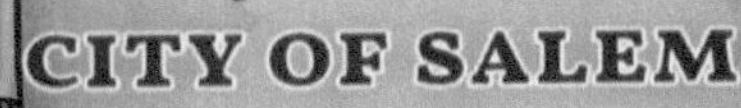

Mohra
The Sephiran
South Salem
River
Collins Cove
CITY OF SALEM

ALL WE
KEEP
HIDDEN

1

SHE'S FOUND ME, yet again.

The woman in white.

Cloaked, nonetheless, but formidable all the same.

Waiting. Watching. Scrutinizing.

Always waiting, watching, and scrutinizing.

If only I could see her face.

Ask her a question.

Speak.

But that's asking too much. I know it is.

She lurks just outside my bedroom door, white fading to grey and then black, until she's merely a shadow. A haunting that's been following me ever since I was sixteen years old. A phantom I can't seem to shake.

I wouldn't say I'm afraid of her. Not necessarily.

Is her presence unnerving? Yes. Quite.

But do I feel fear? No.

If anything, she's more familiar than she is foreign. Perhaps that's because she's visited so often and for so long— or perhaps it's for a different reason entirely. One that might constitute an illness of the mental variety.

That's neither here nor there.

But then . . .

Recognition takes hold—and not the welcome kind.

Just as she's been observing me, I've been doing the same to her . . . but how? I *am* asleep, after all, but this isn't a dream. Nor is it a nightmare.

No, it's something much, *much* worse.

Terror grips me as my heart races, throat going bone dry. I open my mouth to speak, to finally settle this once and for all, but my body won't move. *Can't* move.

Not this again.

Reality takes hold, rather quickly this time. I should be impressed that I might finally be getting the hang of this; but, in all honesty, that's far from the truth.

Unhinged, I claw at my insides, doing everything I can to force my body to respond to my mind's commands. Sleep paralysis will do that to your neural functions. Not quite here, not quite there, but completely and utterly aware—the body stuck in a frightening limbo for what feels like an eternity before finally shaking free.

I always manage to—shake free, that is—but others haven't been so lucky. And, one day, I fear I might become one of them.

2

CRISP AUTUMN AIR greets me as I push open the gates to the cemetery, macchiato in hand. Fallen leaves of varying colors crunch underneath my russet riding boots—worn for leisure, not for sport—as the small heel clacks against the damp pavement. Morning dew still sits on the grass, glimmering in what little sunlight is visible through the fog. It dulls in the cloud cover, marking its permanent residence for the day. I don't blame it.

The sun is for the living.

That isn't to say I'm not living. I am. Flesh and bone, right here. A beating, if not brittle, heart. But when it comes to *living* and the feeling of being alive? Well, I just can't seem to recall.

Or maybe I don't want to.

I step over a small crack in the path, catching a glimpse of myself in a nearby puddle—all five foot, ten inches of me, clad in a cream-colored dress with a plaid waistcoat and a camel-colored beret that matches my eyes and only further accentuates my pin straight midnight hair. After the night I've just had, even I'm surprised at how effectively I was able to pull myself together this morning.

The coffee's definitely helping in that department.

I sip the steaming beverage, my breath visible in the chilled air, as I keep to the path, passing headstone after headstone. Most people get the creeps being in a cemetery, regardless of the time of day—but I'm not most people. And neither is the person perched on one of the larger headstones just ahead of me.

My rival. My "sworn enemy", as it were.

Or so it was stamped on our contracts.

"Maren," he calls out, waving, as if I haven't already spotted him.

I continue to walk in his direction, passing by the antiquated shed in the northwest corner of the property. The groundskeeper usually forgets to lock it, which, I'll admit, has come in handy more than a few times.

"You're looking quite pedestrian today." He frowns, his aquamarine eyes narrowing in disapproval. "I see you didn't think to bring a beverage for your dear old friend?"

I ignore the jab about my outfit. "Friend?" I scoff. "No way. And certainly not after last night."

His brows furrow in concern. "Again?"

"Again," I confirm with a nod, finishing the last of my drink. "But at least I'm still here to tell the tale, right?"

"Unlike these lucky bastards," Brant mutters, his eyes roving the hallowed grounds.

"How many?"

"Six."

"Jesus." I pull a pack of cigarettes from my pocket before striking a match and taking a deep inhale. "Only growing by the day."

"That it is." Brant eyes my cigarette before gesturing for me to fork one over. I roll my eyes, handing over the already lit cigarette before lighting another—which might matter if the so-called "deathstick" could actually do what it's intended to do. But not for us.

Believe me, we've tried.

We sit in silence, processing the recent deaths in our own way, the rustling leaves the only soundtrack to an already gloomy day. I've never minded it, though. The cemetery. Autumn. The thunderstorms and their accompanying nightmares. I find it comforting, in a way.

A home away from home.

Brant looks at me. "Do you ever . . . worry?"

I search those sea-filled eyes for his meaning.

He runs a hand through his chestnut hair, pushing the strands just far enough so that they're out of his chiseled, angular face. "I mean, do you ever worry that we're going to hell?"

I take a long drag of my cigarette. "Hell is for believers," I say, exhaling a train of smoke, "of which I am not."

"Then what *do* you believe?"

I tilt my head back and forth, considering, before dropping the butt of my cigarette into the small beige puddle that remains in my coffee cup. "I believe we'll know only when we're not here anymore."

"Cheap answer," he says with a shake of his head.

"Cheap question," I shoot back.

"You do realize that what your nightly visitor is doing to you is exactly what you're doing to all the others." He gestures to the burial grounds before us. "How you haven't wound up like the rest of them is beyond me."

"The same could be said for you," I point out, wanting to change the subject. "When was your last visit?"

Brant stills, clearly having to think back a ways.

"Well, if it's been *that* long . . . I don't want to hear it."

He gives me a wolfish grin.

"Brant fucking Colborn." I shake my head and laugh.

"Didn't realize I had such a foul middle name, Maren fucking Cordeau."

I raise my hand to my chest in mock offense. We burst into laughter at the exact same time. As always, it feels good to banter with him, even if we *were* pegged to be adversaries for more than one go-around. And when I say that, I just mean that we've been around for more than a few incarnations. How we always seem to find each other is a mystery (and a curse), but it seems the powers that be are determined to keep us together, on the same timeline.

How delightful for neither of us.

"Seems you showed up right on time," he says, breaking my train of thought. "But when don't you?"

I follow his gaze, noticing the hearses pulling up.

Six. Just like he'd said.

I swing my legs and hop down from the short wall, then grab the empty coffee cup.

"Wait. Don't you want to see who's in there?"

I shrug. "Seeing as I was a bit preoccupied last night, I know they aren't mine, so no."

Before he can object, Brant joins me, attempting to link his arm with mine—at which I push away—before starting for the other end of the cemetery, away from all the commotion. We walk in silence until he ruins the streak by asking, "We still on for tonight?"

With a loud sigh, I toss my cup into a nearby trash bin, refusing to break my stride. "Only if you have the stomach for it." I look him up and down. "Which I'm not entirely sure you do."

"Pray tell, Miss Cordeau." Brant's eyes widen with a mischievous glint. "And don't leave out a single detail."

3

I ARRIVE BACK at my third-story apartment, having managed to shake Brant off somewhere along the way. That man, I swear. He's like a long-lost puppy sometimes. I fling off my beret and coat, not bothering to remove my boots as I track little bits of fallen leaves and dirt across the carpeted floor.

It's all temporary, anyway.

I poke my head into the refrigerator and grab the leftover takeout boxes along with a two-liter of soda. One bite in has me nearly cringing at the taste—not because it's gone bad, but because with each incarnation on this damn planet, the food keeps getting worse. *Care for a side of chemicals with your toxins? Pollutants? Contaminants? Not to worry, we have it all!*

Disgusting.

I set the barely touched carton down on the counter, then head into my makeshift apothecary . . . aka the left side of the pantry. The late 16th-century version of myself would be equal parts proud and horrified. I sift through the varying sizes of cork-topped glass bottles when it dawns on me that I don't have everything I need for tonight. Most notably, mugwort, for its hallucinogenic properties.

I lean back into the doorframe, resisting the urge to knock my head against it. If I'm going to dredge up any terror later this evening, stocking up should be at the top of my list. Especially seeing as I'm a Noire whose job it is to both visit and invoke nightmares for the scum of the Earth.

Wouldn't want to break my contract, no sir-ee.

But that's a topic for another day.

I slink around the door and back toward the entryway where my waistcoat is hanging lifelessly on its hook. I dig around in the pockets in search of my phone. *Ugh. And I'd just shaken him, too.*

Just as I'm about to draft a quick text to Brant, I realize that he's one step ahead of me, as per usual. *Got everything you need for tonight?*

I can't help but scowl at the screen. Of the two of us, he's definitely the more organized one—which I both appreciate *and* despise.

Come on, now. You already know the answer to that, otherwise you wouldn't be asking, I type back.

It takes him no time to reply. *Meet you at Madame Viessa's?*

I briefly glance at the mess on my countertop, the still open pantry door. Even though I've just arrived back "home",

I'm already itching to leave again. And, even though I'd rather go alone, I know better than to lie to Brant or try to ditch him. I don't know how, but he always knows. *See you there in fifteen,* I type somewhat reluctantly.

I reach for my coat and remove it from the hook, shaking it out before throwing it around my shoulders. I debate wearing the beret again, but instead throw my hair up in a messy bun. It's a short distance, so at least I can walk. I look down at my boots, cracking a smile for the first time today.

I knew there was a reason I didn't take these off.

☠ ☠ ☠ ☠ ☠

When I arrive at the storefront, Brant's already there, lighting up a cigarette as he leans against the sturdy red brick building. I glance at my watch, then at the sign in the window.

"It's past ten," I point out. "Where is she?"

"Hell if I know."

For some reason, glancing at my wrist gives me pause, but I can't figure out why. For a moment, I swear I'm wearing a bracelet instead of a watch. I blink and the feeling passes.

Brant studies me curiously. "You look like you've seen a ghost or something."

"I'm fine." I shake my head as I pass in front of him, snatching the cigarette from his mouth. "For earlier. You owe me."

"Ruthless little bitch, you are." He clicks his tongue against the roof of his mouth but doesn't complain further. We're able to enjoy the entirety of our nicotine fix when, finally, Madame Viessa comes waddling up the sidewalk.

"My dears," she purrs, the plum-hued feathers in her headscarf ruffling in the breeze, "how long have you been waiting? I hope not too long."

I open my mouth to respond, but Brant elbows me in the side, ever the gentleman. "That's nothing to concern yourself with. We'd wait however long it took."

She looks between the two of us, not quite convinced, so I slap a smile on my face, hoping it'll help our case. It seems to, and I try not to lose my patience as she rattles around in her oversized bag for her keys. It probably only takes her a minute or two to find them, but it may as well be an hour. The whole time, I'm clawing into Brant's arm, which I'm sure will leave a mark—not that he's ever minded.

I nearly maul her over as we enter the shop but, thankfully, Brant holds me back. She takes her time getting sorted behind the counter, the register dinging as she punches a slew of codes into them. A framed picture of her granddaughter is prominently displayed so that all paying customers have no choice but to ask about her. I haven't bothered to, which might explain why she seems to prefer Brant over me.

"So, is there anything I can help you with?" she finally asks.

But I'm already in the back of the shop, making a beeline for the herbs, ultimately leaving Brant to deal with the questioning. I'm sure he doesn't mind, seeing as Madame Viessa prefers his company over mine—over anybody's, really. I've never understood why she's so chummy with him. Maybe it's his looks? His sense of humor? His youthful demeanor?

Speaking of, that's just one of the tough things about this particular incarnation—everyone getting older and more or less "losing it" when both Brant and I are capped at a certain age. *Thirty, flirty, and thriving.* Ugh. I'd never realized just how little patience I had until coming here and doing the work that I do.

It can be its own version of torture at times.

I thumb through the small packets of herbs, trying not to get frustrated by the fact that they aren't in alphabetical order, which is something I've mentioned to *the Madame* on multiple occasions. But, seeing as she's the only one who works here and can't keep a store clerk to save her life, it is what it is.

Knowing better than to shout from back here, I trudge to the front, briefly locking eyes with Brant as he continues his conversation with her.

"I take it Lisette is doing well?" he asks.

Madame Viessa stops what she's doing. "I'm afraid she's going through a bit of a rough patch, the poor dear." She folds her hands in front of her, squeezing her wrists. "I'm doing everything in my power to help her."

Brant frowns. "I'm sorry to hear that. If there's anything I can do . . ."

Ugh. Spare me.

I'd originally planned to let the conversation reach a natural pause before interjecting, but the last thing I want to do is hear about the petty troubles of dear old Lisette. I impatiently tap my fingers on the glass counter, drawing the Madame's attention, although unwelcome.

"Forgive me," I say as sweetly as I can muster, "but it seems you're out of mugwort?"

Madame Viessa glances past me, to the back of the store. "Are you sure? I could have sworn I just—"

"I'm positive," I interrupt, trying to keep my voice pleasant. "I went through each of the packets quite carefully."

"Perhaps if I were to—"

"That won't be necessary," I snap. Out of the corner of my eye, I can see Brant take a sharp inhale before setting his hand over mine.

"Madame, I do apologize. It's been a long morning," he says with actual sincerity. "Would you mind checking the storage room in the back? I'd be happy to assist if you'd like."

Madame Viessa gives him a curt nod, then waves for him to follow her, but not before shooting me a look that should send me running for the hills.

It doesn't rattle me in the slightest.

"Thanks a lot," I murmur sardonically as I pick underneath my nails with the letter opener I'd swiped from the register. I sigh, knowing they'll be gone for a bit, so I push off from the counter and begin to wander the store. My eyes travel along the many shelves of trinkets and odds and ends— miniature cauldrons, statues of deities, bowls of assorted crystals of every size, shape, and color, and books.

Lots of books.

A cabinet with two giant glass doors catches my attention—as does the keyhole underneath one of the knobs. Judging by the dust and cobwebs covering nearly every inch, I'm guessing it hasn't been opened in ages. Without thinking, I blow on it, realizing that it's holding a collection of ancient texts. I immediately regret my decision as dust particles fly all around me. In an attempt not to sneeze, I hold my breath and close my eyes. When I open them, I'm relieved to find that the dust has mostly dispersed, with some of it settling on the lower-level shelves.

Gently, I pull on the knob, wincing as the cabinet creaks open loudly. I glance behind me, but there's no indication that Brant and the Madame have returned or will return anytime soon. I take a step closer, running my hands along the spines of the books, my black-tipped nails in stark contrast to the worn burgundies, forest greens, and ambers of the exteriors.

I can see why the Madame normally keeps these under lock and key, but it seems her age is catching up with her. I slide one of the books from its spot, not all the way, but just enough to see its front. The title is in another language—Latin, I think—as are most of the books kept in here. I'm able to confirm this assumption as I tilt a few of the others toward me to get a better look. It's then I notice that there's one, tucked away in the very back, with a deep amethyst cover. A crest with three crows, each carrying a different item in their beak— a key, a ring, and a serpent—stares back at me.

The title reads *Legends & Lore of the Sable Coven*.

The name sounds vaguely familiar, but . . .

"Found it!" Brant yells from a close distance. "Maren?"

Caught off guard, I slam the cabinet doors shut, nearly taking off my fingers in the process. "Fuck," I murmur to myself, shaking my hand out.

"Maren? Where'd you go?"

"Coming!" I respond, cringing at the faux cheerfulness plaguing my tone. I poke my head around the wall that leads to the register, stuffing my trembling hand into my right coat pocket.

"Will this do?"

I can feel my eyes widen at the size of the canister Brant currently has tucked underneath his arm.

"Umm, I think that's plenty. More than enough—like, do we actually *need* that much?"

"This time around? No, probably not." A hint of a smile tugs at his lips. "But this is the one thing you're always running out of, so I imagine it couldn't hurt to have a little extra on hand." He winks and, before I can argue his very valid point, he turns away from me and tells Madame Viessa to ring it up.

I sigh, readying my payment, but Brant stops me. "This one's on me."

I shake my head. "I've got it."

He steps in front of me, blocking my view of the register.

"Brant!" I say, smacking him in the shoulder.

"We already owe each other," he quips, glancing back at me. "What's another . . .?"

"Sixty-five dollars," Madame Viessa confirms.

Brant's face pales. "It seems I may have made a terrible miscalculation," he whispers to me.

I can't help but laugh. "I've got it. Really. And you make a good point about having extra on hand." I smile as I hand Madame Viessa my card.

She eyes me warily. "Are you sure that'll be all?"

At first, I wonder if she's even more hard of hearing than I thought, but when her gaze flicks to the very area of the shop I'd been perusing earlier, I realize I'm sorely mistaken. The woman's as sharp as a whip. I narrow my eyes at her. "Just the mugwort," I say tersely.

She looks almost disappointed as she clicks her tongue against the roof of her mouth, shrugging. I watch her, carefully, as she runs my card before handing it back to me. "I'm sure I'll be seeing you again very soon." She places the canister in a brown paper bag and slides it across the counter. "Don't be a stranger, now, you hear?"

Suddenly feeling perturbed by the whole encounter, I swipe the bag and make for the door without another word. From behind me, I can hear Brant bidding the Madame adieu with his usual pleasantries, but I don't bother to wait for him. The little bell above the door dings as I step outside and take a giant gulp of fresh air.

I take to the street in a half jog, waving away Brant's shouts as I head in the direction of my apartment. He should be used to my outbursts by now without needing an explanation each time. If he really needs me, he knows how to reach me.

It doesn't even take two minutes as I turn the corner onto the street that leads to my apartment complex for my phone to start buzzing. With my free hand, I silence the call, knowing that there will be more to follow.

But, for right now, I need to prepare. Alone.

Brant, of all people, should understand that.

4

AS IT ALWAYS does, night rolls around with a vengeance. I've spent the entire afternoon (and some of the evening) preparing the incense and other provisions for my excursion. I'm nearly finished when a knock sounds at the door. I push myself up off my knees, adjusting the gold-plated holder before heading to the door. I open it, not the least bit surprised to find Brant, clad in black, on the other side. I glance at my watch, then flick my wrist at him. "Right on time," I say with a raised brow.

"Would you expect anything less?" A coy smile tugs at his lips. "I see you haven't wasted any time since our trip to Madame Viessa's." He doesn't bother taking off his boots as he walks into the living room, eyeing the circle of items I've carefully set up. "Let's get this show on the road, shall we?"

I close the door and lock it, making sure to secure the extra deadbolt. "Not so fast," I say, joining him in the living room. "Don't you want to know who we'll be visiting tonight?"

"Who *you'll* be visiting?" he corrects me.

"It's just as important for Sigards to know who we're dealing with as Noires." I place my hands on my hips. "And, seeing as you're the former, it's your duty to know how to protect me."

He sighs, conceding as he falls into an oversized armchair, haphazardly kicking his feet up onto the coffee table. "Then what do you have for me, oh powerful one?"

I scowl, then swipe the nearby stack of parchment before nudging his feet off the table. For as long as I've known Brant, he usually doesn't give me a hard time when it comes to my duties as a Noire. As my assigned Sigard, he's essentially the gatekeeper to the portal that allows me to both access and invoke nightmares upon the living. Every Noire has one, although whether they travel together in as many lifetimes as Brant and I have is yet to be determined.

I toss the stack of papers onto his lap, scrutinizing him as he rifles through each one.

"Only one bastard tonight?" he says, thumbing through the pages. "And all this, just for him?"

I nod.

"Nathan Sharpe," Brant reads. "Disorderly conduct, vandalism, breaking and entering, four counts of aggravated assault." He scans the lengthy list of crimes before getting to the ones I know will get under his skin. "Domestic abuse, child abuse—" He glances at me. "I've seen enough."

"Keep reading," I say firmly.

He pauses, not wanting to speak the word. "Filicide." He flings the papers back at me. "This sick fuck killed his own kid?"

"Not just killed. Tortured and dismembered—"

He holds a hand up. "I've heard enough."

I angle my head at him. "It's pretty fucked up to say I've dealt with worse."

"Most nights, I don't know how you do it, but then I read something like that . . ." We lock eyes.

"I know," I whisper.

Glassy eyed, Brant leans back in the chair and clears his throat. "I'm sure whatever you have planned will be punishment enough."

"That's just it, though," I say, leaning forward so he can hear me. "I called you over a bit earlier than usual because I need your help."

He perks up, then, clearly surprised. "With what?"

"Before I visit Mr. Nathan Sharpe, I thought we could take a quick trip to the Sephiran."

Brant's eyes grow wide. "You mean . . . *together?*"

I nod, reveling in the shock on his face. Normally, Noires visit the Sephiran alone. It's akin to the Black Market or the Dark Web—only, it's specific to the type of work I do. And, believe me, invoking nightmares is nasty business, especially when you're dealing with criminals of horrendous proportions. I've never minded it, though. As the old saying goes, *karma's a bitch.*

And I'm the lucky bitch who gets to deliver the blow.

"I just figured, what with your past and all, that you'd want to . . . *hand-select* some of the items."

Brant blanches at the memory, as he should. Only a deranged individual would take the life of their own offspring. He hadn't, off course. But his wife in that particular incarnation had.

Brant pushes up from the chair, brushing his hands against his overcoat before pulling on a pair of black leather gloves. "How much time do we have?"

"Two hours." I grin.

He makes for the door before opening it and gesturing toward the hallway. "After you."

☠ ☠ ☠ ☠ ☠

Fifteen minutes later and we've arrived at my favorite pub. Just a couple blocks down from Madame Viessa's sits *The Ivory Stallion*—which is quite the deceptive name, given its backdoor dealings. The booths are colored a deep jade with ivory tabletops, giving the place a grandiose atmosphere while somehow still maintaining that "local pub" feel. I tip my beret at the owner, Charlie, who begins to serve up my usual cider when he notices Brant at my side.

"I see you've brought company," he says, stroking his salt-and-pepper beard.

I make a show of looking around at the empty bar before turning to face him. "Seems you haven't," I tease.

He guffaws, nearly spilling my drink as he sets it on a coaster with a white horse on it. "And for your friend?"

I'm about to order for Brant when he says, "I'll have whatever she's having."

Sensing my annoyance, Charlie looks between us and smiles as he serves up another tall glass of cider. "So, what can I do ya for? Business or pleasure?"

"I suppose a little of both." I lift my glass before clinking it against Brant's. "But as soon as we're done with these, it'll be more business than pleasure."

Charlie nods in understanding before vanishing to the back of the pub, no doubt readying the gateway that'll take us to the Sephiran. It's my guess that that's how this place stays in business, which is a pretty solid assumption since I seem to be one of the only patrons in here, time and time again.

Brant finishes his drink with a loud gulp. He sets the empty glass back on the coaster before turning so that he's no longer facing the bar. He leans in, whispering, "This isn't at all what I expected."

I stifle a laugh, knowing exactly what he means. "I like to think it's by design—getting a drink before diving into the underbelly. Gotta do something to shake the nerves."

"Haven't you been—?"

"Hundreds of times?" I finish for him. "Sure have. That doesn't mean it gets any easier." Even though he nods, I can tell that what I've just said has rattled him some. "Nothing to worry about," I reassure him. "Not when you're with a pro like me."

Before either of us can say another word, Charlie reappears. "It's ready when you are."

I throw some cash onto the counter to cover our drinks before slinking around the end of the bar and ducking underneath the countertop door. I can feel Brant nearly walking on top of me as we follow Charlie back, back, back, passing unopened supply boxes, kegs, and piles upon piles of empty liquor bottles.

"Recycling," he says with a huff, pushing past one of the curtains.

Well, at least he's trying.

An eerie orange glow is cast onto his face the minute he opens the cellar door that leads to the basement. "Here we are," he says.

I nod at him in thanks, grabbing two hooded cloaks from a nearby shelf. "Put this on," I say, tossing one to Brant. I throw the heavy material around my shoulders, securing it across my chest with a single brass button, before removing my beret and pulling the hood taut over my head. I toss it aside and offer to help Brant, but he slaps my hand away as if I'm an overprotective parent. *Rude.*

Charlies watches us, his russet eyes shadowed. "How long you two planning to be gone?"

"Two hours at most," I answer. "You'll leave it open?"

He checks his watch, the wrinkles around his eyes creasing. "Just be back as soon as you've finished, yeah?"

"Deal." He's about to turn to leave when I ask, "Want me to bring anything back?"

His expression darkens. "There is absolutely nothing I want from that place." His eyes meet mine and I immediately understand his meaning, something that wasn't clear to me before. *This* is his eternal sentence—helping people like me.

Like us.

I shrug. "Takes one to know one, Charlie," I say as I grab hold of the top of the ladder. "The sooner you accept that—"

"Two hours, Maren." His voice is bleak. "And not a minute later."

"Understood." Brant and I watch in silence as Charlie retreats, walking back the way we just came.

"Fuck me," Brant says under his breath. "It can't be that bad, can it?"

"Whatever you're imagining," I say as I begin to descend the ladder, "it's worse. *Much* worse."

5

MERE SECONDS LATER and we're wholly engulfed by a luminescent orange glow. The ladder seems to vanish from beneath our grip, Brant shouting the entire way down—an endless fall that may as well land us in the depths of hell. It's a good thing I don't believe in such a place. How can I when what I've seen is so much worse?

Having done this a few times before, I land on my feet and manage to catch Brant by his arms before he lands face-first on the slick asphalt. He mutters incomprehensibly until finally regaining his balance. He whirls around to face me, scowling as he dusts off his cloak. "You know, a warning would have been nice."

"Yeah, but where's the fun in that?" He shoots me a look that's borderline lethal, but it only makes me smile wider.

"Come on, Brant. Pull yourself together. This is not the place to show emotion." I pause. "Or anything of the sort."

Brant gapes at me but, thankfully, doesn't argue or ask questions. He tugs on the lapels of his cloak to straighten them and sets his shoulders back. I look him up and down and give him a nod of approval, then set off down the street with my head down and hands in my pockets. If Brant's smart—and I know he is—he'll follow my lead.

Small shops line the narrow street, each more dismal looking than the last. Buildings constructed out of chipped brick, weathered by natural causes—and its careless tenants, no doubt—crowd what should be wide open alleyways. Overhead signs creak and sway in the musty breeze, hinting at the overall atmosphere of the place.

Muffled screams and groans fill the air, growing louder as we pass by certain shops, and I can't help but notice when Brant finally meets my quickened pace. Honestly, I don't blame him. I wouldn't want to be snatched off a street like this either.

We pass by several people who also seem to be in a hurry—heads down, cloaked from head to toe in black. That's the thing about a place like the Sephiran. Unless you reside here full-time, it's not exactly a place you want to loiter. In fact, that's precisely how the vast majority of its current inhabitants became residents—unwillingly, I should add. There's something about this place that messes with the mind . . . . enraptures it in such a dark and twisted way that it somehow manages to warp the very concept of simplicity into an impossibly daunting maze; desires and fears so distorted, you're unable to tell the difference. For what *is* fear, really, if not desire shrouded in the illusion of guilt, shame, and rejection? Once you arrive at that realization, well . . . there's no telling what's bound to reveal itself.

My thoughts scatter as Brant reaches for my arm, murmuring so quietly that I'm forced to strain my ears just to hear him. "How much farther?"

I point just up ahead. "Fourth building on the left."

We pass by more terrorizing screams, more deafening bangs that leave the walls rattling, before stepping foot into a quieter, albeit slightly more eerie, shop. Only then do I remove my hood and motion for Brant to do the same.

"Conall?" I call out, brushing the splatter of raindrops from the front of my cloak. "Conall, are you back there somewhere?"

A gruff voice sounds to my right. "Where else would I be?" A towering oaf of a man, Conall emerges from the shadows, the shackles around his ankles clanging against the uneven concrete floor. His unkempt red hair is the only lively aspect of the place, save for his eyes which are a stunning shade of amber. He steps behind the counter, grunting as he says, "What do you want?"

"Hey, now," I say, tossing him a rare gold coin, "is that any way to greet your favorite customer?"

The offering has him perking right up. "Maren Cordeau, is that you?" He narrows his eyes in the dim light, then looks to my right. "And who's this?"

"No one you need concern yourself with." I slink over to the counter and give him a smile not even the most enticing temptress could master. "I'm sure you can guess why I'm here."

Conall eyes Brant in sheer disapproval, but it doesn't take long for his gaze to trail back to mine. "Haven't seen you in a while. Thought things had slowed down."

"It never slows down," I say, my voice sultry, "but I ran out of the good stuff."

He snorts. "Have they been that bad?"

"Despicable." I smirk. "My friend here is helping me with an upcoming case." I lower my voice to a whisper. "His methods are even worse than mine, if you can believe that, so I brought him here as counsel."

"What're we dealing with this time?"

"Filicide," I say, the word sending spikes of ice through my veins. "Among other things."

A sickening grin spreads across Conall's deeply scarred face. "Well, you certainly came to the right place." He angles his head at Brant. "And any friend of Maren's is a friend of mine." He picks up his shackles and tosses them aside as he lifts open a trap door that leads underground. "All the good stuff is kept down here—none of that rookie shit." He gestures to the gaping hole beneath us. "Follow me."

I walk around the counter, making sure to carefully step over the thick chains so I don't trip.

Conall's not even halfway down the ladder when he says, "Do me a favor and toss those down to me, will you?"

"Another ladder?" Brant murmurs from behind me.

I choose to ignore him. I heave the metal links into my arms—what'll fit, at least—and drop them into Conall's outstretched hand. "Thank you kindly."

"Are those new? They look . . . retractable." I step onto the top rung of the ladder, waiting until Conall's reached the bottom before descending the rest of the way. "What'd they get you for this time?"

"Selling to a Sigard."

My pulse quickens. I look up to see if Brant's heard the response, but, thankfully, he's preoccupied with his cloak, which seems to have gotten tangled in something on the main floor. Eh, he'll figure it out.

"I'm sorry to hear that," I say, hoping my voice comes across as sincere and not guilt-ridden. There's a part of me that's second-guessing what it is we're about to do, but if Conall's already facing the punishment, then what additional harm is there? Not to mention, he isn't selling directly *to* Brant. He's selling to me, a Noire, who just so happened to bring her Sigard along with her. For . . . moral support.

Yeah, let's go with that.

I hop from the last rung onto the dirt floor, wiping the metal flakes from my hands, which is pointless, seeing as they leave a streak of rust across my palms anyway. I sigh, looking up to see what's taking Brant so long. When he reaches the final rung and jumps off, Conall's already more than halfway down the shadowed hallway, chains dragging noisily behind him.

"You good?" I ask.

"Fine." Brant shoots me a concerned look. "Why?"

His response is confirmation that he didn't hear Conall's answer to my question earlier. "No reason. Just . . . keep up the whole silent act, would you? I think it's making you more trustworthy in Conall's eyes."

"Normally, I would ask how that's even possible, but it seems anything's possible in a place like this."

"Like you wouldn't believe," I mutter before slapping him on the shoulder. "Come on. We're about to get to the best part—or need I remind you of the crimes committed against an innocent child?"

Brant grits his teeth. "You just did. Regardless, I couldn't forget, even if I tried."

We reach an enormous metal door that Conall swiftly opens after punching a code into the keypad. I'd thought we'd left the agonizing screams behind us on the upper floor, but it seems I'm sorely mistaken. As soon as the door opens, we're greeted by shrieks and yelps, and it's then I realize just how soundproof this room must be. The hair on my arms stands on end as I enter the room per Conall's instruction, with Brant trailing close behind me.

The room is surprisingly large and flawlessly circular in shape. Every few feet or so are masked men and their . . . *test subjects? Victims?* It's hard to be sure. But each holds a different device, some I've seen before—brass knuckles, a branding iron, a cattle prod—and some that must be brand spankin' new.

We slowly make our way across the room. I nod at each of the masked men as an acknowledgement of sorts, and briefly consider doing the same to the . . . *others*, but most of them are either passed out, keeled over, or unconscious and unknowingly flirting with death. I glance over my shoulder, noticing that Brant is intentionally keeping his gaze cast toward the floor, unwilling to look anyone in the eye.

I stop walking and turn to face him. "You know, in order to pick your poison, you actually have to look at what's going on."

Brant keeps his stare on my boots but says just loud enough for me to hear, "It's different when they're actually being *used* on people."

I grab hold of his chin and jerk his face upward so that he has no choice but to make eye contact with me. "What is it you think I *do* when I visit these assholes, hmm?"

"But those . . . those are just nightmares . . ."

I give him a lupine smile. "Are they, though?"

Brant yanks his chin from my grip, unable to keep his focus separated from our surroundings any longer. "What about that?" he says, pointing to a man whose arms and legs are strapped to a chair. Just above each of his thumbs is a metal contraption that slightly resembles a corkscrew.

"Thumbscrew," I say nonchalantly. "The screw drives right into the nailbed. It's the twisting motion that really—"

Brant holds his hand up. "That's enough information, thank you." He straightens his cloak, continuing his stroll of the perimeter. He doesn't bother to say anything when he happens upon a man who's being forced to stand upright, his upper leg shredded to mere ribbons. Brant just points, face paling.

"Hamstringing," I confirm. "The way in which the hamstring tendons in the thigh are severed essentially incapacitates the victim and renders them incapable of moving."

Brant shudders. "So that you can torture them further, I suppose?"

I shrug just as Conall leans down to growl in my ear, "Is this his first time?"

I respond with a smirk. "What gave him away?"

Brant blanches with each step he takes—past the waterboarding, dry-boarding, flagellation, compression—but what really gets him is the flaying. Strips of skin hang from what *should* be a corpse, but if the screaming is any indication, that poor soul is most definitely still alive and feeling every last scrape of that serrated knife.

"I've seen enough," Brant says, covering his mouth as if he's about to involuntarily release the contents of his stomach. "An oral description would have sufficed. I can't focus, can't *think*, with all this—"

"Remind me to never again bring you along with me," I say with a roll of my eyes. I step next to a masked man who's holding pliers and a couple of finger splints. "May I?"

The man grunts, waiting for Conall's approval before handing them over. I don't bother asking if I can use his apron to wipe the blood and remnants of skin tissue from the tools, I just grab the corner and quickly swipe them along the cloth until they're mostly clean. I raise them into the light for further examination, then test them for their durability. "Oh, yes. These will do nicely."

"Is that it?" Conall asks, sounding annoyed.

"We'll take a thumbscrew, too. For good measure." I wink at Brant who's already standing just outside the giant metal door. "Pick something," I say to him.

Brant gives me a look that says he'd rather not, but I'm sure he's figured out that if he wants out of here, he'll have to participate in one way or another. That is, after all, why I brought him with me. "The mallet," he says.

"For breaking or crushing?" I ask.

He lets out an exasperated sigh. "Why not both?"

"I like the way you think." I turn to Conall. "One mallet, and *oh*"—I point to a nearby tray that holds a gleaming blade—"I'll take that dagger, too."

"Great, so, can we shut this door now?" Brant says a little too eagerly from his post. "I'm getting a migraine."

Trying not to feel annoyed by my time being cut short, I stalk through the space with Conall on my heels. I stand with Brant in the hallway, watching as more numbers are punched into the keypad. The door seals shut and with it, the incessant screaming.

Brant's shoulders sag in relief.

Conall brushes past us, leading us back down the corridor to the ladder.

"How long do you keep them in there?" I ask.

"As long as is necessary." He glances over his shoulder at me, clearly wanting to end this transaction and get on with whatever it was he was doing before we'd arrived. "I'll take your payment upstairs."

"You got it," I say, securing the dagger in my belt and the thumbscrew and splints in my pockets. I place the handle of the mallet between my teeth before following Brant up the ladder. He reaches the top rather quickly, kneeling by the opening to offer me a hand. "That's barbaric," he says when he catches a glimpse of my teeth baring down on the tool he'd chosen. "You are a force to be reckoned with, that's for damn sure." He extends his arm to help me up, which I graciously take.

Brant heads straight for the exit while I wander back over to the counter, waiting for Conall to finish securing the basement door. I dig in my pocket for the remainder of my coin, discreetly counting what remains in the tiny drawstring bag. It should be enough to cover everything.

I hope.

Conall presses an eyeglass against the ridge of his nose, but before he can give me the total, I toss the small bag onto the counter. It lands with a satisfactory thud.

"Will that suffice?"

Conall grabs it and shuffles it between his hands, the coins clinking with the movement. He doesn't bother to count it before giving me a slow nod.

"As always, it was a pleasure doing business with you."

I turn on my heel, mallet in hand, when he says, "Come alone next time, will you?"

It's spoken loud enough for Brant to hear, who answers for me, "Happy to oblige."

I meet my Sigard at the door, stifling a laugh as I breeze past him and out into the dark night sky. He joins me shortly after, the bells on the door jingling as it shuts. I don't bother saying what I'm thinking because I know Brant's thinking the exact same thing and will likely say it for the both of us.

"Please tell me that that was our only stop?"

"Our one and only." I flash my watch at him before giving him a toothy grin. "You lucked out with the time constraint. Next time . . ."

He shoots me an appalled look. "*Next* time? Did you not hear him? There won't *be* a next time. This was the last and final—the *only* time."

I shrug. "Have it your way."

Before he can utter another word, I take off down the street, swinging the mallet wildly until I'm skipping with sheer glee.

"I swear, if you fucking leave me here, you'll never hear the end of it!" Brant shouts. "Do you hear me? Maren fucking Cordeau!"

Hearing Brant nearly lose his shit more than makes up for our close call at the shop. I don't bother slowing down, and I can't help but laugh the entire way in what little time remains for us here. A rare sight for the Sephiran, indeed.

6

WE ARRIVE BACK at *The Ivory Stallion* with just minutes to spare but, if I'm being completely honest, I wasn't the least bit worried, even if we had ended up being a few minutes late. Charlie may talk some tough game, but he'd never leave anyone to suffer *overnight* in the Sephiran—least of all, me.

Brant and I remove our cloaks, placing them back on the shelf we'd originally taken them from. I secure the beret over my hair, grinning at the fact that he's still out of breath. Even skipping, it'd taken him a while to catch up with me—probably because I'd looked like a mad-woman swinging that mallet every which way. *Very Harley Quinn-esque.*

Charlie bids us adieu as I tip my hat and exit the pub, Brant two steps ahead of me. He starts down the sidewalk, muttering what I think are profanities to himself. I remain a few paces behind him, just waiting for him to whirl around and viciously interrogate me—and whirl around he does.

"So, even after all that, I still have to perform my Sigard duties tonight?" His eyes are so wide I can nearly see the whites around them. "I don't know if I have the energy for it."

"That's what coffee's for." I jog to meet up with him until we're walking stride for stride.

"You better brew a big ol' pot because after all that?" He makes a frantic circular motion in the air with his hand. "I'm going to have nightmares for weeks—months, even. Probably for the rest of this damn incarnation."

"That makes two of us." I hate how my voice drops as I finish saying it, but it's no use hiding how I really feel.

Brant regards me with a bemused expression. "You? Really? But you seemed so calm and collected back there."

I shrug, tugging my coat tighter at the cool breeze that's nipping at the back of my neck. "I'm more or less numb to some of the . . . *tactics*, so to speak, but that doesn't mean there aren't some that lurk in the darker corners of my mind."

"Like what?"

I try to hide the shiver that creeps down my spine. Do I really want to disclose this information? A fragment of vulnerability he could potentially use against me? I chew on my lower lip, debating. We've already been through this many incarnations together, and I'm sure we'll be together for many more. Who's to say he'd even remember what was said or done in this one? I can hardly remember the last one—and, based on prior conversations, he can't either.

"Anything with the neck," I say quietly. "Strangulation. Hanging. Slitting."

"Sounds like you had a pretty nasty hand dealt to you at one point or another."

"Probably more than one," I admit. "That particular brand of execution cuts pretty deep."

He chuckles. "No pun intended."

I smile, having gotten so wrapped up in our conversation that I'm just now realizing where we are. We've reached my apartment—I glance at my watch—and in record time, too. I don't even recall climbing the stairs.

"Think fast," I say as I toss him the mallet. Thankfully, he catches it right as I grab my key to turn it in the lock. Just as I had earlier that day, I toss my beret and coat on the counter along with my keys. "Go get cleaned up and I'll get your *big ol' pot* of java started."

"On it." Brant gently sets the mallet down next to my coat before removing his own. "And make the dark roast, will you?"

"Not a problem, seeing as you'll be the only one drinking it."

He stops in the hallway, just outside the bathroom door. "What? Since when?"

I stick a filter in the coffee maker and start filling it with water. "Since I realized it gives me the jitters when paired with mugwort. And believe me, you do not want a jittery Noire when dealing with criminal scum."

"Huh. Guess I'll have to take your word for it."

I throw a filter at him in jest, though it doesn't get very far. It flops onto the ground like a deflated balloon.

"For the sake of your assignment tonight and the poor sap you're dealing with, let's hope your aim *and* range are a bit more accurate."

"Will you stop delaying?" I press the *Brew* button with an exasperated sigh. "We're on a schedule, remember?" I point to the clock on the wall that's hanging just above his head.

"Yeah, yeah, don't get your panties in a twist."

I raise my hand to my chest in mock offense. "That's derogatory and sexist. Plus, who said anything about wearing panties?"

His gaze flicks to my legs, a sinister smile crawling across his face. We may be so-called "enemies", but that doesn't mean we don't find each other attractive. Have we acted on it? No. Definitely not in this incarnation. The others? Well . . .

Your guess is as good as mine.

"Eyes up here, Colborn," I say, unsheathing the dagger from my belt. "Unless you want to join the ranks of the poor souls unfortunate enough to be in my wake this evening . . ."

He stiffens, his face growing serious. "Fuck it, you win."

"Shower," I say, pointing the dagger in his direction. "Now. Don't make me say it again."

His eyes fall to my legs once more, albeit briefly, but it's just long enough for me to catch him in the act and fling the dagger across the kitchen and down the hall. He manages to anticipate the attack, disappearing behind the bathroom door just in time. The dagger slices into the wood, the handle bouncing from the impact.

Bulls-eye.

☠ ☠ ☠ ☠ ☠

I greet Brant with a cup of coffee as he emerges from the bathroom. He finishes drying his damp hair with a towel before tossing it in the sink behind him, then greedily takes the mug from me with both hands. He takes one large swig and lets out a guttural sound that's somewhere between a sigh and a moan. "Now this," he says, holding the mug up in the air as if it's the holy grail of liquid concoctions, "*this* is where it's at. Best cup of coffee I've ever had."

Interesting, seeing as it's generic, no-brand coffee. I decide to leave that part out. "Glad you like it. That means you'll be able to drink it fast so we can get started." I gesture to the floor, everything still in its place before we'd left.

Brant scoffs. "All work and no play. Some things never change, do they?"

I lift a brow. "Respectfully, I disagree. I'd consider what we just did to be 'play'."

Disgust etches into his expression. "In what bleak world is visiting the Sephiran considered 'play'?"

I shrug. "I suppose that depends on who you ask."

Brant plops down on the floor, covering his mug with his palm so as to not spill, before gently setting it beside him. He then picks up the miniature mortar and matching pestle that contains the incense I'd ground up earlier, taking a large whiff of it. "Yep," he says, making a face, "that's mugwort all right. And what else is that I detect? . . . Copal?"

I nod. "I'm impressed. Seems you've been paying attention."

"Trying to, at least." He sets the mixture back down, watching me like a hawk as I get settled in the center of the makeshift circle I've created. As I lay down, he scoots a pillow underneath my head without my even having to ask.

Color me even more impressed than before.

He waits until I'm fully situated before covering the bottom half of my body with a weighted blanket (it helps me with recall—the ability to differentiate between the astral realm and reality), and then begins fastening the openings in the large cloth into the hooks that are dangling from the ceiling. It ends up forming a tent-like structure where nothing can get in—and, more importantly, nothing can find its way *out*. We're shrouded in darkness until I hear the strike of a match, followed by its dim light, which is now illuminating Brant's face.

"Ready?"

I'm about to nod, but I quickly sit up and double check that the items from the Sephiran are next to me. "Remember, I need to make contact with each of these once I'm in, otherwise I can't use them."

There's a glimmer of amusement in his eyes as he says, "Maren, this isn't my first rodeo."

"And you'll pull me out . . . when?" I prompt.

"When I hear you start humming." He tosses my mask to me. "I don't know why you insist on going over this every damn time."

"Because it's worth going over," I snap. "Or need I remind you—?"

He holds up a hand. "You're right. Forget I mentioned it." He glances at me apologetically. "Sorry to get you all worked up."

"Don't be daft," I say, securing the mask over my face. "You're just giving me more to use." The howlite stones embedded within the fabric feel smooth, heavy, and oh so familiar against my skin. I sigh, immediately feeling at home.

I can hear Brant transferring the mixture of mugwort and copal into the golden cone-shaped incense holder. I peek through the mask as he drapes it over the hook in the very center of the tent, the only one that hangs lower than all the rest. Much like a pendulum would, it swings above me, and I can already imagine the sweet smell that's about to drift downward and put me under.

"Looks like we're all set," Brant confirms.

"Then what are you waiting for?" I say with a relaxed smile. "Light it up."

7

IT TAKES LESS than a minute for me to fall into the familiar oblivion. As I have so many times before, I find myself standing on a translucent bridge, surrounded by streaks of slate gray and indigo. Ahead of me lies a shimmering gateway, its gold and silver sparks beckoning me to come closer. But first . . .

I shift my focus to my arms and hands, waiting for that tiny *zap* to let me know that Brant's done what I've asked—that the items from the Sephiran are locked in and available for use. As if on cue, the sensation arrives shortly after.

I ball my hands into fists before splaying my palms out at my sides. In my mind's eye, I envision the thumbscrew and call it forth. It first appears in holographic form in my right hand before taking its tangible form. I pocket it and then imagine the pliers and finger splints. Two different items at once—*why not challenge myself a little?* Within seconds, the pliers appear in my left hand, the two finger splints in my right. I pocket these as well, knowing that it's enough to get started. I'll get the rest later.

And now, for my least favorite part.

I gingerly remove the scroll of parchment that I'd prepared earlier from my breastplate, unfurling it as I march toward the iridescent gateway. My eyes scan the text, my mouth whispering what's written, as the words I speak morph into images—into *visuals*—all around me.

A real-life horror movie playing out on the big screen.

I speak aloud Nathan's full name. His date of birth. His place of birth. His face appears in the vast nothingness to my left, along with a "highlight reel" of his life, if one can even call it that.

Next, I speak aloud his last known address, which just so happens to be a supermax prison in New Jersey. Street signs indicating Third Street and Federal Street appear to my right, along with a red brick building that I can tell, with just a single glance, is one of the oldest correctional facilities in the United States. The visual zooms in, taking me directly to his cell, in which he appears to be in solitary confinement.

Good. The less people around, the better.

Last but not least, I say the victim's name. *His* victim. His four-year old daughter. Annabeth Sharpe. Murdered just before her fifth birthday at the hands of her own father. I seethe at the visual that begins to appear, but I don't dare stop. This pure, innocent soul deserves justice.

And I'm going to be the one to deliver it.

I watch as a body of water—a river—comes into view, along with doll-sized body parts strewn carelessly at the bottom and around the bank. An arm. A foot. A kneecap, I think.

I grit my teeth, hands curling around the weapons that are pocketed at my sides. I grip the splints even harder as a finger comes into view, still painted a unicorn pink. How long had she sat there, conscious, while her own father tore her apart?

Limb by limb.

Finger by finger.

For her sake, I hope it was swift, but for Nathan, it won't be. I'll make sure of that. This may only be a nightmare, but it'll be one he'll never forget. I know just the right buttons to push, just the right nerves to touch, to ensure that he'll be feeling this when he wakes up—*all* of this.

I bow my head to honor Annabeth's memory, saying a silent prayer in my head that her next incarnation is a long life well-lived and a father who isn't a worthless piece of shit. Not that I have any control over that, but it can never hurt to wish someone well, especially someone as deserving as Annabeth Sharpe.

I blow a kiss at the image above me, a photo that was taken when she was still alive—face scrunched in a giggle, pigtails tied taut with purple ribbons, in a matching purple leotard and tutu. In her arms, she carries a doll, one that looks and is dressed just like her. It's heart-warming and gut-wrenching all at the same time.

"For you, Annabeth," I whisper as I stalk toward the portal. "And for all the other children who didn't live to see past their fifth year on this god-forsaken planet."

Pliers in hand, I glance to my right at the visual of the prison before hurtling into a full-on sprint down the bridge. Arms pumping at my sides, I can feel the darkness fall all around me, the forest of nightmares taking root and sprouting in the fertile void beneath me. Snaking vines and branches criss-cross their way overhead to form an archway of pure contempt and vile disillusionment. I can feel them growing, intertwining, connecting, and binding, as if their swift appearance has suddenly rained down upon me a spike of adrenaline and a rush of pure determination.

I'm mere steps away now, the gold and silver sparks threatening to blind me, but I keep my eyes focused, ready and willing to be thrust into the defunct world of Nathan fucking Sharpe. The portal pulls me in like an electric current I'm unable to resist. I blast into the portal with only three words lingering on my lips.

"Knock, knock, motherfucker."

☠ ☠ ☠ ☠ ☠

A split second later, I find myself standing just outside the New Jersey correctional facility. The doors open on a phantom wind and I don't waste any time strolling through them. Normally, when I invoke nightmares, I like to include some background characters—in this case, a guard or two, some other inmates, the administrative staff responsible for processing—but, seeing as Nathan is in solitary confinement, I felt there wasn't a need for that. What I have planned for him will be plenty terrorizing enough *without* the presence of others.

I wind through the corridors, this maze of a place, before happening upon cell block D. I check my pockets once more, just to be sure I still have the necessary items. The cold metal greets my fingers, begging to be put to good use. *Soon*, I promise.

I turn another corner, my boots clacking ominously against the rust-stained concrete floor. I don't even have to guess which cell he's in. I can sense him at the very end of the block.

I take my time, imagining the mallet in my mind's eye until it appears in my right hand. As I pass each of the doors on either side, I bang against them, loud enough, I'm certain, for Nathan to hear. There aren't any windows on the doors—in fact, the only opening is a small slit the size of a mail slot. I reach the door—*his* door—then bang on the worn metal before sliding the small grate to the left. A set of near-black eyes appears almost immediately.

"There you are," I taunt. "I've been looking for you. I must say, you were much easier to find than I thought."

Those soulless eyes roam up and down, down and up, before narrowing. "You ain't Francis."

"The guard?" I give him a chilling smile. "Afraid not, Mr. Sharpe. But, pretty soon here, you're going to wish I were." I search my memory for the prison staff roster, scrolling through the identification cards in my mind until I land on one Francis Jean Miller. I use the image to conjure up a decapitated version of him, imagining my left hand grasping his straw-like ginger-colored hair. I feel the weight at my fingertips before I see it. I don't even bother to look down at the gruesome head before lifting it up for Nathan to see.

"What the fuck . . .?" Nathan says in horror as he shuffles backward, away from the slot in the door. "Who the hell are you? What do you want?"

Well, that was easy.

"This?" I say wryly, dangling the head for emphasis. "If I'm not mistaken, isn't this a mild version of what you did to your daughter?"

His face falls, white as a sheet.

"Let's get one thing clear. I'm not here to offer you mercy." My voice is cold, unfeeling as I stare into those traitorous eyes. "I'm here to exact the vengeance your daughter so desperately deserves."

"Please, it . . . it wasn't what you think. I've done my time—I'm still doing it!"

I can sense his pulse quickening, see the sweat beading along his brow. *Good. He has absolutely no inkling that this isn't real . . . that he's dreamt himself into this nightmare—one that I have full control over.*

"I think rotting away in this cell is letting you off a bit too easy, wouldn't you agree?"

Panic lines his eyes, but still, there's something . . . *off* about him. "You don't understand what it's like, having been in here all these years," he protests. "All I do is think and think and think . . . reliving that day over and over again."

Is that remorse I hear? Surprising. But is it genuine?

"I wasn't well, you see. In the head, I mean. Something in me . . . it had snapped."

Having heard enough, I slam the mallet against the door three times to silence him. "Unfortunately for you, Nathan, none of that matters. What *does* matter is the life you took.

The one you cut short for absolutely no reason, other than your disgusting need for . . . *what*, exactly?"

It's then I see the disturbing shift in him. His pitiful woe-is-me act is suddenly replaced with something bordering sadistic. It happens almost instantaneously. His eyes darken even more, which I hadn't thought possible, before his mouth curls into a menacing snarl. "She was a mistake, that one. All children are. Her wretched mother wouldn't do anything about it, wouldn't 'take care of it', so I did it for her."

Feast your eyes right here, ladies and gentlemen. A true psychopath in the making.

"You *waited* until she was nearly five years old." I should be inside his cell by now, drilling through each of his thumbs and splinting his fingers so far back that only his agonizing screams remain, but I can't help myself from asking questions, from seeking clarity. Sometimes, I like to play with my toys. Other times, I want answers.

It seems tonight we'll have a little of both.

"She deserved to feel what I felt all those years raising her," Nathan continues. "Pure, inexhaustible pain. Bathing her, feeding her, caring for her, putting her first, *before* myself. I couldn't do it any longer," he sneers. "I didn't *want* to fucking do it in the first place!"

I move closer to the door. "She was a *child*," I hiss, my rage building. "You should have just left. She would have been better off without you, that's for damn sure." It's then I realize that I'm still holding Francis's head. I toss it to the side where it lands with a sickening thud. I inch closer and closer to the door, bending my knees just enough to where only my mouth is visible from his vantage point. I run my tongue along my upper row of teeth before smiling in a way that would have even Pennywise running. "Open up, Nathan."

"What's wrong? Don't have a key?" he taunts. "I didn't think so. Why don't you go ahead and fuck right off?"

"Oh, Nathan," I say softly. "Since when would someone like me need a key?"

I lower my gaze so that I can see inside his cell, so that he can see the look of absolute assurance on my face. At the sight of it, he begins to inch further and further away from the door until his back is flush against the wall. I grin even wider, then swing the mallet at the handle—once, twice—until it finally shakes loose on the third hit. I set my boot adjacent to the busted lock and kick with all the force of a titan on a good day. The door swings off its unmalleable hinges—which should be a major indicator to Nathan that there is *no way* that this could happen in real life, that this is an illusion— but, as I was counting on, he's too terrified to see it for what it is.

Fear will do that to a person.

I eye the bolted-down metal chair to the right of where he's currently cowering, feeling proud of myself for not forgetting that minor, but very important, detail. It's all in the preparation and planning—there's nothing worse than invoking a nightmare without the necessary provisions, like a chair to hold the bastard in place while I wreak havoc on his soon-to-be corpse. Good thing, too, because if this short interaction has revealed anything, it's that Nathan's bound to be a squirmer.

Slowly, with calculated precision, I enter the cell, one step at a time. I remain facing him even as I shut the door behind me. "Sit," I command, angling my head at the chair.

"Go to hell," he spits, trying to put on a brave face. Too bad his eyes tell a completely different story.

"No need," I say dryly. "Isn't it obvious? We're already there." I level another steely gaze at him. "Now, sit."

"Make me," he drawls.

God, I was hoping he'd say that. I shrug. "Your choice, not mine," I say as I lunge for him, swinging the mallet with full force. I direct it at his left kneecap. A deafening sound cracks at the blow, the middle of his leg inverting in a sickening, non-human way. He shrieks on impact, grasping at the wall, but there's nothing to hold onto. I don't waste any time before striking again, this time at his right kneecap, to which he leans backward, wanting to fall to his knees, but is unable to do so because of the new direction his legs are now pointing, courtesy of Brant's weapon of choice. He wails in pain, which has me wanting to smash his face in, but I refrain. That would be far too easy—and way too quick.

I gently set the mallet next to the chair before grabbing hold of his arms and dragging him over to it. He flails and shouts, mistakenly thinking that someone out there can hear him. Little does he know, there's *no one*—not a single soul. Not like anyone would care, anyway.

With brute strength, I left him up onto the chair, which is no easy feat, let me tell you—because he weighs at least two-hundred and eighty pounds, if not more than that. He lands with a thud, unable to stop running his mouth and yelling profanities at me while I strap him in. He's so distracted by his own yelling that he doesn't even notice I'm doing this until I've finished.

"I swear, if you lay another finger on me—"

"You'll what?" I give him a faux pout. "You didn't do anything the first time," I say glancing at his left knee. My gaze moves to the right. "Or the second, for that matter." I cross my arms over my chest in outright arrogance. "I wonder what you'll do about this?" Before he can utter another word, I slam my fist into his nose, feeling the bone and soft tendons as they shift underneath my knuckles.

"You fucking bitch!" he sputters, blood oozing from his now crooked nose. "When I get out of here—"

"You won't," I say, stepping back from the chair to admire my work. "Ever. Not as long as I'm still living and breathing." I dig into my pockets and flash my various metal toys at him. "But enough with delaying the inevitable, right?"

He shakes his head adamantly as I walk toward him in calm, measured steps, blood streaking his upper lip all the way down to his chin. "Fuck this," he says, a clear tremor in his voice. "Where are the fucking guards?" He tries to look around me, but I'm so close now that I'm all he can see.

"It would seem that, like me, *fuck* is your profanity of choice." I pick underneath my nails with the edge of the thumbscrew. "But, I'm afraid that's about all we have in common." I lift my gaze, stalking toward him with such speed that he startles back into the chair, eyes wide as I drop to my knees and grab his right hand. I hastily pluck his middle finger from the fist he's failing to make and secure it in the splint.

"You're wrong," he says, eyeing the tool that's mere centimeters from absolutely decimating his finger. "You're just as bad as me—worse, even."

I test the durability of the splint, pushing his middle finger back. Not enough to break it, but just enough for him to produce a yelp. I look at him with lethal calm as I process what he's just said. "Worse than you? Oh, I'm betting on it."

I give him a diabolical grin before snapping his finger back into a position he should find rather fitting—a permanent, overextended "fuck you".

He screams, eyes watering, yelling more profanities.

"I'd save some of that energy if I were you," I say without a hint of remorse as I ready the next tool, "because we're just getting fucking started."

8

"THAT WAS BRUTAL."

When I come back to, Brant is standing right over me.

"As brutal as visiting the Sephiran?"

He offers me a hand to help me up, clearly weighing each experience in his head. "It was a close second, I'll give you that."

"Really?" I shake out my arms and legs in an effort to get reacclimated to my physical body again. "I actually feel like I went a little easy on him."

Brant stares at me, gaping. "Maren, the guy couldn't even walk. He now has no use of *either* of his hands. You smashed his face to a pulp, so he can't breathe—or see, for that matter."

"At least I left his mouth intact."

Brant raises a brow. "Did you, though? I'd hardly count pulling his teeth out as *intact.*"

"I left some of them," I muse, walking to the kitchen to grab a glass of water. Invoking nightmares isn't for the faint of heart and often leaves me feeling parched. "He's lucky I didn't slice his tongue straight from his mouth, however tempting."

"Why didn't you?"

"Gotta save something for next time, I suppose."

Brant shakes his head in mock disapproval. "So, I'm assuming he'll become one of your regulars?"

"Oh, yes. I've already saved him a slot in my mental schedule." I chug my water before setting the glass in the sink. "Speaking of, was there any interference tonight?"

"Nope," he says reassuringly. "All clear."

"Good." I meander back into the living room and plop onto the couch next to him. I raise both of my legs and set them on his lap, then wiggle my feet at him.

He grabs my foot with a roll of his eyes, massaging it through my sock. "Astral projecting is hard work, huh?"

He says it in jest, but I know exactly what he's insinuating . . . that my physical body can't actually hurt or be sore because, *technically,* it didn't come with me on my little trip to the prison. "Maybe it's from our stroll in the Sephiran earlier?"

"Ugh," he says, dropping my foot immediately. "Don't remind me."

"Keep rubbing and I won't."

He sticks his tongue out but does as I say. I lean my head into the throw pillow and close my eyes. Just as I do, Brant begins to hum a familiar song, Chopin's *Nocturne* in B flat minor. I smile, rolling my head from side to side. He's about thirty seconds in when I ask, "Do you think that was one of your incarnations?"

"What? As Chopin?"

I sigh, but don't open my eyes. "You really go for it, don't you? No, I mean the time period. You know, the 1830s."

"Oh." I can hear the disappointment in his voice. "But if I *had* been Chopin—"

"You weren't," I cut him off. "But I'm not surprised that you'd entertain such a thought. And to think, I'd pegged you as the simple-minded one." I peek at him out of the corner of my eye. Just as I'd expected, I've stirred something within him. I feel it in the change in pressure on my foot, the slight dip and frown of his mouth.

"You can't tell me you've never at least *wondered* about them? All your past lives?"

"I don't," I say honestly. "But *whatever* I did, it got me here."

"Is that a good thing or a bad thing?"

I chew on my lower lip. "Some days, I don't really know."

Satisfied with my answer, Brant switches to my other foot. "Good. For a minute there, I was starting to think you really were dead inside."

For some reason, his response makes me snort. "I think when it really comes down to it, we're all a little dead inside."

"What makes you say that?"

I give him a knowing look. "Well, for starters, I've never met anyone who enjoys going to cemeteries as much as you do—*and* waiting for the hearses to be unloaded."

"It's a part of my job description, you know that."

"Brant, of all the places we *could* meet up, cemeteries and graveyards undoubtedly top the list. And it's always *your* idea."

"What can I say?" he says with a wink, "Salem's got a lot of cemeteries."

"That it does," I agree. I sit up, pulling my legs back into my lap before crossing them. "Well, next time, we're going to meet at the library."

"You know we can't smoke in there." His tone is matter of fact. "At least with *my* choices, we can be who we really are, without shame."

"Fine," I counter. "Pickering Wharf, then."

He considers my proposal with narrowed eyes before sticking his hand out for me to shake. "Deal. But if the smell of fish is too overbearing, I need you to agree that we'll resume meeting in our original spot."

I clasp his hand firmly. "Deal."

It's in that moment he catches a glimpse of my watch and, subsequently, the time. "Well, I'll be damned. We're well into the witching hour." He pushes off from the couch and grabs his coat. "I should get going."

I can't explain it, but something tugs at my insides, wanting him to stay. "Really? You usually stay later than this."

He finishes buttoning his coat before winding a wool scarf around his neck. "Is that . . . *desire* I detect?"

"Brant," I say, running a hand down my face. "We've been over this." And we have. Many, many times. Yes, there's an undeniable attraction between us. Yes, there's familiarity. And comfort. It gets lonely merely existing, but when that existence is so vastly *different* from everyone else's in your reality? Sometimes the very human need for connection surfaces, threatening to take over . . .

Like it seems to be doing right now.

Brant meets my gaze, holding it steady. I can tell his eyes want to roam across the couch and over all of *me*, but he doesn't do either as he whispers, "Just say the word, Maren."

Hearing my name when his voice lowers an octave sends a shiver down my spine. I bow my head and break eye contact, simultaneously fighting every stupid hormone in my body. How primitive these "needs" are. It's quite rare that I get wrapped up in them—or pulled under, for that matter.

Brant takes a step toward me, slowly starting to undo the buttons on his coat. I watch as he releases the first one, then the second, but when he gets to the third, I press my hand against his stomach. It may be a silent rejection, but I can still see the hurt flash in his eyes. It only lasts a second before it's gone.

"Right," he says, clearing his throat with a shake of his head. "It's been a long night. I should let you rest—"

"And I should do the same," I add, hating how chipper my voice sounds. "I'll see you in a couple days, yeah?"

"Yeah. Until then." He swipes his phone from the table and nods. "Goodnight, Maren."

He turns to leave, but not before backtracking and planting a kiss on my forehead. For a minute, I'm convinced that he's going to move lower, to take it further, but he seems to be just as taken aback by his actions as I am. It's so out of character, so *unlike* Brant, that we both just freeze. I'd been warned that Noire-Sigard relationships can run into some . . . *complications* from time to time, but Brant and I have always been solid. Nothing to worry about. I mean, we're fated to hate each other.

His eyes flick to mine—searching, but I don't know what for. He looks like he wants to say something, and, for a brief moment, I think I want him to; but then a wave of common sense seems to crash into us both at the exact same time.

"Well," he says, shuffling toward the door, "goodnight."

I toss my hand up in a small wave, watching as he opens and closes the door behind him. When I'm certain that he's a good distance from my apartment, I let out a loud sigh. I raise my hand to my forehead, fingers brushing the very spot where his lips had just been. I smile, hating myself for doing so.

"Goodnight, Brant," I whisper.

9

WHEN I WAKE, I experience only a split second of peace before the events of last night blaze into my awareness like hellfire. And when I say "events", I don't mean my one-on-one time with Mr. Nathan Sharpe; but the awkward exchange that had taken place between myself and Brant . . . The depth in which his eyes had searched mine. The unexpected kiss he'd planted on my forehead. The undeniable sexual tension that had sparked between us—not for the first time, either. And, most notably, *wanting* him to stay . . .

Immediately feeling a migraine coming on, I light the cone of palo santo incense that's sitting on my nightstand, watching as the smoke begins to cascade over the blown-glass fixture. I waft some toward me and take a big inhale. It instantly relaxes me. The journal entry I'd written last night stares me in the face, beckoning to be reread, contemplated, and analyzed, but I'm not in the mood. I don't feel like writing today either, so I close the notebook and secure the ends with its pre-stitched-in black ribbon.

One glance out the bedroom window indicates that it's my favorite kind of day: overcast and slightly gloomy, making it an ideal day to scour the county library, which I've been meaning to do for some time. That might *also* be why I'd recommended it to Brant as a potential new meetup spot. Alas, it looks like I'll be going alone . . . but after last night, that's probably for the best.

The clock reads 10:04 A.M., which is earlier than usual for me to wake up and start the day. I usually sleep in until the early afternoon, especially on the days where I've *ovetyred*—the fancy term for invoking nightmares—the night before. My line of work requires *a lot* of sleep and a very open, flexible schedule. It's a good thing I have both.

I grab a chunky russet sweater that's stitched with overlays of beige, maroon, and pumpkin hues, and pull it over my head. My hair instantly picks up on the static, somehow managing to make my bedhead look even more unkempt. I slip on a matching pair of pants that are a shade darker than the sweater before heading into the bathroom to fix my hair. At this stage, I'm not sure a comb can even make a dent, but I give it a try. I spritz some dry shampoo into my roots and work it in. It helps the situation some, albeit not by much.

A dash of makeup and touch of jewelry later, I'm in the kitchen, desperately trying to find something at least semi-nutritious to eat. Seemingly out of nowhere, I get a craving for egg white bites. I decide I'll stop into the café that's next to the library once I'm on my way . . . if my stomach doesn't eat itself by then.

My phone's only halfway charged, so I swipe the cord from the wall and toss both into my bag before doing a onceover of my apartment. My gaze tracks to the couch, where Brant and I had been sitting last night.

Nope, don't even go there. Leaving now . . .

As if he can read my mind—which, some days, I'm convinced he can—my phone buzzes with a text. I peek at it to make sure it's not an emergency. It isn't. I tell myself I'll text him back later because right now I need to focus.

And find something to eat.

I lock my apartment door and bound down the steps, hoping that the doom and gloom outside is just that and won't suddenly transform into a full-fledged thunderstorm. I'm pleased to find that there's just a light drizzle, which is sure to flatten my hair right up.

The library is about the same distance as Madame Viessa's, just in the other direction. My pace is brisk as I nod at passersby, hoping that the weather will hold out just a little while longer. If the darkening clouds above are any indication, I might find myself in some very wet clothes sooner than anticipated. I pat the outside of my bag, hoping to feel the elongated shape of an umbrella, but I'm dismayed when I realize I'd forgotten it at home. I suppose it's what I deserve for getting distracted by an unnecessary reminder that I'm attracted to my Sigard, as I most certainly was this morning.

The raindrops grow larger and with it, so do my steps. I approach the café, luckily still mostly dry, and just as I'm about to pull the door open, someone nearly runs into me. My shoulder collides with something bony and sharp—an elbow. I whip my head to the left, taking in a tall woman with an elongated face who's dressed entirely in black. She peers down at me from her wire-rimmed glasses—and that's saying something, because I'm quite tall myself—before asking in a sultry tone, "Coming or going?"

As if the question isn't confusing enough, seeing as I'm clearly pulling on the *outside* of the door, that's not what causes a chill to lodge in my chest. No, it's the *way* she'd said it. Almost as if she'd meant to cause confusion.

"After you," I say, hoping that she'll take the bait so I can study her even closer.

Gray eyes search mine, so light that her irises might as well disappear into the whites surrounding them. She tilts her chin, her jet-black hair swaying with the movement. "If I startled you, it was unintentional."

Honey laced with poison. That's exactly what her voice sounds like. Just as I'm about to respond, a phone starts ringing. The woman frowns, digging in her crocodile-skin purse for the buzzing object. Honestly, it's the ugliest bag I've ever seen and doesn't seem to match her otherwise very put-together ensemble, so it's hard not to take notice. Growing impatient, I'm about to walk into the open door I'm currently holding when she breezes right past me, Cruella de Vil style. I walk in behind her, not bothering to hold the door for the other patrons who are now swarming the sidewalks.

She continues to walk in front of me, completely engrossed in her conversation. I'm not sure what I was expecting, but I thought she'd at least let me go ahead of her— which, now that I'm thinking about it, is totally out of character for this woman I've only just met and will probably never see again.

My stomach growls and I can't help but tap my foot at the slow-moving line. When "Cruella" gets to the counter, she orders a black coffee. That's it. No cream. No sugar. No pastries, bagels, or muffins. Again, I don't know what I was expecting.

"Can I get your name?" the barista behind the counter asks.

I lean in, curious to hear her response.

Stark red lips curl around the word. "Lilith."

I nearly choke on my own saliva. *Um, are you fucking shitting me right now?*

Oblivious, the barista writes the name on the cup with a flourish, then directs Lilith to the counter at the opposite end of the store. I watch as she glides across the floor in an effortless fashion. It's only when I hear the barista say, "Ma'am?" for the second time do I finally approach the counter.

"What can I get for you?" she asks.

"I'll have a cinnamon dolce latte," I say somewhat absentmindedly, my gaze still pointed across the store.

"Will that be all?" A pause when I don't respond right away. "If you'd like, I can upgrade your drink to our larger size and you can take half off any of our hot breakfast items."

Ah, capitalism, my brain retorts.

Food! my stomach screams.

"Right," I say, snapping my head back so that I'm finally looking at the barista and not at the woman across the store. "Yes, I'll have a large coffee and egg white bites, please."

She gives me the total to which I hand her my payment. Just as she'd directed Lilith, she instructs me to pick up my drink at the opposite counter. With my head down, I stuff my wallet back into my bag, simultaneously walking along the beige tile floor; but when I arrive, Lilith is nowhere to be seen. *She did only order a black coffee*, I realize. I'm not sure why I feel disappointed, but I do.

I wait impatiently for my name to be called, all the while checking over my shoulder and out the window, hoping to maybe catch a glimpse of her walking by. I'm fully aware that my actions border on creepy and weirdly desperate, but I can't help it. There was just something so . . . *magnetizing* about her. Like I could stare at her for hours without blinking. Or talk to her for days and *still* have questions I'd be dying to know the answers to.

"Marr-in?"

I sigh as I approach the counter. "It's pronounced Mare-inn," I say, taking the cup from a tattooed hand.

"Isn't spelled that way."

I look at his nametag. "Okay, Jay-cob." I make sure to accentuate the *o* instead of the usual *u* sound.

"It's . . ." He glances at his nametag, then looks up at me with an amused grin. "Nice, I see what you did there. Hey, I know this is kind of random but would you maybe want to—"

"Nope," I say bluntly, "but I applaud the effort."

Still grinning, he slides my order of egg white bites across the counter. "Your loss."

"Or my gain?" I say, popping one of them into my mouth. "Alas, it seems we'll never know." I grab the small tray, winking at him, then make for the door.

"I'll never forget you, Marr-inn!" he calls after me in mock infatuation.

Well, at least he got that part right. That's what they all say after I'm done with them, for better or worse. Not bothering to look back, I push the door open with my hip, eating the remaining muffin-shaped eggs before tossing the tray in the trash receptacle. I take a couple swigs of my coffee, savoring both the taste and the warmth of the cup between my palms.

I spot an open bench just outside the café but, seeing as the storm clouds are moving *with* me and not away from me, I decide I may as well keep on the path to the library. I walk two more blocks, turning the corner as the monstrous building comes into view. I climb the steps, finishing the last of my beverage before going inside.

I enter through the double doors into complete and utter silence—it's so quiet, I swear you could hear a pin drop. The woman behind the checkout counter doesn't even look up. In fact, I think she might be asleep on the job.

As I usually do when I come here, I slink to the back aisles that lead to a separate room where the historical archives can be found. *Everything you ever wanted to know about Salem is right here, folks.* Researching my victims' victims is something that doesn't get old.

I don't think it ever will.

I browse the collections of documents, knowing that most of them have been scanned into a database, but there's just *something* about physically combing through old newspaper articles for information. The feel of aged paper against your fingers, the smell of it . . . it's the high of all highs, if you ask me.

While I don't have my next "assignment" just yet (I'm usually given a couple days to recoup), I continue to aimlessly roam the aisles. Libraries are an ideal place to let your thoughts wander—amongst the greatest writers, thinkers, philosophers, and innovators of not just our time, but of *all* time. So, why then, do my thoughts keep circling back to Brant? Speaking of . . .

I hear something.

I stop mid-stroll with my hand outstretched near the top shelf. I angle my head and close my eyes, removing as much sensory input as possible so I can truly listen.

"Will that be all?"

I'd recognize that voice anywhere. It belongs to Brant.

What is he doing here? Especially after completely rejecting my idea to meet here in the first place?

I don't get the chance to ponder these questions further because the voice that responds is enough to make my blood run cold. This one I also recognize, but I wouldn't be able to say that had I not stopped into the café earlier.

Lilith.

"I'll contact you again in one month, no sooner," her sickly-sweet voice croons.

"A month?" I can hear the concern in Brant's voice. "But what if—?"

"It won't," Lilith cuts him off, seemingly without remorse. "Because you'll see to it that it doesn't."

Mentally, I'm kicking myself for not having gotten here earlier so I could hear the entirety of their conversation. Then again, I had no idea I'd even be stumbling upon something like this. I'm peeking through the shelves, enraptured by my internal tantrum, when Lilith turns to leave.

"Shit," I murmur, realizing that she'll have to pass by the aisle I'm currently using as cover to reach the exit. I book it in the opposite direction and lurk behind one of the endcaps, hoping that Brant will decide to follow Lilith's path and not stroll down the other side—the side I'm now on.

Padded footsteps approach as they pass each of the aisles. I dare a glance just as Brant is walking by. I hear him stop, which has me holding my breath and sucking in every body part imaginable, but he doesn't explore any further.

I wait and wait and wait until I'm absolutely sure that they've both left and are as far away from the historical archives room as possible. I blow out a long breath, sagging against the endcap until I slink to a sitting position. I run a hand through my hair, shaking my head at how immensely close that was. I have half a mind to run after them and flag them down, depending on who I'd reach first, but I'm much more of the "debate in silence" type.

I know Lilith is a . . . *semi*-popular name, especially around here. I also know that the vibe I'd gotten from her in the café earlier had been enough to trigger my fight-or-flight response, and yet I'd chosen neither. And the fact that she's talking to Brant, who's a Sigard, is uncanny. Part of our "contract" in the line of work we do here involves keeping ourselves at a distance from the "common folk". Can you imagine doing what I do and realizing that the person you just fell for is the same person you'll have to torture?

Hey, I don't make the rules . . .

But that's definitely a risk I'm *not* willing to take.

It's also highly unlikely that Brant would take that risk, which tells me that Lilith must be in on his role here.

That, and her fucking name is *Lilith,* for crying out loud.

I don't know how long I've been sitting here, running the same hand through my hair, over and over again, but it's clear a librarian must have passed by me a few times, because with the way she's now approaching me, I can't help but envision the way a predatory cat would approach a mouse.

"Excuse me?" she asks, pushing thick tortoise-framed glasses up the bridge of her nose. "Is everything all right?"

I nonchalantly wave my hand in the air. "Everything's fine, thanks."

Doubt clouds her face. "Is there anything I can help you find?"

"No," I say, rather curtly. "I'm just thinking."

She looks at me as if that's the strangest response she's ever heard.

I can't help but add, "Isn't that what people do at a library? *Think*?"

"I—I suppose so." She glances down the aisle, not knowing what to say or do next. "If you need anything, I'll be at that desk just over there." She points in the direction she was just looking.

I give her a brief nod before casting my gaze downward at the oddly patterned carpet; but as she turns to leave, my head suddenly snaps back up. "Actually, I take that back. There *is* something I need help with."

Her face lights up. "What's that?"

"What kind of information do you have available on Judaic mythology?"

She eyes me curiously. "I believe we have some records, mostly in the Mythology and Folklore section. Although, there may be some in the Philosophy and Theology section, but I'd have to check to be sure. What exactly are you looking for, if I might ask?"

I push myself to my feet. "I'm looking to learn more about Lilith."

The librarian's face falls. "As in the female demon?"

Oh, how I pity those with preconceived notions of a history they know nothing about. I grin, pleased to do my civic duty for the day. "Demon . . . or goddess?" I challenge.

10

I DECIDE THAT my library search has rendered nothing useful—at least, nothing that I didn't already know. Downtrodden, I return the small stack of books, some of which are uncatalogued, to the librarian with a forced smile before heading toward the exit.

It's been a weird day. A weird day, a weird night . . . as I step outside, I'm disheartened to find that what little sun had decided to appear is already setting. *How long had I been in there?* Long enough for the day to pass without my realizing it, apparently. Libraries are like that, though—their own special breed of wormholes, especially when you're locked in a room with no windows and only pages upon pages of books and archives to keep you company. Not that I'm complaining. I'm actually surprised to see that there even *is* a sunset after such a gloomy morning. I guess it had cleared up at one point or another, but I'd been too preoccupied to notice.

As I stroll by the café windows, I glance inside, surprised to see that the barista from earlier—the one who'd gotten my name wrong—is still working. We awkwardly make eye contact, and his eyes grow wide before a huge grin spreads across his face. He waves to me hysterically, although I can't tell if he's joking or if he's just as surprised to see me as I am him. *Poor kid. That's a long shift.* I give a small wave back, taking note of the day and time so that I don't accidentally run into him on future coffee runs.

Is that a little harsh? Yes.

But, as I said before, I don't make the rules.

I take my time walking home, knowing that what awaits me is yet another night alone of ordering takeout and watching movies I've already seen one too many times . . .

Oh, the human experience. Isn't it grand?

I keep to the edge of the sidewalk, waiting for the streetlights to kick on, yet enjoying the slowly fading sunset all the same. I've almost reached my apartment when I see the cemetery, not realizing that I'd taken a slight detour from my usual route. I approach the wrought-iron gates and give them a little shake, realizing that they're already slightly ajar. When I look up, I see a shadowed figure sitting on a bench near the back. A lighter flicks on and I know immediately who it is.

Follow the sunset, they said. *It'll be like following your bliss,* they said.

Ultimately, I have two choices: 1) I can hope that Brant's too far away to spot me and just keep walking until I get home, or 2) I can assume the more likely scenario, which is that he's already seen me if I can see him, so I better buck up and join him for a smoke. I already know what's waiting for me at home, and even though I technically hid from Brant earlier today, I'd much rather partake in what he's doing. And so, my decision made, I push open the gates, knowing that if he hasn't spotted me by now, the creaking will surely give me away. I see him raise his left hand, the one that's not holding his cigarette, as he calls out, "Oy, Maren! Is that you?"

"In the flesh," I shout back.

I round the cobblestone path to where he's sitting and plop down next to him. "Fancy meeting you here," I say, snatching the cigarette from his mouth before taking a long drag. "This is mine now, thank you very much."

He rolls his eyes but doesn't fight me for it. He produces a small white pack from his coat, flipping it open before grabbing one with his teeth. The lighter blazes, illuminating both our faces in the growing darkness. "Good thing I have plenty, then."

I drop my shoulders, instantly feeling relaxed being here, with him—but then my brain does that thing where it starts replaying things I wish it wouldn't. *Fucking fantastic.*

"I didn't think I was going to see you again so soon," he says through a long exhale, the smoke curling around us. "To say I'm surprised is an understatement."

"Is it a *pleasant* surprise?" I say, unable to stop myself from asking.

He angles his head, a dark glimmer in his eyes. "Of course it is. Why wouldn't it be?"

I shrug, suddenly feeling a thousand times guiltier for not being upfront about seeing him at the library—and essentially *spying* on him—earlier today. "I don't know. Just after last night, I thought you might need a break."

He waves his cigarette in the air as if that's the most ridiculous thing he's ever heard. "If I recall, *you're* the one who's always taking breaks. Not me." He must realize how callous he sounds because he quickly adds, "Not that I'm saying you shouldn't. You totally should. Especially after what you go through, night after night." He gazes longingly at a nearby headstone. "I'd need an eternal break after just *one* of your Noire sessions, that's for damn sure."

"I suppose you and I are just built differently," I tease, feeling grateful that my playful self is beginning to emerge again; but the feeling quickly dissipates as I note the somber expression on his face.

"I suppose we are," he says quietly. "Here for different reasons, ones that are out of our control . . ." he trails off, even though I desperately want him to finish his train of thought. I realize that his sudden change in demeanor might have something to do with that little chance encounter I'd witnessed today . . . but how can I get him to openly talk about it without revealing that I already know about it?

"I take it your day was eventful," I say, prodding him along. "What happened today that was out of your control?"

He snaps out of his daze, shooting me a sidelong glance that's riddled with suspicion. "What an oddly specific question that is."

"Is it?" I say, trying to keep the heat from rising to my cheeks. "Because you literally just mentioned things being out of your control. So, I'm asking about it. Isn't that what 'friends' do?"

Any ounce of suspicion in his expression fades almost instantly. "You're right. I'm sorry. It's just been an off day."

I'm inclined to agree with him, but then that means I'll have to open up and share more about *my* day . . . which I'm not quite willing to do at present. Best if he goes first.

Spoken like a true sociopath.

When he doesn't elaborate further, I ask, "How so?"

I can see the contemplation in his eyes, the lines that form along his jaw and forehead . . . Brant's always been truthful with me. And I with him. But it looks like he's about to break that streak—*or have I already broken it?*

Some people would say withholding information is just as bad as lying. And I would say . . . fuck those people.

Then again, maybe they *do* have a point.

"It's . . . complicated," he starts, my heart jumping at the admission. "I don't know if it's something that's lingering from last night from our visit to the Sephiran or what, but I've just felt off today." He casts his gaze ahead, and I can't help but notice it's in the direction of the library. "Tomorrow will be better, though. *A new day*, or whatever it is the normies say. Nothing for you to worry about, I promise."

He gives my shoulder a pat which only causes my heart to drop further into my stomach. He straight-up *lied*. Brant just *lied* to me. His Noire. The one person he's sworn to protect and keep safe. I bite the inside of my cheek to keep from saying something I'll regret. I look away, hoping he won't notice, but he does.

"Hey," he says, pulling me into him. "Everything okay?"

"Yeah," I say, forcing the budding anger from my voice. And then, to change the topic, "Think you could point that thing elsewhere? The smoke's drifting into my eyes."

"Oh, shit," he says, switching the cigarette to his other hand. "My bad."

"All good," I say, even though I'm feeling far from it.

"So, got any riveting plans for the evening?"

Even though my brain is a jumbled mess of betrayal and confusion, I somehow manage to answer, "I wouldn't call them riveting. Just another rewatch of some old favorites, maybe I'll get crazy and order some Chinese."

"How very basic of you," he jokes.

How I wish that were true, but after this conversation—and this day as a whole—tonight will be anything but. "If *I'm* considered basic, then the vast majority of the human population should be scared," I say as I rise from the bench. "Very, *very* scared." I dig the butt of my cigarette into the ashtray.

"Want some company?" Brant asks, mimicking the motion.

Oh, how I did. How I really, really did.

But this conversation has changed everything.

And what's worse is that he doesn't even know it.

"Maybe next time," I offer, hoping he can't hear the disappointment in my voice.

"I'll take you at your word," he says. "Don't think I won't hold you to it."

"I know you will," I say with a strained smile, turning my back to him before he can see me shatter. Because all we've had *was* our word, but without that . . .

Without that, we're just like the rest of them. Two people who hide behind the truth and tell white lies until we create our own inescapable web of falsehoods. Until we can't distinguish the ceiling from the floor.

But who are we now? And an even more terrifying thought . . . *what might we become?*

11

I'M BACK HOME, stuffing my face with more lo mein and orange chicken than I know what to do with. With greasy fingers, I grunt as I struggle to open yet another bottle of cabernet. When the cork is finally free, I do a little dance in my seat and pour myself a glass, then grab the remote and stream the next horror movie in the lineup of classics.

The opening scene pans across the front of a mental asylum, and that's all I need to see to remember that it's one of Brant's favorite titles. Not quite sure what that says about him, but what can I say? We're suckers for the dark and twisted. When the opening credits begin playing across the screen, I choose to distract myself by swiping a fortune cookie from the table. The plastic wrapper is hastily discarded as I crack it open.

It could be better, but it's good enough, it reads.

"What in the actual fuck? I thought these were supposed to be uplifting!" I shout, throwing the cookie at the television. It *plinks* against the screen before falling to the floor. "Why did it have to be so accurate, though?" I murmur, picking up the red and white takeout container. I situate the chopsticks between my fingers as the opening credits end and the first scene of the movie finally begins to play. This is my second movie of the evening . . . or is it my third? I probably shouldn't have downed an entire bottle of wine over those first showings.

Oh, well. Too late now.

My hope is that the gore, terror, and psychotic breaks will make me feel less alone as the understated "villain" of my own existence, but somehow, it only seems to be making it worse. Not to mention, I'm nearly bored to tears at what is considered "gore" by industry standards. This shit doesn't even come *close* to what I'm doing on a weekly basis. Perhaps they should make a movie about me. Now wouldn't that be something?

I'm mid-noodle-slurp when my phone vibrates on the table. The sound is only amplified as my phone dances a short distance and touches the bottle of wine. I reach for it, even though I know I shouldn't.

How's that takeout treating you?

I swallow a mouthful of food, then cleanse my palate with a large swig of wine. I quickly brush my fingers against a napkin before typing, *Stalker.*

Ouch, he replies. *I can't check in on my favorite person?*

"Oh, your favorite person that you straight up *lied* to earlier?" I scowl, wishing I had the guts to actually type it.

Instead, I write, *My fortune cookie shit on me.*

Brant's response is instantaneous. *Umm, come again?*

It said, 'It could be better, but it's good enough.'

A slew of random letters comes through, which I've come to learn is his way of expressing hysteria and maniacal laughter. *I'll have to see it to believe it.*

I'm about to respond when something gives me pause—and oh, how I hate my brain when it's been poisoned with even the slightest bit of alcohol. *Maybe you should,* I type back, a plan formulating in my head.

Is that an invitation?

My fingertips hover over the glowing letters. If I'm ever going to get to the bottom of that stupid conversation Brant had with Cruella—*er,* Lilith—today, it'll likely be with wine, takeout, and horror movies . . . and maybe something more?

"This is a bad idea," I say, talking aloud to myself as one does after one too many glasses of vino. *Strictly professional.* We've kept things strictly professional for a reason.

But he lied. *He lied. He lied. He lied.*

If he can lie, then why can't I use a little manipulation to get to the truth? The truth he should have shared openly to begin with?

"That's some sound logic to me," I say, pressing send on a text telling him to come on over.

There's a noticeable pause before the next message comes through. *Wait, are you being serious?*

You want to see this fortune cookie or not?

A hurried reply. *Okay, I'm just going to take a quick shower and then I'll head over.*

I know I *should* think twice before responding, but I don't. *I have a shower here. Hurry up, before I change my mind.*

I'm already out the door. See you in five.

Five? I question, knowing it'll take him at least fifteen minutes to walk here.

I'm fucking sprinting, Maren.

I've hardly registered that I'm grinning from ear to ear when a knock sounds on my door. *Holy hell, is he here already?* I stumble over the pillows that are spread haphazardly across the floor, feeling like an idiot for not freshening up first *before* sending him the green light to come over. I check my teeth in the first reflective surface I can find, which is pointless, seeing as I can't exactly see straight anyway.

I take a deep breath before another knock sounds, then open the door to find Brant, in a fitted white t-shirt and gray sweatpants, waiting on my doorstep. My lips are probably tinged a deep purple, as are my teeth, but that doesn't stop me from smiling. It also doesn't stop him from grabbing me around the waist and pushing me into the doorframe as he presses his mouth against mine. He tastes like hickory, leather, and smoke and I can't help but pull him closer to me as he explores every inch of my mouth with his tongue.

We trip over our own feet as we stumble the rest of the way into my apartment. I hear the door click, knowing by his body movement alone that he's kicked behind him to shut it. The horror movie's still playing in the background, people screaming as ominous music plays, but Brant and I are in our own world, our own movie. His hand travels up my silk pajama top, cupping my breast as he flicks the hardened peak. I moan against his mouth, tugging his hair back just hard enough for him to echo the sound.

I can feel the length of him growing beneath his sweatpants as I press further into his legs, so I'm not at all surprised when he picks up all five foot, ten inches of me and sets me on the counter. I may be tall, but he's taller, and with the way he towers over me, his hair brushing my forehead as he continues to kiss me, it's everything I ever thought it would be. I could try to deny the fact that I've imagined this exact scenario with him many, *many* times before, but here we are, doing it, *living* it.

His hands drift to the sides of my face while mine move lower and lower. I want his shirt off *now*. I want *everything* off—now. My hand lightly brushes against his bulge, and I can tell by the way he bucks forward that he wants, more than anything, for me to grab it. I tease him once more, then pull away from his mouth, chest heaving.

His eyes search mine, but not in their usual contemplative way. Instead, he's looking at me with pure, unadulterated desire. "Why'd you stop?"

I gently nudge him away from me so that I can hop down from the counter. He obliges, watching as I stand before him, then slowly begin to lower myself to my knees. "To give you what you really came here for." I can hear his breath hitch in his throat, which makes this moment all the more enticing. "Now close your eyes."

"Maren . . ."

"Eyes. Closed." I gaze up at him through thick lashes, waiting until he does exactly as I've told him. Once they're shut, I break away, crawling to the television where the fortune cookie had landed. I pull the wadded-up strip of paper from the ground, then crawl back over to Brant. When I'm back in position, I slowly run my hands up the front of his sweatpants, noticing how he shivers when I graze *that* spot.

"Whatever it is you think I came here for, I'm ready for it," he says. "I've *been* ready for it—"

Smirking, I stand, holding the fortune directly in front of his face before telling him to open his eyes. "Well, it could have been better," I say, reciting what I'd told him earlier, "but it's good enough."

At first, I can tell he's confused, but then it registers.

"You little shit!" he says playfully, snatching the strip of paper from my hand. "You stopped for *that?*"

"That *is* what you came here for, is it not?"

His eyes darken. "Looks like you're about to find out."

I shriek as he scoops me up and throws me over his shoulder, lightly smacking my ass before tossing me onto the couch to continue what we've started.

Yep. I'm calling it.

As Brant and Maren, this was bound to happen.

But as Sigard and Noire?

Well, we're completely and utterly *fucked.*

12

Fuck me, *Brant fucking Colborn* spent the night.

I wake from my wine-induced haze, careful not to disturb the one person I *swore*, up and down, to keep it professional with. The potential implications of this are bad.

Very bad.

Ever so cautiously, I climb out of bed and tiptoe to the bathroom. I'm so mad at myself I could scream. What was the point? What was the *reason*?

I fish underneath my sink, completely distracted by my thoughts, until my hand grasps the familiar bottle of mouthwash. I'm in the middle of gargling when I remember the answer to my question. I'd wanted more information about Lilith . . . and I'd gotten it. I nearly gag on the acidic rinse as

I recall our conversation last night after we'd finally fulfilled our primal urges and peeled ourselves off of one another. Much like my movie marathon last night, the scene plays out as if it's on a film reel . . .

"Maren, there's something I need to tell you."

Fingers laced. Deep breath. Voice full of regret.

"I wasn't completely honest with you earlier."

No shit. I muster a look of curiosity. "About what?"

"When you asked about my day . . . I lied."

I prop myself up on my elbow, flattening the pillow beneath me. "Why?" It's not so much this question I want an answer to, but the *what*. Or maybe it's both. Or maybe I don't really care right now because of the euphoric high I'm currently experiencing after a night like tonight. Seems the fortune cookie did have some truth to it after all: It *could* be better. And it was. It really, really was.

"Something . . . out of the ordinary happened. I received a visit I don't normally get." Brant studies my face. I'm not sure if he's looking for a flicker of recognition because, honestly, it kind of feels like it. Too bad I'm hell-bent on acting totally oblivious. "Maren, I had a visit from . . . the person who visited me . . ." As if his expression doesn't already indicate that this is hard to talk about, the cracking of his voice really sends it home.

"Who visited you, Brant?" I press gently.

He casts his eyes toward the ground. "Lilith."

"Oh?" I feign ignorance. "That's . . . surprising."

"Yeah. It is." Brant blows out a sharp breath. "She wanted to discuss my . . . my ovetyr sentence."

At first, I'm certain I haven't heard him correctly. An ovetyr sentence occurs when those who sell their souls for unspeakable horrors have those very same horrors inflicted upon them for the rest of eternity—never able to escape, never able to start over, never able to find peace. As a Noire, I serve those ovetyr sentences in one form or fashion. "But you're a Sigard. You're Sigard-*ing*," I counter, making up a new word. "Therefore, this lifetime, this *incarnation*, can't possibly be your ovetyr sentence."

His silence speaks volumes.

What's worse is that he can't give me any details about it. Eternal sentences are strictly between the Ovetyr Agent, which is Lilith, and the recipient, which, in this case, would be Brant . . . as well as the Noires assigned to carry out said sentence. If this somehow *is* true, it would mean that *I'm* an integral part of Brant's ovetyr sentence . . . regardless of the fact that I'm not one of the Noires carrying it out.

Squinting from the glare of the bathroom light, I try to shake the memory, a shudder running down my spine. I spit into the sink again, watching what's left of the aquamarine liquid swirl down the drain before splashing some cold water on my face. How can such a perfect night go from life-changing to earth-shattering in such a short time—and with *one simple admission*? I crack the bathroom door open, peeking through it to catch a glimpse of Brant. His mouth is open, arm thrown over the side of the bed, still out cold. When he wakes, will he even remember what he told me last night?

What we *did* last night?

Furthermore . . . will he regret it?

I can't be here. The thought digs a tunnel across my mind, filling it with all the reasons I should just call it quits and leave now. *I have to get a new Sigard. Is that even possible? Can I be reassigned? I wonder if it'll have to be for a different timeline, maybe even a different reality? Staying here is too dangerous.*

We're both at risk.

And I put us here.

Fuck.

How could I have been so careless?

How had I not even *considered* the possibility?

I put the mouthwash back underneath the sink, trying to formulate a plan. Brant's still asleep, so perhaps I could just leave . . . but where would I go? One thing's for certain, though, I definitely can't think straight and hope to figure things out here.

I browse the bathroom for any item of clothing that looks more presentable than my pajamas. There's nothing discarded on the floor, nothing thrown over the shower curtain . . . I check the hook on the back of the door where I've hung a large winter coat that won't fit in my closet. It's a bit excessive, but it's the only choice I have if I don't want to accidentally wake Brant. I throw the thick wool coat around my shoulders and begin to button it, trying to sneak across the room at the same time. I recall that I have some boots sitting by the door—but no socks—so not only is this about to be wildly uncomfortable, but also slightly embarrassing to the public eye.

I slip the boots over my bare feet (which is an *atrocious* feeling, by the way) and, just as I'm lacing them up, I can hear Brant's groan from inside the bedroom.

Shit. Move faster.

With my coat half buttoned and only one boot laced, I straighten and slip the keyring off its hook, then slide my phone off the counter. My hand is on the doorknob, *so close to freedom*, when I hear Brant clear his throat. I don't even have to turn around to know that he's wide awake now, standing in the bedroom doorway with what is likely a look of stark disapproval on his face.

"Going somewhere?"

I squeeze my eyes shut, silently berating my hungover brain to do its job and think of a reasonable excuse. "Breakfast," I say before turning over my shoulder to look at him. My voice is surprisingly casual, even to me. "I figured you'd be hungry when you woke up."

"Is that so?" He raises a brow. "Turn around then."

Ugh. He knows me too well.

"Really," I say, trying to stall the inevitable, "I'll be back before you know it."

"Maren," he says, crossing the threshold into the kitchen. "Turn around."

I drop my shoulders and sigh, knowing that the minute he sees my shoddy shoe-work and my half-buttoned coat, he'll know I had no plans of returning. That my plan had been to leave and never come back.

Okay, so *never* might be a bit of an exaggeration, but after the bomb he'd dropped last night . . . again, I haven't had time to think things through. Slowly, I turn around, afraid to look him in the eye. I hear a stifled laugh as he takes in what I'm sure is an absolute mess.

"Either you're *really* hungover, or you're trying to get out of here as fast as you possibly can."

What are the chances he'll believe it's the former? I sigh, finally making eye contact. His expression is hopeful, but once our eyes meet, that hope fades. Probably because I feel as despondent as I look. My voice cracks as I say, "Which one do you believe it is?"

He bows his head. "I think you already know the answer to that."

"I just . . . need some time," I say, feeling even worse now that I've been caught. "We may have talked about things last night, but trying to process it this morning—*sober*," I add, really emphasizing that last word, "well, it isn't easy."

"So, you figured you'd just . . . leave?"

I know better than to try and lie again by saying I'd planned to grab us breakfast, so I just bow my head in response.

"Were you going to come back?"

I release a long breath, hating how we can go from pure bliss the night prior to . . . *this*. "Honestly, I wasn't sure."

"Maren."

"No," I admit, fighting against my raging guilt. "I wasn't going to come back."

He sucks in a sharp breath. "Well, I guess *I'll* be leaving, then."

I watch in roiling shame as he begins to collect his things. Once he's grabbed his phone, keys, and shoes, he sets them on the counter and pulls his wrinkled t-shirt over his head. He doesn't even bother to put on his shoes, which somehow makes this already crass situation sting even more.

He brushes past me, not bothering to give me a hug, let alone look me in the eye. "See you," he mumbles, reaching for the door.

I don't know why, but I let him. I don't stop him as the knob turns in his hand. I don't stop him as he pulls the door open. I don't stop him when he crosses the threshold from my apartment into the hallway. In fact, the moment some sense is finally knocked into me is the *least* opportune moment because he's already halfway down the hall, standing at the stairwell.

I won't let him take that first step. *I can't.*

"Brant, wait!" I shout, throwing the door the rest of the way open and darting into the hall. I step on something that feels both solid and flimsy at the same time, but don't bother to see what it is. My focus is on Brant and Brant alone. "You can't leave," I say breathlessly, joining him at the edge of the stairwell. "Please . . . not like this."

His tone matches his eyes. Cold, distant. "Why not? *You* were about to."

Even though the truth in his words cuts through me like glass, it doesn't hinder me from trying to rectify the situation. "You were right. I . . . . I wasn't thinking straight. We had so much wine and I, well, I just wasn't expecting that you could potentially be facing the types of things that I'm inflicting upon others on nearly a daily basis, not to mention *protecting* me while I'm doing it—" I break then. I can feel it in my throat and chest, the churning of tears desperate to claw through, forming their very own hurricane inside of me. I begin to sob, making what is probably the ugliest sound known to man, realizing that Brant has *never* seen me cry. Ever.

Which is probably because I don't do it often.

He immediately softens at the sight. Desolate and shaking, he pulls me into his chest. "Hey," he says, coaxing me. "Hey, it's fine. You're fine. It's all fine."

I press my face into his shoulder, desperate to shove the tidal wave of emotions back down, deep into the yawning void where not even I know they exist. I remain in his warm embrace for I don't know how long—him, shoeless, me with only a coat and one laced boot—linked together as if we're each other's lifeline. And, in some ways, I suppose we are.

When I finally pull away, I can't look at him, but he forces me to all the same. He takes my cheeks in his hands, making slow circles with his thumbs to brush away my tears. "There's so much I want to tell you," he whispers. "But you know I can't."

"I know. Which makes this even harder since we tell each other everything."

"If I could, I would. *But,* because our relationship is strictly professional . . ."

I manage a half-smile. The movement feels like it's cracking through the tear stains on my face. "Is? Or was?"

'It *was* strictly professional, yes." His use of the past tense fills me with subtle hope, and the way he looks at me reminds me of our very first meeting in this incarnation—when we realized we somehow already *knew* each other without actually *knowing* each other. "I suppose we can't exactly say that now, can we?"

I shake my head. "I'm not sure we could go back, even if we wanted to."

"I wouldn't want to." The words are sincere, heartfelt. "Would you?"

"No," I say quietly. "Especially now that I know what you've got hiding under there." I waggle my eyebrows as I glance at his sweatpants then back up at him, which leaves him howling with laughter. The sound echoes in the corridor, surely waking my neighbors; but it's a relief to see him smile.

It's the first thing that's made me feel decent all day.

"Well, good thing, then, because it seems you already have your next assignment." His gaze tracks back down the hall to my still-open apartment door. The solid-yet-firm thing I'd stepped on earlier . . . I see now that it's a manila folder.

I look back at him, suddenly feeling nervous. "You don't have to . . . I mean, I understand if you need to take a break. I can go at this one alone."

He squeezes my shoulders in response, then presses a kiss to my forehead. "Don't be a martyr, Maren. We have a contract, one we both swore to. I will continue to fulfill my duty, regardless."

While I admire the loyalty, my heart plummets at his choice of words. *It's a contract. That's all it is. An obligation.*

He seems to sense what I'm thinking. "And," he says, wrapping me in his arms, "because I *want* to. I'd never let you do something dangerous, especially not alone. I'm here to protect you."

Hope sparks in my chest as we walk back to my apartment, stride for stride. I swipe the folder from the ground and clear my throat. "Do you want to read it, or should I?"

"That depends. Can you see through your tears?"

I gasp in mock offense and punch him playfully in the shoulder. "That settles it. I'll read."

"Good," he says, with a lighthearted laugh, "because, to use your words, I don't think I'd have the stomach for it, anyway."

13

IT'D TAKEN ONLY a moment or two to browse the immense stack of paperwork before tossing it onto the coffee table in defeat and heading for the shower. I hadn't even made it past the first page. As much as I'd acted like I hadn't wanted Brant to join, I ultimately let him. His insistence on the matter only made it easier for the both of us. Much to my surprise, though, we'd actually *showered*—without any funny business—and chatted, mostly about the case. It felt oddly similar to our usual meetings, just in the nude with hot water and soap.

I've just finished putting myself together as I wander into the living room, running a comb through my hair. I quite like my hair in this incarnation. It's pin-straight which means both my hair and fringe dry in the same way after brushing them, no heat required. Saves me a lot of time and effort, that's for damn sure.

Brant's on the couch, his shirt sticking to his back from his still-damp hair, leafing through the folder's contents. Something metallic drops from an inner crease and clinks as it lands flat on the table. Brant's so preoccupied with what he's reading that he doesn't even notice it . . . or me, for that matter.

I walk over to the table and kneel, picking up the small fishing hook and turning it over in my hands. After examining it for a solid two minutes, I clear my throat to get his attention.

He peers at me from over the folder. "Going fishing?"

"Very funny." I roll my eyes. "Did you really not hear it fall from the folder?"

He lifts the file up and looks beneath it as if he's going to find the hook magically sitting there, even though it's clearly in my hands.

"Ever the observant one, aren't you?"

He closes the folder rather dramatically, then throws it onto the table with so much force, it nearly flies off the edge. I manage to catch it just before it does.

"I'm pretty sure you've spent more time eyeing that hook than reviewing the paperwork when the latter is likely to tell you much more about your next assignment."

There's an edge to my voice as I say, "Maybe for you, but who says our minds work even remotely the same?"

His glance at the bathroom door is intentional *and* obvious, as if to say that our minds work in *exactly* the same way, but I'm determined to prove him wrong.

"Confirm it," I say, sliding the papers back to him.

"Confirm *what*?"

"Open the folder and confirm the details I'm about to give to you." I give him a pointed look. "And before you say that this is unfair—that I've already looked at them—I only glanced at the first page."

Brant opens the folder. "The cover page? It doesn't even tell you anything—"

"Exactly."

Brant sighs. "All right. Have at it."

"My target is a murderer," I say, going easy on him.

"Most of them are," he derides.

"More specifically, a serial killer," I continue, ignoring the jab. "Male. Late twenties. Caucasian."

Brant's mouth falls open. "That's—"

"His victims were women, every single last one of them," I interrupt. "Various methods of torture were used. And not only did he kill them, he raped them, too." I shudder, my rage spiking. "He's serving a life sentence and is likely in line for Death Row, depending on the state that incarcerated him." I squeeze the hook in my hand, nearly drawing blood.

Brant sets down the open folder and leans forward, his eyes wide with shock. "How could you possibly know all that from looking at a single *fishing hook*?"

I hesitate before answering, trying to remember if this is one of those things I'm supposed to keep to myself, but honestly, Brant and I seem to be *way* past any "rules" at this point. "It's like a key in a legend. Specific items are sent along with the file to help with profiling, just in case there's not enough time to read"—I gesture to the massive folder—"all of *that.*"

Brant scratches his head. "But everything you said . . . it was oddly specific."

"It was." I drop the hook onto the table, noticing the deep imprint it's left on my palm. "Sadly, there are a lot of people who fit that same profile—more than you might think."

Brant whistles, leaning back into the couch. "I take it you've dealt with a lot of these scumbags?"

I grimace. *You should know,* I think. But Brant's always preferred to keep his distance from the details. Our recent visit to the Sephiran is proof of that. Instead, I just say, "I guess so."

"Right, then. So, what's the plan? Do we need to swing by Madame Viessa's again? Or go back to the . . . Sephiran?"

I can't help but notice the way his throat bobs at the end of his question. I force a smile, knowing that he's going to like *and* hate my answer at the same time. "No, not this time. Like I said, I've dealt with his kind before. I already have everything I need."

His shoulders sag with relief. "So, in two days' time, then?"

This is the part he won't like. I shake my head, my eyes flickering with malice. "We take care of this asshole *tonight.*"

☠ ☠ ☠ ☠ ☠

I know Brant's concerned about me. I would be, too, given the night we've just had . . . and morning after. But this vile prick has already spent too many nights *not* getting visits from me, so I feel I must rectify that immediately.

Have I had time to process the fact that Brant is likely serving his very own *ovetyr* sentence and that every night he closes his eyes, he has his own twisted brand of torture inflicted on him for hours on end? No, I most certainly haven't. And I'd be lying if I said that it wasn't fucking with my head a little (or a lot)—wondering *what* could have possibly been worth selling his soul for, and if it might be anything like what I've encountered during my time carrying out these horrific sentences . . .

Keeping my head lowered, I glance at him from across the room. It's no wonder he looks like shit all the time—with dark bags under his eyes and the permanent exhaustion that's seemed to settle into his features. It refuses to fade, regardless of how much caffeine he drinks. If I were him, I'd do everything in my power to not sleep either.

Oh, shit.

Had a Noire visited him last night?

After we'd . . .?

I steal another look at him. *No, there's no way that happened last night. I mean, I would have known, or at least sensed it . . . right?*

"All set," Brant calls to me from the center of the living room. I'm in the kitchen, holding a glass of water that's still full because instead of drinking it, I've allowed my thoughts to consume me. I snap out of my spiral, guzzling down the water before joining him. More second thoughts about the timing of all this come crashing in, but it feels too far gone now. Everything's set up, thanks to Brant. He's here. I'm here. We have the file.

I eye the insanely large hook that's been placed on the edge of the circle. Every time I see it, it reminds me of *The Texas Chainsaw Massacre.*

Brant follows my gaze. "I'm guessing that'll be the main course tonight?"

I make a hook with my finger and touch it to my right shoulder. "Left side could hit the heart, center could hit the spine. It has to be believable," I say, not taking my eyes off the metal monstrosity. "It'll leave him off-kilter, too."

Brant nods silently, gesturing to the array of weapons opposite the hook. "And then you'll use these?"

I can't bring myself to look at him. Knowing that this very well might be a rendition of one of his *own* sentences threatens to tear me apart. *But you don't know that*, I remind myself. *And he's taking all of this quite well. Really well, actually.* I close my eyes and take a steadying breath. *You're not doing this to Brant, you're doing it to Mark Nolan. Who deeply, deeply deserves everything that's coming to him.*

I open my eyes in a flash, feeling sick to my stomach—and not because of the wine we'd had last night. I lower myself to the floor, sitting back on my heels. "Show me the pictures," I say hoarsely.

I can sense Brant's concern even without looking at him. "Maren . . ."

"The pictures, Brant," I demand, speaking louder this time so that my voice doesn't crack. "Now."

He shuffles away from me, moving things around on the coffee table that we'd shoved aside earlier to make room for the session. He returns, standing before me, with the folder in hand. I keep my gaze lowered as I stick my arm up, waiting for him to drop it in my outstretched hand, but he doesn't. I know exactly where this is going before he even opens his mouth.

"Look at me."

I grit my teeth. "You're wasting precious time."

He doesn't budge. "Look at me," he says again.

"Just give me the file, Brant."

"Maren, look at me right now."

I can hear the anger rising in his voice just like it's rising in my chest. "Give me the fucking folder," I hiss.

There's a brief, short-lived moment of peace before he implodes, collapsing to his knees and gripping my chin with such force that I have no choice but to meet his fierce gaze. His eyes burn with rage, yes, but there's something else there, too. Something I'm all too familiar with.

Anguish.

"You can't do this tonight," he says, his voice on the verge of shaking. "Not in this condition. It's too dangerous and—"

"*I* can't do it, or *you* can't do it?" I shoot back, matching his intensity. "I only need the pictures to do my fucking job."

His mouth turns up in a snarl as he slaps the folder onto my lap, but he doesn't let go of my jaw. "You're lying. You need those pictures so that you can work yourself up to do it in the first place! Well, here you go," he shouts, finally releasing his grip, "take a look at all of these horrendously mutilated bodies. Hide your own shameful actions behind his. Go ahead, then!"

I stare at him, wide-eyed, suddenly paralyzed by the thought of what could possibly warrant *this* kind of a reaction from him. Could this mean he'd done something worse than Mark Nolan? Than Nathan Sharpe? Than the hundreds of other convicts I've invoked nightmares for over our years of working together? And if so, how had he been able to hide it this whole damn time? Moreover, what brand of *fucked up* would you have to be?

I glare at him, suddenly wanting nothing to do with him, with *any* of this. He's right about one thing—we *can't* do this tonight. Our emotions are too high as it is and, quite frankly, I can't trust him. Not with this reaction. Not until I can get more information and *really* process this.

Even though blazing anger churns inside me, I manage to push myself to my feet in a rather controlled way, letting the file slide right off my lap. I don't say a word as I walk by him, straight into my bedroom and turn the lock.

Less than thirty seconds go by when I hear him gather his things and the front door slam shut. I crouch and check underneath the door to ensure there are no shadows—but Brant wouldn't trick me like that. With the coast clear, I emerge from my bedroom and walk to the front door. I slide the deadbolt into place. Then, I collapse onto the floor in a heap of limbs and cry for the second time that day.

14

I'M JOLTED AWAKE on the couch by yet another dream, this one even shorter than the last. Heart pounding, I reach for my phone on the coffee table, the glaring numbers coming into focus. 3:33 A.M. I groan, tossing my phone back onto the table before curling deeper into the blankets. For the past two hours, I've been waking up in twenty-minute intervals. I should just get up and start the day or perhaps do something that'll make me tired, but the effort feels far too great. I just want to lay here, without cause, until the sun comes up.

At least when I close my eyes, the thoughts dissipate, fading from my consciousness and my reality entirely—but, damn, the minute my eyes open, it's like my brain picks up right where it'd left off. If only I could figure out how to use this brilliant capacity in *other*, more self-serving ways . . .

I close my eyes again, waiting for sleep to whisk me away, but this time, it doesn't. Frustrated, I flip onto my back and reach for my phone again. No calls or texts. I'm surprised—and, admittedly, disappointed—to discover that Brant hasn't tried to make contact since he'd stormed out.

Not even once.

The realization pulls me upright as I attentively scroll through my emails, texts, my phone log . . . nothing. As if that whole fucked up situation hadn't even happened. I recoil at the thought, knowing that my budding anger will only continue to build if I don't distract myself—and quick.

Looks like we're getting the day started before four o'clock in the morning. *Oh, joy.* I wrap the blanket around my shoulders, wearing it like a cape, as I head toward the kitchen. Tea sounds nice. As does a danish. I only have one of the two right now, so I fill the kettle with water and place it on the stove. The burner glows bright orange and then a deep red, mirroring exactly how I'm feeling inside.

I lean against the counter, drumming my fingers against the side. Brant's face, flushed with rage, floats across my mind, his grip tightening ever so steadily on my chin. I jerk my face away, even though it's only a memory.

Keep yourself busy, Maren. Don't let it get to you.

But there isn't much to do at this ungodly hour *except* for think—which is exactly what I *don't* need to be doing right now. It's then another thought collides with the memory of Brant, pushing his face aside to reveal an idea that isn't any better but, honestly, how could it get worse?

I don't give myself a chance to talk my way out of it. I turn off the stove and move the kettle from the burner, foregoing my tea, then head straight into my bedroom. I pull a black turtleneck from my closet and pair it with black pants and black boots. The hastily discarded file from last night sits idly on the floor, in the exact same place it'd slid off my lap, taunting me, like a well-kept secret. I flip through it, taking only the one-page summary of the case and the crime scene photos. I fold each item until they're small enough to fit in my back pocket, then stuff my phone into the other.

It's a good thing *The Ivory Stallion* is open twenty-four hours—well, not for *all* patrons, but for my kind it is. As per usual, when I arrive, it's a ghost town, save for Charlie. He straightens from behind the counter, a bottle of whiskey in hand.

"Back again so soon?" He scans the area around me. "I see you decided to come alone this time."

Guilt begins to coil in the pit of my stomach as I recall our previous visit and the potential danger I'd put us all in without their knowledge. But that's not why I'm here.

"The usual?" he offers.

I shake my head. "Not this time." I head straight for the back of the bar without waiting for him to take the lead. My ill manners seem to irk him.

"I take it you're in a rush."

"Something like that," I say, not bothering to slow down.

We're only a quarter of the way into the cellar when he says, "You know, try as you might to do this alone, you *need* me—"

I want to tell him that I don't need anybody, because that's exactly how I feel right now and what got me into this whole mess in the first place, but I clamp my mouth shut. It won't do any use to drag him into this—in fact, it'll probably complicate things even further. I hop off the ladder and wait for him to do the same, then gesture for him to go ahead of me.

"That's more like it," he mutters.

"Say, Charlie," I muse as I follow behind him, "am I the only patron you do this for?"

His hazel eyes glimmer in the dim light. "You know I can't tell you that."

"Why not? What happens if you do?"

Charlie sighs loudly. "Can't tell you that either."

I mimic his frustration, exhaling a loud breath through my nose. "Do you know how lonely this gets?"

"You certainly didn't *seem* lonely the last time you were here."

Even though there's an edge to his tone, I can't help but smile. "Touché, Charlie. I must admit, you're a sharp one."

"I'm afraid I've gotta be, doing this line of work and all."

I watch as he readies the portal, noticing how much quicker he is this time around, as if he hadn't previously closed it. *Clue number one.* The second clue dawns on me when I reach for the cloak—as I always do before visiting the Sephiran—only to realize that there's just one cloak and not two. The backup cloak, the one Brant had worn last time, seems to be missing. Missing . . . or is it, perhaps, currently in use?

I can't help but smile, knowing that I've just answered my own question. And what's even better is that Charlie is completely unaware. I've almost finished buttoning my cloak, wondering who might be wearing the other one, when I notice something incredibly familiar on the lower shelf. I swipe my phone from my back pocket and quickly flash a light on it to reveal scales of a greenish-brown hue in the shape of a purse. My mind reels back to the encounter in the café and the hideous bag "Cruella" had been carrying.

Lilith's bag, to be more accurate.

I'm on fire today. My smile grows even wider when I realize that I've managed to answer *all* the questions I had by simply observing my surroundings.

What are the chances I run into Lilith while I'm wandering the streets of the Sephiran? Rather slim, actually, but not impossible. At the very least, perhaps I can ask around, maybe even trace her steps. Seeing as Brant and I aren't exactly on speaking terms right now, this is my best chance to get more information—on his soul contract, this particular incarnation, and what his ovetyr sentence might entail—and, wouldn't you know it, the pieces seem to be falling right into my lap. *Oh, how I love it when a plan comes together.*

15

THE SEPHIRAN APPEARS even darker and more shadowed than usual. Regardless of the time of day on the other side of the portal, it's always night here. Fortunately, that doesn't pose a problem for me, seeing as I now know exactly what I'm looking for—a woman donning an exact replica of the cloak I'm wearing. *Thank you, Charlie.*

But what to do when I find her? If confronted, would she even remember me from the café? Or was I merely in the background amongst the others, like the barista, the librarian, and other patrons? I don't know why, but the thought irritates me. That I might be "just like the others".

Is she who I think she is? And, if so, why has she been meeting with Brant? What does she know that I don't?

That last thought has me stopping in my tracks. Upon my incarnation as a Noire, I've only been given information on a need-to-know basis—the manila folder is a prime example of that. Come to think of it, I don't know the specific names of the council and committee members who oversee my line of work. Much like the Sephiran, they're very much kept in the dark, as am I. I've always believed there was a reason for it, but perhaps it's more by design than anything else. A way to guard their identities and safety along *all* timelines.

Knowing not to stay in one spot for too long, I continue onward, passing by the shop Brant and I had entered during our last visit. I'd originally decided to come here to distract myself—to perhaps browse the selections in some of the other storefronts—but after seeing that atrocious crocodile bag, my plans had shifted rather quickly.

I make a quick left into a familiar alleyway, which is one of my favorite shortcuts to get to the next street over. I don't know what Lilith would be doing in the events district, but I suppose her presence in the shopping district would be just as strange. The events district is chock full of illegal activity: we're talking gambling, proxy crimes, trafficking, drug and weapons trading, but with a bit of a twist—the ability to trade one's soul in exchange for fulfillment of their deepest, unspoken, innermost desires. Turns out, it's where most people pick up their ovetyr sentence without even realizing it. Ever heard of someone "making a deal with the devil"?

Consider the Sephiran the origin story of that phrase.

I usually spend most of my time in the shopping district, picking up tools that will best suit my needs for whatever sentence I've been called to attend to, but I hardly ever walk the streets of the events district. Everything about it makes my stomach turn. With that said, though, I care more about finding Lilith than my potential discomfort, so I slip out of the alleyway and onto the cobblestone street. I haven't even walked a block when I dodge some seedy characters trying to lure me into another—much *darker*—alleyway, as well as some pools of blood that haven't been hosed down yet. At second glance, the difference in color tells me that the street has probably *never* been hosed down. I make a mental note to throw these shoes away the minute I return to *The Ivory Stallion.*

My stroll takes me past gambling tents, fighting rings, grow operations, and warehouses full of weaponry with armed guards stationed around the perimeter. All the while, I keep my eyes peeled for any sign of Lilith. It doesn't help that nearly everyone is wearing black, or some variation of it, so I'm forced to strain my eyes more than I'd like. I catch a glimpse of a cloaked figure emerging from one of the tents, but quickly come to discover it's a man. My pace is just fast enough to keep anyone from speaking to me, but also slow enough to observe my surroundings.

It doesn't take long to reach the end of the street, and the district as a whole. I look to my left, back toward the shopping district, then to my right which is . . . well, I'm not sure, actually. But it's lined with dim, flickering streetlamps and there's a road that leads *somewhere.* Knowing that it can't be worse than what I've just ventured through, I decide to walk it.

The curve of the road throws me for a loop, seeing as the district streets are straight and quite narrow, but as I wind along the pathway, a sense of ease and familiarity washes over me. When I arrive at what appears to be a park, that feeling is only heightened. While it may not be your average park and more of a Tim Burton-esque graveyard for plant corpses, I'll take it over the Sephiran's events district any day. I stick to the outskirts of its rectangular shape, realizing that it's maybe half the size of a football field. Through the leafless branches of the trees and bushes, I spot an odd structure at the opposite end of the grounds. Curiosity pulls me forward, but not enough to have me walking straight down the middle in plain sight.

I remove the hood of my cloak and turn over my shoulder every few steps, just to be sure I'm not being followed. Paranoia is not something I usually entertain, but tonight is different knowing that Lilith is also here.

Only when a strange fog rolls in does it dawn on me that, of all the times I've visited the Sephiran, I've never noticed any "weather". To me, it's always felt like a veil between our so-called "reality" and the otherworld—a liminal space of existence. There are times when it doesn't feel real here, just as it doesn't feel real *out there*. Our senses will have us believe that because we're able to observe our physical surroundings while having the capacity to also experience them, that life *must* be real when, in fact, it's the opposite. Individual experiences are only perceivable by the person experiencing them. In that sense, perhaps "reality" is actually just *conditioned familiarity.* Remove the familiar conditions and creature comforts and what really remains?

I make my way through the dense fog, hoping that wherever I'm headed will lead *somewhere* and not just dump me out at a dead end. What lies ahead only grows darker and more ominous with each step I take, which is something I didn't think possible in a place like this. I narrow my eyes, doing my best to focus on the oddly shaped structure that's slowly coming into view.

Inch by inch, it reveals itself, nearly convincing me that it has a consciousness of its own. Like weathered wallpaper, each layer has been stripped away to ultimately unveil its original condition. It's a mausoleum of epic proportions—if I had to guess, it's been here for hundreds of generations . . . *thousands*, even. Most mausoleums I've seen are made of granite but, as I draw closer, I can see that there's something different about this one. It seems to be made of mud-brick and stone, and is quite reminiscent of the architecture of Egyptian tombs.

Captivated by its beauty, I decide to venture inside. I pull my lighter from my pack of cigarettes and flick it on, unable to hide my gasp as I observe the walls to the left and right of me. Hieroglyphs cover every inch of the space. I'm tempted to run my hand over them, to really *feel* the history, but preservation wins out. I'm moving in a circle, investigating, when I hold my arm out in front of me. The flame from the lighter flickers then steadies, revealing just how massive this chamber actually is. Not only that, but it looks like it . . . descends.

Holy shit. It's a crypt.

I continue my trek along the hallowed hall, careful not to accidentally brush up against anything. I intend to leave it exactly as I found it—as one should do with *any* ancient artifacts. Along the way, I notice a point in the walls where the hieroglyphs are no longer visible but seem to have been replaced by runes. *Gaelic runes.* I bring the flame closer, recognizing Norse symbology that then leads into Celtic sigils and Neo-Pagan references. As I climb down the surprisingly sturdy staircase, it's clear that this isn't just a crypt from a singular period in history, but an inclusive time capsule of them *all*.

I try to recall from my hours of research at the library what this place might be, but the texts I've managed to get my hands on have all said the same thing: that each era has its own unique location, its corresponding artifacts having been discovered at the site to further substantiate the claim. Never have I heard of, seen, or even remotely *imagined* that a smorgasbord crypt, such as the one I'm currently exploring, could even exist. It seems physically impossible.

Which brings me back to my original question . . .

What is actually *real?*

Now that my curiosity is piqued, I pick up the pace, intrigued by the prospect of what awaits at the end of this stairwell. Tombs? Caskets? Even more seemingly never-ending chambers? The possibilities are endless.

What I *wasn't* expecting, by any stretch of the imagination, was an immense cavern filled with water. The stairs lead to a pier, of which there is only one, that overlooks the near-idle pond. At the edge are two torches, which I light immediately to reveal an intricately carved canoe that's tied off at my feet. Off in the distance, I'm able to make out dozens of monument-like structures.

"What the hell is this place?" I whisper to myself. I move in a slow circle, gazing at my surroundings in complete awe, the boat beckoning the potential voyage ahead, should I choose to take it. I'm seriously considering it when I hear something.

Footsteps.

With all my senses on high alert, I quickly scan the area for a potential hiding place. My choices are slim: either I can try to blend in with the background behind the pier, *or* I can dip into the water and hide underneath it. If I turn back now, there's a good chance I'll run into whoever's approaching—and I'm too curious to see not only what happens next, but *who* this person is.

Having made my choice, I blow out the torches and step to the edge of the pier before gently lowering myself into the water. I don't bother to remove my cloak, my shoes, or any other item of clothing—again, where would I hide them?

Luckily, the water is lukewarm and not a temperature that would have me risking hypothermia. It's also just shallow enough to where it only reaches the middle of my neck. I duck underneath the wooden beams, feeling around in the dark for the center. I gingerly grab the rafter above me and take a deep breath. The footsteps draw closer.

I'm expecting them to continue onto the dock when there's a pause. Silence falls around the cavern, save for the lapping of water against the boat. *Shit.* When I'd arrived, the water had nearly resembled glass—a regular visitor here would certainly sense that something's amiss.

I continue to hold my breath, hoping that whoever's up there will carry on with their plans, regardless. The footsteps start up again, but they're slow, measured . . . *calculated.* A shadow passes over the slits in the beams. I strain my eyes, but it's still too dark to see anything. There's a *tink* of metal— a Zippo lighter, I realize—as light suddenly floods the front of the pier.

The stranger is so far ahead now that there's no use looking through the beams. As much as I want to monkey-bar my way closer, the sudden movement in the water would surely give me away. So, as much as it pains me, I stay put.

The rustling of rope and subsequent *thud* on the dock indicates that whoever's above me has done this before—and is about to take a ride. I lower my shoulders into the water even more, until my chin and lips are fully submerged. At this level, I'll be able to catch a glimpse of whoever's in the boat, so long as they row straight. That'll also give me the opportunity to move to the front and hopefully get a closer look.

I watch as one foot lands in the boat, followed by the other. They're pushing off now, but not before a long-winded whisper—a chant? While I may not be near enough to hear it, I am close enough to *see* what happens next. The carvings on the boat begin to illuminate in a magnificent display of indigo and violet. In that moment, all the symbols I'd observed on the walls instantly come to life in a way that can only be described as mesmerizing. Transfixed, I begin to draw closer but stop myself when I realize the canoe hasn't moved yet.

Patience, Maren.

There's an audible sigh, as if disappointed the trap hadn't yielded its prey, but I still can't tell if it's a man or a woman. Finally, the canoe leaves the dock, the symbols shining on in their brilliance, leaving their temporary mark in the water's reflection. I wait for the ripples from the oar to reach me before moving forward. When I do, I stay back just enough so as to not poke my head out and blow my cover.

As I'd hoped, the slender frame steering the boat is cloaked in the same garb as I am, which can only mean one thing: like me, Lilith is one of the Sephiran's regulars. *But,* it would seem she's a bit more experienced in this arena, seeing as, until today, I didn't know a place like this even existed. What remains unclear is *what* this place is and why she's here . . . two things I doubt mere observation will yield the answers to.

The canoe glides across the water, headed directly for one of the stone monuments. It stands at least ten stories tall and, while I can't see as clearly as I'd like from my current vantage point, if I had to guess, there are probably markings etched into them, too, just like everything else in this place.

Lilith arrives at the edge of her chosen monument. I'm glad it's near the front and not the back, otherwise I'd be shit out of luck. She raises her left arm into the air, followed by her right, and then throws her head back. I can tell she's speaking aloud by the way her chest and shoulders move, but, of course, I can't actually hear what she's saying.

It doesn't take long, however, for the monument to begin to shake, as if the crypt itself has suddenly been hit by an earthquake. Light streams up, up, up from the seemingly endless body of water, illuminating the structure's symbols in the same indigo and violet hues as the boat.

I'm not sure what to expect next, but certainly not this: the monument essentially cracks in half to allow her through before stitching itself together again. It dawns on me that each monument must be a portal—and, if the hieroglyphs, runes, and other symbols are any indication, that would mean each monument is a gateway to a specific period in time. *I'm in a time-traveling crypt.*

This is how Lilith got here. This is how she was able to reach Brant. And either she's gone back to where she originally came from, *or* she's continuing her business meeting with others who are in a similar position . . .

Is it possible, then, that I, too, could visit other timelines? Parallel realities? Other dimensions? Past lifetimes, even? Time is merely a construct, so I don't see why not. And if *Lilith* is who I believe her to be . . . then the answer to these questions is a resounding *yes*.

A flicker of hope sparks in my chest. I swim to the edge of the pier and, after a few efforts, heave myself onto it. I'm lying face down, trying to catch my breath, when I notice the boat heading back in this direction, captain-less. Based on what I've just seen, I'm assuming it's enchanted, which means that as much as I want to board it *right now*, I probably shouldn't. I don't know the incantation, nor do I have any idea what each monument stands for. All things considered, it isn't enough to stop me. I step into the boat, gazing at the vast chamber. As I'd suspected, it doesn't move, not even when I grab the oar and try rowing. It doesn't light up either.

Determined not to feel disappointed, I hop back onto the pier. I take a mental snapshot of the monument Lilith had disappeared into. I have no idea how I plan to accomplish a feat like this, but I trust that I'll figure it out.

I always do.

I hop down from the wooden pier, kicking up dust once I'm back on the dirt landing, then climb up the stairwell. I take my time passing by each of the walls—or the different eras of time, rather—just in case something jumps out at me. But the symbols are just as cryptic as the crypt itself.

When I finally reach the main section of the mausoleum, I take one last look at its interior, but there's nothing hinting at how to access the portals—nothing I'd recognize, anyway. It's on my way out, however, that I do notice something familiar. Something I've seen recently. At the top of the mausoleum is a crest . . .

With three crows.

I examine each of the beaks.

A key. A ring. A serpent.

The crest belongs to the Sable Coven.

This is who I need to find if I want answers. And even though I may not personally know any of their members or where to find them, I know someone who might. I check my watch and smile. Lucky for me, Madame Viessa opens shop in just a couple hours' time.

16

I ARRIVE AT Madame Viessa's storefront thirty minutes before opening, surprised to see that the sign that hangs on the front door has been flipped to "open". I pull on the handle to find that the door is indeed unlocked, and that this isn't one of the Madame's typical harebrained moments. The little bell jingles as I step inside, the door swinging shut behind me.

"Be with you in a moment!" a familiar voice shouts from the back.

I don't waste any time as I make for the area of the shop that holds the book about the Sable Coven. I search far and wide for that deep purple cover, the crest imprinted on my brain, but it seems to be missing . . . or worse, sold.

I'm so engrossed in this possibility that I don't even notice Madame Viessa's presence until she says, "Seems you have something quite particular in mind."

My hand snaps to my chest as I make a sound that falls somewhere between a wheeze and a gasp. "You startled me."

Madame Viessa surveys the shelves, her glassy eyes full of contempt. "What is it you're looking for?" She steps in front of the shelves that house the ancient texts, her frame so wide, it blocks my view of the titles. It doesn't take a genius to figure out that the movement is intentional.

"Something caught my eye during my last visit. It was in passing." I bite my lower lip at the half-truth. "It was a book. About the Sable Coven." I revert to that moment in my mind as best I can, trying to recall the exact title of it. "It was called *Legends of . . .* or *Sable Lore . . .*"

"*Legends & Lore of the Sable Coven,*" Madame Viessa says without hesitation. "What about it?"

I peek around her, but she instantly straightens in an effort to maintain eye contact. "I'm interested in purchasing it."

The woman raises a brow, then clicks her tongue against the roof of her mouth. "You're not the only one, it seems. I'm afraid you're too late."

"Someone else has purchased it?"

She nods.

"Who was it?"

She tilts her head curiously. "Do you really think that's something I can disclose?"

I stare her down, willing her to reveal what she knows, but she doesn't budge in the slightest. "Well, then, do you happen to have another copy in stock?"

Madame Viessa laughs—no, not laughs . . . *cackles*. "I do. But it isn't for sale."

As it always does with this woman, my patience is wearing thin. "Why not?"

Madame Viessa takes me by the arm and leads me away from the bookshelves and toward the door. "My dear child, I don't think you understand. That book is not mass produced nor is it available for just anyone to buy."

I stop walking, forcing her to do the same. "But it's in your shop . . . and you *sell* things here, including books."

"That I do," she says, lowering her voice, "but there's a reason why some things are under lock and key." She angles her head back in the direction of the bookshelves. "I have agreements in place where I sometimes . . . *hold* items for my patrons. Items that aren't explicitly for sale but are more for safekeeping."

I scoff. "And you just leave them out in the open like that? For everyone to see?"

"Did you leaf through it?"

I think back to my last visit. "No, but I assumed—"

"Well, you assumed wrong." The woman's tone is curt.

I lower my voice an octave to match hers, nearly gritting my teeth as I say, "But you *do* have another?"

"A copy, yes. But it's currently in the process of being transcribed and rebound with additional information."

"By whom?"

"By me, of course."

I blink, mouth agape. If there's one thing I know about witches and covens from all the lifetimes I've incarnated in, it's that their grimoires are *sacred*. No one outside of the coven is granted access to read it, let alone transcribe it. Which has me thinking only one thing . . .

"*You're* a member of the Sable Coven?"

The Madame's eyes glimmer with delight. "I am an Elder, yes."

Jackpot. I nearly jump out of my boots to hug the woman, suddenly feeling an urgent need to retract any disrespect I've shown her today or in the past. "I'm honored," I say, quickly changing my tune. "Truly honored."

The woman doesn't say anything as she releases my arm and begins walking back to the register. Her response has me feeling very out of place and quite unwelcome but, even so, I force myself through the discomfort and follow her.

"Actually," I say, knowing that I might be pushing my luck, "I was hoping that you might be able to help me."

Her eyes flick to me, razor sharp. "With what?"

My breath hitches in my throat at the realization that I don't know how to even begin to *approach* that question with everything I've experienced in the past forty-eight hours. Can I tell her about what I do for a living? About Brant? About *Lilith?* And what about the Sephiran and the time-traveling crypt? Yes, this woman might be an Elder of her coven, but what I'm about to lay on her is so far beyond comprehension that not even her stature can make it make sense. Hell, *I'm* still trying to make it make sense.

The front door jingles. *Shit, another customer.* I need to think fast *and* play my cards right. "Have you ever been to *The Ivory Stallion?*"

Madame Viessa eyes me warily. "A time or two."

"So you know Charlie?"

She nods. "I do."

I lean into the counter, lowering my voice to a whisper as I ask, "And has Charlie ever given you a tour of the place? Taken you into the cellar, perhaps?"

The way her mouth curls into a smile tells all.

"The Sephiran," she murmurs, pointing her finger at me before shaking it in the air. "I suspected as much. Hard not to with your exceedingly large and frequent purchases of mugwort."

"Then you know of . . ." My voice trails off as I realize I don't know the name of the crypt, or even the district it's in.

"The park," she says, seeming to read my mind. "You entered the park."

"I entered more than just the park," I say, egging her on.

She blanches. "You . . . entered Mohra?"

Mohra. They must be the same thing. As far as I know, there's no district or shop or event in the Sephiran by that name.

"The mausoleum?" I say to clarify.

Her eyes are wide now, but she doesn't leave me hanging. She nods. "But how?"

"I sort of just . . . stumbled upon it. I—"

She doesn't wait to hear more before grabbing my arm, yet again, to pull me toward the back of the store.

"What about your other customer . . .?"

She lets out a small hiss before dropping my arm and hurrying to the front. I watch in amusement as she rushes a woman, who's about my age, out the door. A string of apologies follows before she locks it and flips the sign from "open" to "closed". She scurries back to where I'm standing, rubbing her palms together as she says, "Follow me. And keep talking."

"That's just it, I don't know much about it—"

"But you traveled the waters? By canoe?"

"I *saw* the canoe," I clarify. "And the water. And all of these beautiful, intricately carved monuments—"

"You did not travel, then?"

"I couldn't," I say, not sure whether to bring Lilith into this. "I stepped into the boat, but it wouldn't budge." Another half-truth. Let's hope this one works in my favor.

Madame Viessa stops just outside the plum-colored curtain that leads to the back of the store. She narrows her eyes at me. "Did you just expect it to . . . float on its own?"

I nearly recoil under her gaze. "There was an oar that I tried to use, but I'm telling you, the boat wouldn't move." I don't dare mention how I know that the whole place is enchanted and that I saw Lilith herself speak an incantation to activate said enchantments. Especially because I haven't the slightest inkling if there's any history between Lilith and the Sable Coven. It feels like I'm actually getting somewhere with Madame Viessa—that I'm talking to someone who *knows* something—and I'm not about to fuck that up.

The Madame's gaze only grows more lethal by the second, so I quickly formulate how to reveal what I know without *actually revealing* what it is I know. "The reason I'm here is because I saw your crest. At the top of the mausoleum. I noticed it on the way out." All truthful. "I recognized it from my last visit here, the emblem that was on the book I asked about. I thought that, perhaps, the two were connected somehow—that the Sable Coven either built or presides over the mausoleum and everything inside of it."

Madame Viessa is silent, but her eyes don't leave mine. She wants to see if I'm lying. It's a good thing I'm not.

Finally, after the most intense staring contest of my life, she says, "It is true. My coven bears great responsibility over Mohra."

There's that word again. "What exactly *is* Mohra?"

"It is the gateway to all time," she says simply. "Past, present, and future—all existing at once."

"And the boat is a means to . . . travel through time?"

"In a word, yes."

Her response is like music to my ears. "And can anyone travel? Or just members of your coven?"

"We may be the Gatekeepers of Mohra, but we do not travel. That was part of the deal."

"But someone like me?" I try to keep my tone even. "Could I travel?"

"Potentially." I expect her to elaborate, but she doesn't.

"What would be required of me to do so?"

"Well, first, we'd need to know *why*—what your intentions are."

Which is exactly what I've been afraid of. Having to reveal my status here and what I do . . . it's not something to be known by just anyone. But, then again, I'm not talking to *just anyone*—I'm talking to an Elder of the Sable Coven, the very gatekeepers of Mohra.

"Well?" she presses.

I can't lie to her. Not about this. Not when Brant's livelihood is at stake . . . or mine. *No more half-truths, Maren.* With that in mind, I launch into the story I've never dared utter to a single soul.

Madame Viessa stares at me in complete silence. She hasn't said a word since I finished my entire life story—about being a Noire, about Brant being my Sigard, and about how Brant himself might very well be serving his ovetyr sentence in this lifetime . . . I'd decided to omit Lilith's role in all of this, at least for now. And that's probably because not even *I* know what it is.

We're sitting near the back of the store at a circular table where the Madame reads fortunes, surrounded by crystals, tarot decks, pendulums, and an array of other divination tools I'm only partially familiar with. The lengthy silence that drags on between us is becoming increasingly uncomfortable, so I reach for a blue and gold gilded deck, but not before the Elder swats my hand away.

"Don't touch," she orders.

"That's it?" I glare at her. "After everything I've just told you, that's all you have to say?"

Her tawny eyes grow shadowed yet unencumbered by my words. "I'm thinking."

I want to tell her to *think faster* but, by the grace of some unseen force, I manage to keep my mouth shut. Insulting this woman won't do me any good, this I know; but the longer she takes to respond, the more I'm questioning what I've just done. Everything I've just told her.

She reaches for an obsidian-tipped pendulum, the chain sliding through her wrinkled fingers. After it spins clockwise, counterclockwise, and a few other directions that are difficult to determine from where I'm sitting, she finally says, "If you travel, you must declare that you will not, under any circumstances, change *anything.* You will also need permission from the other Elders, as well as the High Priestess. There will be a ritual involved, one that is not for the faint of heart."

Did this woman not just hear what I do for a living?

"As long as you meet *all* of these conditions, you will be permitted to travel through Mohra, to any five timelines you desire," the Madame finishes. "But, be warned that what you find may change the very fabric of this reality upon your return."

I nod, just wanting to get on with it. "How long until I can travel?"

Disdain radiates from her lifted brow, as if my choosing not to heed her warning will be the end of us both. "That depends entirely on you. Behave like this, and I can almost guarantee safe passage will not be granted at all."

I sit back in my chair. "If my behavior is that atrocious, then why are you helping me?" A risky question, but the need to assert myself boils violently beneath my veins.

Much to my surprise, though, her brows fall and her expression softens. "Because an ovetyr sentence is eternal. You seek answers, as any sane person would. Without trust between a Noire and a Sigard, what is there, really? It would cause a collapse in your line of work, and what happens in one timeline affects them all." She pauses, smirking before she adds, "Not to mention, I can't keep you from walking the path you're already on. No one can."

"Except for the other Elders and the High Priestess, apparently."

"There are many ways a path can be taken. Walk. Run. Fly. Row. Detours and shortcuts often circle right back to what's already been laid out for each of us."

To me, what it *sounds* like is that my trip to Mohra is a sure thing, regardless of the Coven members, their decision, and this elusive ritual—but I don't dare say that out loud. It seems there is a sort of game to be played here . . . and if it's going to take me where I want to go, then I'm more than willing to play.

"When can I meet with your coven?"

"The Full Moon is in three days. We'll send word then."

"Send word? How?"

"Just keep an eye on your window at dusk."

Before I can get her to explain further, she pushes away from the table and stands. "Now, if you'll excuse me, I've lost enough business for one day." She releases the pendulum, then grabs my wrist and turns it faceup before dropping into my hand a smooth, polished black stone with a rune etched into it. The gold letter is in the shape of an R. I recognize it immediately. *Raidho.*

"Until you receive word, keep this on you at all times," she says as I curl my fingers around the stone. "After that, you can do with it what you will."

Speechless, I watch her walk to the front of the store. Once she's out of sight, I glace at my palm, tracing the gold mark with my thumb. From what my scattered research has revealed, *Raidho* symbolizes motion, transportation, *the journey.* On a larger scale, it is representative of the human path, leading by example, and the power of our actions; the ordered movement of energies in time and space as it pertains to our awareness.

I smile, cupping the rune in my hand before pocketing it. I rise from the table and make a beeline for the front, hardly noticing just how many people I've had to weave through to reach the door. I don't bother to look around for Madame Viessa or bid her adieu, as I'm sure I'll be seeing her in just three days' time. In the meantime, though, I've got some serious Noire work to catch up on.

17

I ARRIVE HOME to an additional three folders on my doorstep, all marked in the upper right-hand corner with thick red tape. I sigh, opening each one of them to reveal the exact same assignment over and over again—the one I still haven't completed due to the fact that I may no longer be able to trust my Sigard.

With the folders tucked underneath one arm, I jimmy my key into the lock and turn it, then shoulder my way into the door. I fling the files onto the counter, cursing as they slide across the slick surface and onto the floor . . . which is honestly where I should have tossed them to begin with.

I remove layer after layer of clothing, feeling the exhaustion settle in as I peel each one off. At this point, I've been awake for more than twenty-four hours. Not only am I physically drained from my visit to the Sephiran, but I'm also emotionally drained after everything that's transpired with Brant . . . not to mention, mentally drained from all the new information I've had hurled at me. Whereas I couldn't drift off to sleep before, I have a feeling that now will be a totally different story.

I throw on a worn, oversized t-shirt and some joggers before crawling straight into bed. I pull the covers tight around me and turn onto my side, creating a blanket cocoon that I never want to leave. No longer am I the caterpillar, desperate to wriggle free, but instead, the corpse of a butterfly that has already succumbed to its fate of eternal rest.

With that image in mind, I let out a long, blissful sigh, knowing that, if I really wanted to, I could stay in this exact spot for the next three days until the full moon waxes. Yes, the folders may pile up even more urgently, and yes, there may be consequences to those actions, but right now?

I don't care.

Right now, all I want is the *uncomplicated* human experience—more specifically, that singular moment just before sleep pulls you under. After you've already wound through the bullshit of the day and played out the probable events of tomorrow before once again reclaiming your peace of mind. That everything is only as it seems and that nothing has meaning except the meaning we decide to give it—and it's that comforting notion that carries me right into a deep, deep sleep.

The pool of crimson at my feet is the first indication that I am not awake, but in a dream. A *lucid* dream.

The blood seeps into the forest floor, transforming flaky dirt into fertile soil. I scan my feet and legs, my hands and arms, looking for the source of the blood, but I am unmarred. Unscathed. I lift my chin and slowly turn my head. Thick, patchy trunks of coniferous trees stand at every corner, swaying at every bend. Pinecones still attached to thin branches litter the ground. There is no one here but me, and yet I can feel their presence everywhere . . .

The Sable Coven.

"I've done what's required," I hear myself say. "I only ask that my request be fulfilled."

Snickering sounds from the brush, but when I scan the dense greenery, not a soul is in sight.

"I have done what is required," I repeat, my voice quaking this time. "I demand what I am owed."

The tree behind me creaks and groans. Above me, the sound of wood cracks like bone snapping after a terrible accident. I step to the side just before a branch comes hurtling to the ground, the pine needles whistling in the wind. It crashes into the earth, but nature holds steady. The forest floor does not bend or quake at the impact but instead rises taller, as if growing hands to hold this new addition.

Raidho, the whispers begin to chant, growing louder and more forceful. *Raidho! Raidho! Raidho!*

I go to dig my hands into my pockets, but quickly realize that I'm wearing a sheer white linen and nothing more. *The rune. I left the rune!* I circle frantically in place, unable to move forward or backward, only side to side.

The chanting grows so loud it threatens to take my sanity along with it. I drop to my knees, the linen doing very little to protect the sharp edges of the twigs and branches that are now digging mercilessly into my skin. I press my palms to my ears and bow my head into my arms, doing whatever I can to regain my focus.

Wake up, Maren. Wake up!

The forest is filled with angry chanting now. Regardless of how hard I press against the sides of my head to shut it out, I can still hear it all, reverberating in the back of my skull like a bad song. I open my mouth to scream, but even that is dwarfed by the sheer magnitude of the voices around me. They engulf my pain, my agony, my despair, as if it were feeding them. Every morsel that I give, they take and take and take.

It's then I sense her.

The woman in white.

She isn't alone this time. No, she's with someone all too familiar. Talon-like nails grip Brant's neck, urging him forward. He looks worried, *afraid,* which is not an expression he wears often—in fact, this might just be a first. His eyes widen as the claws tighten around his skin before he's forced to his knees. He collapses from the sheer force, but his head remains upright, however painful and unnecessary.

I'm about to speak his name when the woman in white lifts her other hand, this one less claw-like and more human-looking. I look from her to Brant, once again wishing that she'd remove her cloak so I can see her face.

Trust, a voice slithers around me, not female or male, but not quite human either. It sounds more like an echo in a vast chamber.

"Please," Brant seems to say, but I quickly realize he hasn't said anything. I've only read his lips, his desperate plea to be removed from this woman's clutches.

I can't take my eyes off him. "I . . ."

In little more than a blink, an enormous oak tree suddenly takes root, towering over me, over *us*. I notice yet another inconsistency that wasn't there before—a hole in the ground right next to Brant. It's rectangular, about eight feet in length . . . I know exactly what it is. It's his grave. What's even worse is that there's no headstone. *An unmarked grave.*

I can't think of anything more demoralizing.

Brant glances at the hollow pit, eyes growing wide as he eventually sets his gaze on mine. This time, he does speak— and it's his voice. I'm certain of it.

"I'm so sorry."

It's a confusing sentiment because I don't know what it is he's apologizing for, but I'm not given the luxury of time to think on it further. The woman in white releases her grip around Brant's neck, but not before pushing him off balance. His right shoulder leading the way, he falls side-first, the void seeming to swallow him whole.

I shout, starting to run toward them, but my legs won't move, as if they've suddenly been encased in quicksand. But when I look down, I see only the same dirt and moss-covered ground. "Brant!" I yell, my voice hoarse.

There's no response.

I turn a lethal gaze onto the perpetrator.

As above, so below, the voice hisses.

I don't have a chance to respond as the earth begins to quake beneath me, the dirt vibrating at a dizzying speed. Before I can really register what's happening, it lifts from the ground and drifts over to the open grave, burying him alive.

"Brant!" I scream again, unable to move. "Brant!"

Just when I think I can't take any more, a loud banging yanks me from the dream. I jolt upright, my neck and shoulders protesting as they cling to the sheets. Sweat beads at my hairline, my upper lip, underneath my arms . . . I'm trying to recall what's just happened when even more banging reminds me why I'm here. How I woke up.

I stumble out of my bedroom, using the front of my shirt to dry my face. A shiver creeps down my spine as I lay a hand on the door and press my ear against it. "Announce yourself," I say, breathless and groggy.

"Maren fucking Cordeau, open the damn door! Now!"

Brant. Honestly, he's both the first *and* last person I want to see right now—how that's even possible, I don't know, but I'm glad he's here and that he's okay. *It really was just a dream,* I assure myself. I unlock the door and swing it open. One look from him tells me that I look *way* worse than I feel.

"Cosmos above, what happened to you?"

"Nice to see you, too." I wave him inside but when he doesn't move, I grab his arm and pull him across the threshold. "I just woke up."

"From death?"

I scoff, wondering how it could possibly be that bad . . . but then I catch my reflection in the microwave door. The image staring back at me isn't as crisp as a mirror, but it doesn't need to be. I'm as white as a ghost—whiter, even—and my raven-colored hair is plastered to my face and neck while somehow also sticking out every which way. I lean in even closer to see that my eyes are bloodshot and that a deep purple hue is settling nicely around my lids. I immediately go to the kitchen sink, turn on the faucet, and splash some cold water on my face.

Brant watches me from the entryway, and I can tell he's waiting for me to get my bearings before laying into me. With my hands pressed against the edge of the sink, I slowly turn only my head toward him. I can feel the droplets of water as they glide down my skin and onto the neckline of my shirt.

"What are you doing here?" It's then I notice what he's carrying—six manila folders. That's two more than I have.

He must notice the pile that's already scattered on the kitchen floor—*I mean, how could he not?*—but he does the respectful thing and tosses them onto the counter. "I've been trying to reach you all day. Why haven't you been answering your phone?"

Still leaning over the sink, I press my chin into my arm, mumbling my response, "It's been a long day."

His eyes widen in bewilderment, but his voice is more concerned than anything else. "Maren . . . how long do you think it's been since we last . . .?" He trails off, but I know exactly what he's asking.

I straighten, swiveling my body toward the microwave to read the time. "Well, seeing as it's 6:30 in the morning, we just saw each other yesterday."

He takes a step toward me, looking even more concerned than before. "Maren, it's 6:30 *at night*. And it's two days after the fact." He taps two fingers against the stack of folders on the counter, then brushes back his hair in a way that's very unlike him. "I thought you were going to take care of this, but these keep showing up on my doorstep like clockwork. I know you need space, but you've never been one to forego your duties." He frowns, looking me up and down. "But I suppose the larger question at hand is . . . are you *okay*? Because you look like you've been on a bender in hell."

I hold up a palm to let him know I need a minute, then glance out the window behind me, trying to wrap my head around the fact that the darkness lingering there is due to the *night* and not the morning. True, I'd been awake for over twenty-four hours, but had I slept that long, too? And just how long had that strange dream lasted, exactly?

But that isn't what Brant's here for. It isn't because of the hassling with the manila folders or even to check in on me . . . it's because something's happened. Something *big*. I can read it in his body language, however odd it may appear to be—the guarded way in which he's standing, the nervous ticks of his hands and mouth, the shadowed expression he's wearing.

"What is it?" I ask, suddenly feeling on edge. "What's happened?"

"When I couldn't reach you, I decided to go to Madame Viessa's." He clears his throat, but it still cracks as he says, "When I got there, she was slouched over the counter, facedown in her own blood."

If it weren't for my firm grip on the counter, the buckling of my knees would have sent me straight to the floor. "She's dead." It doesn't come out as a question, but as an unwelcome realization.

"There's more." Brant shifts uncomfortably between his feet. "I know they say not to touch anything at the scene of a crime, but I noticed something peculiar." He strolls toward me, taking his phone from his pocket as he does. I'm still in shock when he flashes the screen at me.

It's horrendous. And coming from me, that's saying something.

"Whoever did this removed her eyes and wove a pendulum through the sockets. Her shoulders were dislocated, teeth removed, patches of her hair were missing—"

"Yes, I can see all of that," I snarl, instantly regretting my tone. "She was brutally tortured *not* in a nightmare, but in waking life."

Brant's about to lower the phone when my eye catches something it hadn't previously. "Hang on," I say, grabbing the device from his hand. I zoom in on the photo, at a small pool of blood that's separate from the rest . . . as if it were somehow *intentional.* Something had been marked in it and, although small, once I turn the phone upside down, I can see quite clearly that it's in the shape of an **R**.

Raidho.

I bring the phone away from my face and hold it out to the side, desperate to be rid of it. I press it into Brant's chest, causing him to nearly fumble it when I release my grip. "Fuck me," I say, running a hand through my hair as I begin to pace across the kitchen. "Fuck!"

"What is it?" He studies the image on the phone, turning it around as I had. "Why are you freaking out?"

"You really can't be here right now," I say, feeling the urge to throw everything in sight. "I can't risk getting you involved in this, too—" I clamp a hand over my mouth before I divulge too much. "Damn it!"

"Maren, this might be the only time I've said this and actually mean it, but you're on the verge of scaring me shitless. What the fuck is going on?"

I eye the front door, knowing that he's not going to leave until I give him an answer, but that he'll easily block me if I try to get past him. My gaze flicks to my bedroom door. Brant notices. Even so, I dash over to it, hoping to lock myself behind it if only for a few minutes, just so I can think.

But Brant storms after me, shoving past the flimsy barrier as if he were among the gods himself. I don't dare try to skate past him nor do I back myself into a corner, so I instead stand at the edge of the bed, arms crossed defiantly.

"I need you to give me a minute."

"And I need you to tell me what the fuck is going on."

I throw my hands in the air, not knowing where to begin. "Tell me you at least called the police, Colborn."

He bristles at my use of his last name. So casual, so disrespectful for a conversation like this. "I know better than to get involved with the authorities, you know that. But I did wait across the block until another unsuspecting patron entered and ran out of there crying. I heard her sobbing into the phone as she made the call."

My breath shudders. "Well, I'm happy you didn't just leave her there, undiscovered."

"I'm not a monster." Brant meets me in the middle of the room but doesn't touch me or try to console me. "And after what I've told you—"

"Don't," I say, flashing him a feral look. "I can't think about that right now. Especially since *knowing* about it is what got me into this whole mess." I close my eyes, recounting recent events—seeing Brant meeting with Lilith, unknowingly following her into the Sephiran and Mohra, wanting so badly to discover Brant's past (and my own) that I'd struck a deal with a coven of witches . . .

Brant searches my face, studying my every expression.

You need to tell him. You can deny it as much as you want, but he's already involved, a quiet voice tuts.

"That night we . . . well, you know," I stutter, cheeks flushing at the memory of our bodies pressed together, "I also wasn't entirely truthful. I saw you with Lilith. In the library." I let my arms fall to my sides, hoping that it'll somehow help me drop my guard at the same time.

His throat bobs, but he doesn't say anything.

"What I failed to tell you is that, before I saw you, I ran into her at the café, the one right next to the library. When I was on my way there. She gave the name Lilith for her order, which no one seemed to think twice about except for me." I shake my head, wishing I could erase the past seventy-two hours.

"Assuming she's *the* Lilith, when I saw you meet with her in the library, only the worst kinds of thoughts flooded my mind. I wanted to know more, but I knew I couldn't ask you." My heart hammers in my chest, but the words come out surprisingly steady and assured.

"When I couldn't sleep, I went to the Sephiran. Lilith was also there. I came across a place called Mohra, realizing that this is how Lilith had traveled to our timeline and how she probably travels to others." I turn my back to him, ashamed to admit what comes next. "I needed to know what had happened in your previous lifetimes, what you had offered up that might merit an ovetyr sentence. So, I went to Madame Viessa for help, to see if she knew how to travel safely across Mohra. And now—"

"And now she's dead."

I freeze at the familiar silky-smooth voice. I whirl around, hoping that it's just my imagination messing with me, but it isn't. Brant is no longer standing before me.

Lilith is.

A ruby-colored satin gown pools at her feet, its black lace detailing snaking up the sides into a magnificent display at the tops of her shoulders. The raised posterior collar only further accentuates her flawless ivory skin, untouched and unmarred by the elements. Raven-colored hair tumbles over her shoulders in waves, framing her face in a way that demands the utmost respect, regardless of the malevolence that lies beneath. Atop her head sits a horned crown made of bone, scales, and beaks.

She is, hands down, the most formidable woman I have ever encountered.

"I had a feeling I was being followed," she purrs, deviously floating across the room in a ribbon of red. "And by a Noire, no less."

The fact that she knows *what* I am momentarily throws me. "You . . . You're familiar with Noires and Sigards?"

Amused, she throws her head back in a laugh fit for a villain. "Of course. What exactly do you take me for? I'm familiar with every incarnation, every potential sentence, every *line of work* across all timelines." She flashes a lethal grin. "It is under my jurisdiction, after all."

The statement hits me like a freight train. For a moment, I'm disappointed in myself for not seeing just how obvious it is. Much like Lucifer, Lilith delights in the most extreme pleasures in life. Whether they're considered sinful or pure doesn't matter, doesn't even *exist,* actually, as all meanings for all things are merely perception.

"So, it *is* you. You're the one behind the sentencing?" I ask, trying to keep the intrigue out of my voice. "The one who *chooses* the souls gracing my manila folders?"

"Oh no, dear child. If only it were that easy. Alas, I cannot intervene with free will. And to a much larger degree, no one can."

"But you give them the option? To choose an eternal ovetyr sentence?"

A smile snakes across her face. "What is free will, really, without options?"

Hmm. "Is Madame Viessa really dead?"

"Yes." There isn't even the slightest bit of remorse in her voice.

"Were you the one who killed her?"

She looks me directly in the eye. "No. Have you not been listening to anything I've said?"

As much as my instincts are telling me to take everything she says with a grain of salt, there's another *larger* part of me that knows she's telling the truth. How's that for a paradox?

"Who did, then?"

She clicks her tongue against the roof of her mouth, smiling as she says, "Well, *that* is something I'm not at liberty to say. But what I can tell you is that the Sable Coven *will* be out for blood. And, if memory serves me well, Madame Viessa was one to keep *very* thorough records of her transactions." She grabs the glass jar of mugwort from a nearby shelf, shaking it for emphasis. "I certainly wouldn't want my name to be on that ledger. Do with that information what you will."

My name is most certainly on that ledger. And so is Brant's. And the fact that she was going to send word for me to meet with her coven the night of the full moon . . . *I'm going to be their number one suspect. I'm about to have an entire fucking coven of witches after me . . .*

I'm about to continue along that line of thought when it dawns on me that I have no idea where Brant is—if he was actually even here to begin with. "Where is Brant?"

She follows me into the kitchen as I hastily pull some different clothes on. "Why, he's exactly where you left him, Maren. Don't you recall?"

Hearing her say my name is unlike anything I've ever experienced. It makes me want to slit her throat *and* bow before her all at once. "No, I don't recall. That's why I'm asking. I haven't seen him in . . ."

And then it dawns on me, what she actually means.

He's exactly where you left him. Just like in my dream, I turn a lethal gaze on her.

Lilith sighs, completely unbothered as she picks underneath her long, triangular nails. "I've heard that dirt naps are rather nice this time of year—"

I don't wait to hear the rest as I rush out the door and head straight for the cemetery.

18

PLEASE DON'T BE DEAD.

It's the only thought I can think as I race across the slick streets, past the dog-walkers, the joggers, and the lines of cars crowding every traffic light. I push past the gates that lead to the cemetery, frantically scanning the grounds for an unmarked grave.

Was he buried alive?

Did I somehow do this?

Does this mean the dream was real?

Is Lilith the woman in white?

I can hardly focus on the task at hand with the incessant line of questioning bouncing around my head. I walk by plot after plot, headstone after headstone, feeling increasingly more helpless with each step I take. The bright flowers and *happy birthday* balloons mock me, the honoring of loved ones passed. Meanwhile, I'm over here scrambling to ensure that someone with a whole lot of life left doesn't end up suffocating underground.

I check another row. And another. And another.

I bite back a scream that's clawing at my throat, a cry of both frustration and desperation. I refuse to lose hope.

Please don't be dead please don't be dead please . . .

The bizarre dream I'd had was in a forest, not a cemetery. It would have been a hell of a lot easier had it taken place in the latter but, as dreams tend to do, they hardly ever line up with reality. I shouldn't be surprised.

How long has he been buried?

What if I'm too late?

What if he's dead?

The snarky part of my brain answers that question with, *Well, at least he's already where he'd end up anyway!,* causing me to silently sneer at myself and my wildly inappropriate sense of humor.

I switch gears to roaming the outskirts of the grounds, keeping an eye out for freshly raised dirt and patches of grass that have clearly been removed and replaced. I'm not having much luck when I spot the giant oak tree at the northwest corner of the property. *Of course.*

I rush over to it, internally cheering as my feet meet raised ground. I drop to my knees and pull at the patches of grass. They come off easily and in one piece. *This has to be it.*

I look at my hands, preparing myself to dig. Who am I kidding? That'll take all night and time is not a luxury I can afford right now. I'm on the verge of panicking even more when

I remember the old shed Brant and I always crack jokes about. I peer around the tree, spotting it just a few short strides away. I dash over to it, praying that the groundskeeper had his typical harebrained moment and left it unlocked.

He did.

I squeal, finally feeling like I'm making some headway, and grab the first shovel I see. I run back to the oak tree, the shovel swinging wildly at my side, as if I'm the villain in a corny adolescent Halloween special. Breathless, I arrive on the scene and begin digging, grunting with each push of metal into the damp ground. I'm beyond thankful for the recent rain and the fresh soil because I charge through that dirt like a well-oiled snowplow after a severe winter's storm.

Once I get deep enough below ground level, I move to what I hope are Brant's feet, so as to not keep digging and accidentally plunge the shovel right into his chest. I'm working around the edges when I spot a leather sole. I throw the shovel to the side and tug on the boot, just to be sure I'm not imagining things, and then begin digging with my hands, pushing dirt *down* the slope so that I can get to his head.

As the dirt loosens more and more, I can see movement from underneath it. I keep pushing the dirt away, ignoring the burning and aching in my arms. By some fucking miracle, sputtering sounds.

I did it.

I'm not too late.

He's not dead he's not dead he's not dead

I wipe the rest of the dirt from his face, nearly bursting into tears at the sea of green staring back at me. Brant takes in a long, labored breath just to cough and sputter again. Now that he can breathe, I move to where his chest should be, and then his legs, picking up the shovel again to move the dirt as far away from him as possible.

"Maren?" he rasps.

"You're okay," I say, focusing on the methodical strokes of the shovel. "You're okay."

"What the fucking hell . . . what is this?"

I can hear the panic in his voice, but I need to keep him calm so that he doesn't accidentally cave himself back in.

"Don't move," I instruct. "I'm almost finished."

"Did *you* do this?"

I stop shoveling. "Are you fucking kidding me right now?" I toss his saving grace to the side. "Why would I put you in here just to dig you right back up?" I reach my hand out to help him up.

He hesitates, but ends up taking it, shaking his legs before wriggling them free. "So, you *didn't* bury me alive?"

"Of course not," I say. "Although I did dream it."

I hoist myself up onto the ledge, hoping that Brant has enough strength to do the same. He takes the other side and jumps up with ease, not fatigued in the slightest.

"What do you mean you *dreamt* it?"

"Exactly what it sounds like. But your friend *Lilith* gave me a visit. She pretended to be you, actually. Had me fooled there for a second." I look him up and down, wondering if I look as hysterical as I feel. There's dirt in my hair, all over my face, underneath my nails and my clothes—I have dirt in places where dirt shouldn't be. *Try telling that to Brant.*

"Shit, Maren." Brant runs a hand down his face, only further smearing what's already there. "Are you serious?"

His admission answers one of my questions: Brant was definitely *not* in my apartment earlier—that was *all* Lilith. "Look, I'm just happy you're okay . . . which you are, right?" As I say this, I realize that he doesn't exactly look shaken up. He isn't trembling or panting—he isn't even breathing heavily. In fact, he's acting like this is just another common occurrence on a random weekday.

"We should probably get out of here. It's dark enough for us to leave without raising too much suspicion—even if it does look like we spent the evening robbing graves." He searches for a clean spot on his shirt, but there isn't one to be found.

I remove my jacket and hand it to him. "Here, throw this around your shoulders. You look way worse than I do. We'll head to my place since it's closest and get cleaned up."

Brant takes it, then glances at the grave. "What do we do about that?"

"Leave it," I say, already starting for the gates. "If you ask me, we just made their job a bit easier."

☠ ☠ ☠ ☠ ☠

Brant decides to get cleaned up in the sink while I hit the shower. By some grace of the gods, we'd managed to arrive back at my apartment without any nosy bystanders asking questions.

After I've thoroughly scrubbed the dirt from every nook and cranny of my body, I emerge from the bathroom wearing only a towel. I'm about to throw my pile of dirt-ridden clothes in the wash when I notice Brant, in only his boxers, drying his face and shoulders at the kitchen sink.

I clear my throat to announce my presence. "Shower's free." I angle my head toward his discarded clothes. "I'm about to do a load. Want me to add yours?"

He looks at me and nods but averts his eyes rather quickly once he realizes I'm in a towel. I walk toward him and scoop his clothes from the floor, cringing at the sodden mess, before opening the door that leads to the stacked washer and dryer. Once I've loaded everything and started the machine, I turn back around, my gaze settling on the counter—more specifically the rune strung on a length of black cord. Brant doesn't say anything as I join him in the kitchen. If there's one thing I know about him, it's that he does *not* wear necklaces of any kind.

"Where'd that come from?" I ask as nonchalantly as I can while shuffling through one of the cabinets.

Brant snaps out of his daze, then looks at the item to which I'm referring. "I . . . I don't know. Apparently, I was wearing it the entire time I was . . ." His voice trails off, but I can guess the ending of the sentence without him saying it.

Underground. Buried alive. Near death.

"May I?" At his nod, I drop the canister of coffee onto the countertop and slide over to the sink. Gently, I run my index finger over the tawny stone, tracing the indentation of a **Y**. "Algiz," I whisper, more to myself than to him. "It means protection. Defense. Instinct. The shape represents the horns of an elk, so it can also signify guardianship."

Brant lifts a brow, clearly impressed. "When did you become so well-versed in the meanings of runes?"

I shake my head, unable to answer because I myself don't even know. "They're Elder Futhark runes," I say hurriedly, rummaging through various coat pockets for the one Madame Viessa had given me. When I finally find it, I return to the kitchen and place them side by side. "Madame Viessa gave this to me before she . . ." I look up at him, paling at the fact that he doesn't know.

Brant searches my expression for clues. "Before she what?"

"Brant," I say, while turning him to face me and taking his hands in mine, "Madame Viessa was murdered. Earlier today."

He sucks in a sharp breath, his grip loosening. "What do you mean *murdered*? How? By whom?"

"I don't know," I say ruefully. "But I'm probably one of the last people who saw her alive. She gave me this rune, *Raidho*, after promising me that, with the help of her coven, she'd help me travel through Mohra." Déjà vu wraps around me as I recall having this very same conversation with Lilith *disguised* as Brant. "Everything was all set, and I was supposed to meet with them on the eve of the Full Moon—"

"That's tomorrow," Brant murmurs.

"It is," I confirm. "But I'm worried that word never reached the coven after Madame Viessa's death. And that I'm probably their number one suspect."

Brows furrowed, Brant pushes off from the sink, his muscles rippling with the motion. He still hasn't fully showered, but even covered in remnants of dirt and grime, he looks *damn* good. "I think I may have missed something—about Mohra?"

I bite my lower lip. "I suppose Mohra is a new concept to you, as it was to me."

He stalks around me, grabbing the kettle from the stove. "Do you still have those tea packets I left here?"

I nod. "They should be right where you left them." I point to the cabinet across from me. The silence yawns between us, save for the sound of running water.

He retrieves two packets, then sets the kettle back on the stovetop and turns on the burner. "I know what Mohra is," he finally says, "or, at least, I know it's what Lilith uses to visit her Sigards. But, I suppose the larger question is what *you're* wanting to use it for?"

I can't lie to him. Not after what's just happened. "I . . . well, I need more information about your ovetyr sentence."

Shadows cast around his eyes, darkening his entire face. "You know that I can't tell you that."

"I know." I hate how chipper I sound. "Which is why I'm using Mohra to travel to past timelines." The minute I say it, I realize just how creepy and borderline obsessive it sounds. "But not only for that," I add. "I want to know about my past lives, too."

He takes a slow step toward me, his mouth pulled taut. "This is dangerous, Maren. It isn't a good idea, by any means."

The kettle begins to whistle and, much like the water inside, I feel like I'm also on the verge of spilling over. "Don't you understand? I can't fulfill my duties as a Noire without being able to trust my Sigard!"

The pleading in his eyes is unbearable. "We've made it this far, haven't we?" He reaches for my hand, but I hastily pull back. "Can't you trust that?"

I want to. So badly it hurts. But I can't. I bow my head in solemn response.

He sighs, remorse filling the air as he says, "I'm not permitted to say anything about my ovetyr sentence to anyone. That's why Lilith came here in the first place. She foresaw our conversation and came to warn me. But, even so, I didn't heed her warning—at least not entirely." His eyes glimmer with sincerity. "The fact that you're even aware of what we may or may not have discussed goes against every last law and regulation of the Noire-Sigard relationship. Isn't that enough for you to trust me?"

How I wish it were. But what he doesn't understand is that for every nightmare I invoke in the future, the only person I'll be able to see in my well-devised torture chamber is *him*. Which makes it near impossible to do my job the way it's supposed to be done.

I gently lay a hand on his cheek. "I respect your decision. Truly, I do. I'm also asking that you respect mine."

He brings his hand over top of mine, then turns his face inward and presses a soft kiss to my palm. "Whatever you come to discover, please don't forget us. *This*." He squeezes my hand before removing it from his face and gingerly places it back at my side.

Head down, he retreats to the bathroom. I grab the edge of my towel, trying to process what he's just said. It's as if he already knows there's something unpleasant in our history. But how? Why would he remember and not me? Something's off.

And I don't like it at all.

The washer slows to a low rumble before coming to a stop altogether. I throw the load of laundry into the dryer and turn the knob to *high heat* before changing into a fresh pair of pajamas. I'm about to relax on the couch when I decide to circle back to the kitchen and swipe the runes from the counter. A million questions flood my mind.

Who had buried Brant?

Had it been Lilith?

The Sable Coven?

If this protection rune is any indication, I'd assume it was the latter. But why? As a warning to me? He'd been buried alive and left for dead yet also provided a rune to guarantee his protection. Honestly, it sounds like the kind of stunt I would pull. If lifetime after lifetime has taught me anything, it's that there's *always* a loophole.

Padded footsteps pull me from my thoughts as Brant appears with a towel wrapped around his waist. I can't help but stare at his chest, his arms, that lovely V-shape that leads to his—

"Are the clothes dry?" He smirks, knowing he's caught me at the precise moment my mind was entering the gutter.

I flick my gaze to his. "See for yourself."

He sets his hands on his hips, only further accentuating everything I'd been staring at previously, then whistles as he turns to open the door. From behind it, his towel drops to the ground. I roll my eyes and laugh, knowing exactly what he's trying to do.

"What's so funny?"

"Your desperate attempt at wooing me."

He pokes his head out from behind the door, still shirtless. "Who said I was trying to woo you?"

I angle my head toward the ground. "The towel."

"Funny," he says, disappearing again, "I didn't know inanimate objects could talk."

The door closes and I try to hide my disappointment once I see that he's fully dressed. "You're not staying?"

He tilts his head, eyes alight with curiosity. "You want me to? Even after . . . everything?"

Embarrassed, I lower my gaze. I'm being hypocritical and I know it. "I shouldn't, but I do."

"But you don't trust me."

I squeeze my eyes shut with a sigh. "Should I rescind my offer, then?"

He drops his shoulders, in resignation or defeat, I can't tell. "I would very much like to stay."

"Good." I don't know if I mean it, which makes it the most confusing word I've ever uttered.

"There's just one problem, though." He looks down at his clothes. "I didn't come prepared."

I flash a devious smile. "Sure you did. It's underneath all that." I make a circular motion with my hand at the lower half of his body.

"Seems it was a waste of time getting dressed then."

I grin. "Seems it was."

He strips off his shirt, followed by his pants and socks, so that only his boxers remain.

"You know," I say coyly, "I wouldn't be opposed if you were to—"

He snaps the waistband. "Oh, I know you wouldn't." He strips those off as well, baring all in the middle of my living room. My entire body hums at the sight. *Conflicted feelings much?*

Brant turns and stalks toward the kitchen, the sound of mugs clinking and water pouring. I'd completely forgotten about the tea. He reappears a few moments later with two steaming mugs in hand. I can't help but take a mental snapshot as he walks in my direction. Brant serving me, stark naked, definitely tops the list of all-time most unexpected moments.

I scoot over to make room for him. He places the sparsely decorated cups on the table, then unfolds a blanket and sets it over the seat cushion.

"You didn't have to do that, you know. We've done far worse things on this couch."

He grins, leaning back with his arms propped up behind his head. "Of that I am well aware."

I reach for my tea and take a careful sip, blanching at the taste. As an avid coffee drinker, it just doesn't hit the same. My eyes rove up his body, past his chiseled stomach and defined chest and shoulders, up the length of his neck, until I finally reach those striking turquoise eyes.

"Enjoying the view?" he murmurs in that raspy way that turns my core molten.

"Very much."

"Likewise." He leans forward and grabs his mug, every inch of his skin rippling with the movement. "Although, I do admit it'd be better if we were . . . equally dressed."

I bat my lashes at him. "Aren't we?" I tease.

In one swift movement, he takes the cup from my hand, sets them both down on the table, and climbs on top of me.

A gasp escapes me involuntarily.

"You're usually not one to be taken by surprise," he murmurs as he brushes his mouth against my ear. "Does this have anything to do with thinking you'd lost me earlier today?"

What he's just asked should infuriate me, but, for reasons unbeknownst to me, it doesn't. It's actually struck a chord—and a deep one at that. Because I do believe, at some point or another, I *will* lose him . . . especially since I'm embarking on this journey to Mohra against his wishes—and against all common sense. I look up at him, trying to recover from the distraught expression I'm sure is on my face, but Brant is nothing if not observant.

He notices right away. "What is it?"

"You're right. I've been caught off guard what feels like all day. And when I realized where you were, what had happened . . ." My breath hitches. "I really thought I *had* lost you."

"Granted, when one's buried, whether alive or dead, the end result is almost always the same."

"I thought I was too late."

He brushes a tendril from my face. "It seems, even after everything, we've really come to care for one another."

A blush crawls across my cheeks. Brant and I normally don't "do" sentimental, but ever since the other night, when we'd both let our guards down . . . it's curious to think that *this* is becoming our new normal.

"I know we've complicated things," he whispers, moving to my other ear. "Lilith sensed it the minute we met. She isn't happy about it nor does she condone it, but this isn't about her."

"It sure as hell isn't." I loop my arms around his neck, pulling him closer. "And I'm okay with complicated if you are."

He presses into me and I into him, releasing my arms so that he can reach my pajama bottoms. He moves down the couch, slowly sliding them off my legs to reveal nothing underneath. I don't wait to pull my shirt over my head, laying bare before him.

He brings his fist to his mouth and bites down onto his knuckles. "Why the fuck did we wait so long to do this?"

I open my legs an inch wider and flash him a wicked smile. "Why are you stalling, Colborn?"

Shadows dance in his eyes as he grabs my ankles and pulls me forward. I let out a squeal as I try to hang on, but he moves fast. His mouth grazes my calf, the inside of my knee, my inner thigh . . . I let my head fall back, wanting to watch but also wanting to just *feel* it. He takes his time reaching my center, flicking his tongue against the delicate fold. He begins to work me with two fingers, switching back and forth in expertly timed intervals between his hand and his mouth. I groan, thrusting further into the motion, hips undulating to match his pace and begging him to go faster.

He obliges.

I arch my back higher, feeling my release building. I want to look at him, to watch him devour me, but I know the minute I do, I'll only be inviting those conflicted feelings from earlier to return. A double-edged sword.

Fuck it. I'll take the risk.

"Keep going," I pant as he makes eye contact with me.

He gives me a slow blink, my wetness gleaming on his mouth as he continues to suck, lick, and flick. My hands tangle in his hair, pulling him closer, hips circling wildly as the sensation builds. It's the perfect amount of pressure and the perfect pace, but it's the feral look in his eyes that pushes me over the edge. That and when he says, "Let me taste all of you," without missing a beat.

I lift my hips higher, higher still, nearly holding my breath as the pace increases. Stars explode in my vision as my body tremors, stills, then releases. I finally let go of his hair, basking in the feeling of pure, unadulterated bliss.

"Fuck, that was good," I say breathlessly as I prop myself up on my elbows.

"You're telling me," Brant says as he sits upright, licking the remnants of me from around his mouth. "But who says we're finished?" With a sly smile, he climbs back up over me and lines himself up. He pushes inside so quickly, it almost comes as a shock to my body—the good kind.

"You've done all the work so far," I say between thrusts and his grunting. "It's my turn."

He gives me a savage smile but doesn't stop.

I take it as a challenge. I secure my arms around his neck, then tuck my feet underneath me and spring off the couch. He's not prepared in the slightest. I use the momentum to guide our bodies so that he's sitting upright, his back flush against the couch, with me straddling him. I lift up off him, not all the way, but just enough to make him glower at me. He goes to press my shoulders down, but I swat him away.

"My. Turn." I give him a look fit for a commander.

He pulls his arms back in mock surrender, then brings them to my hips, but doesn't press down. His eyes rove my body, just as mine had done to his earlier, so I let him stare. I can feel the length of him twitch just beneath me in anticipation.

I put one hand on his shoulder, tipping his chin up with the other, then slowly slide down. His mouth parts in satisfaction, but he doesn't look down or away. He keeps his gaze locked on mine, his eyes dancing with fervor as he watches me near another release, except this time, *on* him.

When I start to slow down out of sheer exhaustion, he grabs my hips tightly and begins to pump into me as hard as he can. We're moving so fast that I almost feel like a rag doll, my body begging to go limp and enjoy the pleasure that's coursing through me. I perk up, tightening around him precisely at the moment he pulls out and releases himself all over my chest and stomach. I smile as he lets out a string of profanities before collapsing back into the couch.

Chest heaving, he stops me from using my shirt to clean up with and jogs across the living room to where he'd undressed earlier. "Here," he says, joining me back on the couch, "allow me."

I splay my arms out next to me, unable to keep the grin off my face. "Ever the gentleman you are, Brant Colborn."

He finishes wiping me clean, then presses a kiss atop each peak of my chest, and then my mouth. "I'm not one to leave a mess behind."

I laugh. "Well, thank goodness for that."

He helps me pull my shirt overhead, grabbing the wadded up one in my hands. "I'll take that," he says as he strides over to the washer and throws it in for another cycle.

I watch as he clumsily pulls on his boxers and his pants, not bothering to put my own bottoms back on. I eye our mugs of tea, which are still quite full and are probably lukewarm by now. Not like I was planning on drinking it anyway. "Want me to put another pot on the stove?" I offer, being polite.

Before I can grab them, he removes the mugs from the coffee table and follows me into the kitchen. I move the runes out of the way, suddenly getting an idea as they sit in the palm of my hand. "You said the Full Moon is tomorrow?"

Brant's one step ahead of me, already doing what I'd offered by refilling the kettle with water. "Indeed, I did."

I lean my back against the counter, rolling the runes around in my hand. "I need to meet with the Sable Coven. It was very clear, the way Madame Viessa expressly mentioned meeting under the Full Moon. If she didn't get the chance to deliver the message . . ."

"You could be waiting another month until the next one," Brant finishes.

I nod in mutual understanding. "I can't wait that long."

He turns the faucet off and sets the kettle on the stovetop. "What did you have in mind?"

I raise a brow in surprised delight. "Does that mean you're willing to help me?"

He shrugs. "I suppose that depends on *what* I'd be helping with."

"These runes," I say, rolling them off my palm and onto the counter, "they came from the Sable Coven. I'm sure of it. And last time I was at Madame Viessa's, I mentioned a book I saw there during one of my visits. The one on display was gone, but I learned that the Madame kept another one in the back." I chew on my lower lip. "She was quite adamant about no one seeing it, though."

"Do you think the book will help you locate the coven?"

I turn the burner up higher. "I'm not sure, but it's the only lead I have."

He gently takes my hand, interlacing my fingers with his. "Did the murder happen *inside* the shop? Because if so, it's probably going to be covered in police tape."

Shit. I hadn't considered that. "We definitely can't go during the day, then. Too risky."

Brant sighs, turning off the stove. "I take it having tea just isn't in the cards for us today."

"Oh, please," I say sarcastically. "You and I both know we didn't come here for tea."

"Speak for yourself," he jokes. "To you, it might just be an afterthought—"

"Okay, but in all seriousness," I say, laughing, "if we're going to get that book, now's as good a time as any."

Brant glances at the microwave. "At two o'clock in the morning?"

I nod. "So, are you going to help me or not?"

"Even though I know what this is bound to lead to next, I'm finding it hard to say no," he says with a sigh. "As dangerous as it is and as much as I don't want you to do it, I can't deny the fact that my sole responsibility is to *protect* you. That's a vow I'm not willing to break."

I don't give him a chance for second thoughts. "We should get going, then."

He looks me up and down, grinning from ear to ear. "But first we need to get you into some pants."

19

WE MAKE IT out the door a quarter past the hour, knowing that running into the authorities likely won't be an issue, if there even are any. The block where Madame Viessa's store is located is completely taped off, but as far as I can see, there are no police officers, no detectives . . . not even a security guard. More than anything, I wish there was a back entrance, but with the way this old building's laid out, there's only one way out—and it's the same way you get in.

The streets are quiet, which isn't surprising for a weekday at this ungodly hour. Brant and I are dressed in dark attire, fitting right in with the majority of people who've decided to devote their lives to committing crimes. The streetlights above us flicker, which only adds to the already ominous vibe, as we duck underneath caution tape and other signs labeled NO TRESPASSING in bold, angry letters. We shamelessly ignore each one, but make sure to keep an eye out for a well-placed guard or anyone else we'd rather not run into. Luckily for us, the coast is clear.

We arrive at the then-shattered, now-boarded-up, glass door. "Well, this is unexpected," Brant says, running a gloved hand over the wood.

"Is it going to be a problem?"

He gives me a knowing look. "When have we ever come across a problem we couldn't solve?"

I can think of two from today alone, but I don't mention either of them.

"It's plywood," Brant confirms, examining it further. "The thickness shouldn't be a problem for what I have planned."

I lift a brow, completely unaware of this part of our "plan". "I hope that whatever you brought won't make too much noise."

He pulls a drill from the bag I'd forgotten he was carrying. "The quietest one on the market. I figure since there's only one way out, this wood panel couldn't be secured from the inside, only the outside." He points at one of the screws, then lines up the drill.

"That almost seems *too* simple."

"I know." Brant laughs. "Oftentimes, the simplest answer is the right one."

Sure enough, he's able to remove every single one of the screws—and in record time, I might add—to reveal shattered glass . . . and a perfect size hole to reach into to unlock the door. "Care to do the honors?"

He moves out of the way as I step farther to the right and snake my arm inside the opening. The lock clicks. Flabbergasted by how easy it was, I enter the shop, immediately noticing the rank smell coming from within. Thankfully, there's no alarm system to worry about—Madame Viessa was very much a believer of "the Universe being her protector", which, to some degree, holds quite a lot of truth . . . but people are still grade-A asshats with free will to do idiotic things where some of us unknowingly end up in the crossfire. An alarm system may have served her well is all I'm saying.

I tiptoe across the stained carpet, careful not to disturb any equipment or evidence markers. I try to ignore the blood that's still pooled on the glass countertop near the register, shaking the image of how her body was found. I may torture people as a Noire, but 1) it takes place in a dream state and 2) it's never someone I know or hold dear.

This is real life and someone I knew quite well.

She's also someone who didn't deserve that fate.

"Ugh, it reeks," Brant groans. He shines his phone's flashlight in my direction. "How long do we have to be in here?"

"Until we find what we came for. The book on the Sable Coven."

"Which looks like *what*, exactly?"

I roll my eyes, having already told him this on the way over. "The cover is a deep purple, and it has a crest with three crows, each carrying a different item in their beak—a key, a ring, and a serpent. The title will read *Legends & Lore of the Sable Coven*."

"You said there was a copy on one of the bookshelves?"

"*Was*," I emphasize. "That copy was long gone the last time I was here." *The last time I saw her alive.* I gulp. "But

Madame Viessa mentioned another copy she kept in the back."

"To the back it is, then," Brant murmurs, leading the way. We don't make it very far, though, because something catches his eye at the register. I decide to keep moving because the smell is overbearing and it's making my eyes water. I'm nearly to the back of the store when Brant calls out my name in a concerning tone.

"Hey, Maren? Can you come over here? You're going to want to see this."

"Just a sec," I respond, scanning the back shelves behind the curtain. *Purple book, purple book . . . no purple book.* The storage area isn't all that big and I'm certain it would have popped out at me had it been there. Feeling discouraged, I make my way back to the front of the store, joining Brant at the register.

The look of disapproval on his face is enough to make me want to cringe. "Thanks for making me wait in the midst of all this blood," he says sardonically.

"Sorry," I quip. "I wanted to check the back since Madame Viessa made mention of it."

"And?"

My shoulders slump. "I didn't find anything."

"Well, had you listened, I could have saved you some disappointment." He flicks a small circular piece of paper between his fingers before holding it out to me. "I was about to ask if *you* wrote it, until I realized it's actually the information you're looking for, so that wouldn't make any sense."

I snatch the blue paper from his hands realizing there's writing on both sides. At first glance, the handwriting does oddly resemble my own—like, it's *uncanny*—but the message is entirely foreign to me.

"It isn't in English—what's that about?"

"They're runes," I say suddenly, as recognition takes hold. "The message, it's like an anagram, except with runes. We're not rearranging letters to decode it, but instead using the Elder Futhark alphabet."

"Again with these damn runes," he murmurs.

"Find me a book," I say with a snap of my fingers. "I know some of these, but I'm rusty on the order they go in."

"On it," Brant says as he makes a beeline for the bookshelf. "Why do you think the police left it behind? It didn't have an evidence marker."

"They probably just thought it was gibberish. I mean, if you look at it, it's just a bunch of weird symbols that don't actually spell anything." I move away from the blood-ridden counter, wondering if some fresh air will help. "This *has* to be from the Sable Coven, though. Between the rune Madame Viessa gave me and the one you found around your neck after the whole graveyard incident . . . this must be how the witches communicate."

"Found it," Brant says, waving a brown book with gold lettering in the air. "Here's your Elder Fuck-chart or whatever it's called."

"Fu-thark," I correct him. "Can you find a page with the entire alphabet?"

He flips to the index. "There you go. All . . . twenty-four of them."

I grab the book and take it to the sitting chair in the far corner of the room. Brant's slow to follow.

"I don't mean to rush you, but isn't this something we should do back at your place? You know, when we're not breaking and entering at the scene of a crime? I've still got to re-board up the place."

Knowing that he's right, I scan the note, then the page with the alphabet to make sure I have everything I need to decode it; but I guess I won't really know until I actually do it. "You're right. Let's get out of here." I do a quick onceover of the shop. "Is everything exactly as we found it?"

Brant nods. "Everything except for the note. And that book."

I walk over to the shelf where a book is clearly missing and move the remaining texts closer together. "There," I say hopefully, "that looks better." I look up to get Brant's approval, but he's already at the door. I stash the note in the book and tuck it under my arm before heading to the front.

He peeks his head out the window. "All clear. After you, m'lady."

I scoff, rolling my hand into a fake bow, before exiting the shop. I tap my foot against the pavement as Brant drills the wood panel back onto the door, keeping an eye out in all directions.

"There," he says with a grin. "Good as new."

It's still early enough to avoid running into anyone, so I suggest heading back the way we came. With Brant in agreement, we trek back to my apartment, not the slightest bit concerned that the sunrise is nipping at our heels. Strangely enough, this might just be the easiest thing we've done together yet.

20

I'M SITTING CROSS-LEGGED on the bed with a notebook, the runes text, and the cryptic message splayed out in front of me. Brant's across from me, looking at everything upside down.

"Figured it out yet?" he asks, tilting his head to get a better look.

I chew on the edge of my pen, turning both the book and the note around to show him what I have so far. "So, this B-shaped one is Berkana, and it literally means 'birch'."

"And we know this one is Raidho," he says pointing to the middle symbol in the top row.

"We do," I agree, pulling that exact rune from my pocket. "No mention of yours, though, which is interesting."

"Clearly, the note isn't meant for me."

I smile at him, hoping that a momentary break from my intense thought process will yield some clarity.

"This F-looking one is on either side of Raidho," he says, drawing a finger across the paper.

"Fehu," I confirm. "It's the first rune in the Elder Futhark alphabet."

"And where does Raidho fall in the alphabet?"

Stumped, I turn the book back around to face me. "It's the fifth rune."

"So 1-5-1," Brant murmurs. "And you said this next one means Birch?"

I nod, realizing that he may very well be onto something. "This X is the Gebo rune but, to me, it sort of looks like a crossing."

"Birch Crossing," Brant says suddenly, his eyes lighting up. "I know of it. It's on the other side of town, where the railroad tracks are."

"Is 151 Birch Crossing an actual street address?" I ask as I fumble for my phone, nearly knocking it off the nightstand.

Brant beats me to it. "Holy shit." He flashes his phone screen at me. "It exists."

"Okay, okay," I say, trying to contain my excitement while also feeling really stunned that we may have just figured out a key piece of the note. "Now what about these, at the bottom?" I point to a sideways looking hourglass and a weird S-shaped lightning bolt.

Brant takes the book and scans the alphabet. "The hourglass looking thing is Dagaz and it means"—he pauses, flipping to the appropriate page—"dawn."

I wait for him to expand upon what he's just said, but he just looks at me, confounded. "Dawn?" I say. "Literally, *dawn?*"

He turns the book around to show me. "Maren, I think it's a meeting time. At dawn."

I grab the book from him and flip it to the page that contains the sixteenth rune. "This S-shaped lightning bolt one is Sowilo, and it means . . . Sun."

"Sunday," we both say simultaneously.

I throw the book to the side and clasp my hands over my mouth. "Did we just crack the code?"

His childlike excitement lights me up even more. "You better fucking believe we did!" he exclaims.

"So, the Sable Coven wants to meet Sunday, at dawn, at 151 Birch Crossing." I flip the note over, a lone rune in the shape of a jagged parenthesis staring back at me. There's an X drawn through it. I reach for the book, quickly identifying it as Perthro.

Noticing my silent intensity as I study the text, Brant asks, "There's more?"

I nod. "On the back. Perthro. It says here it symbolizes fate and destiny . . . but also mystery and secrets."

"It looks like it was a mistake," Brant muses, tracing the shape of the X with his index finger. "Why else would it be crossed out?"

I shrug. "As a warning, maybe? That, perhaps, this *isn't* my fate? That meeting with the Sable Coven isn't my destiny?"

"*Or* what if X marks the spot?" Brant suggests. "That would mean it *is* your destiny."

All this talk of fate and destiny has my stomach turning. "Regardless, I'd be doing myself a disservice to ignore what is obviously a very intentional note."

"So, you're going to go?"

"What other choice do I have?"

"There's the Maren I know." He puts his hand up for a high-five which is something we've literally never done before. I meet his palm, surprised when he wraps his fingers around mine and pulls me in for a kiss. I nearly fall on top of him as he tugs me even closer, laughing as his mouth moves over mine. We stay that way, tangled in a mess of limbs, for a solid five minutes.

I blow out a long breath, willing my heart to slow down before saying, "I'm not sure why we're this excited. I mean, this *is* a coven of witches we're talking about."

"Dangerous, indeed," Brant murmurs, gingerly running a hand through my hair. "You want me to come with you, right?"

I look at him, searching the depths of his eyes for the right answer—except I know there isn't one. On the one hand, I believe this note was meant for me and me alone. On the other, *they* were the ones who dragged Brant into this by burying him alive in the cemetery . . . assuming it *was*, in fact, the Sable Coven.

"You can say no if you want," Brant says, "but that doesn't mean I'm going to listen."

I punch him in the shoulder. "Then why'd you ask?"

"To give you the illusion of having a choice."

I punch him again. "You're a stubborn one, you know that?"

He flashes me an infuriating grin. "Takes one to know one."

☠ ☠ ☠ ☠ ☠

The weekend arrives with more folders piling up on my doorstep—and, according to Brant, it's been the same for him. *What if it's a trap?* I type into yet another text, having gone back and forth with the decision more times than I can count. *What if they already suspect me as the murderer?*

I thought this whole thing was about trust.

His response nearly sends me into a tailspin. *Initially, it was. And then it became about my own morbid curiosity and needing to know what could have possibly led him to choose his ovetyr sentence. But now . . . now it's about something far greater than Noires and Sigards and exacting justice. It's about our incarnations on a soul level. It's about what happened over those many lifetimes and how we ended up here. The answers I seek will likely open Pandora's box, but I just can't let it go. I need to know.*

It is, I type back. *But I'd be lying if I said I wasn't a little worried.*

His response is quick. *Let's just meet with them and take it from there.*

Fair enough. See you tomorrow, bright and early?

Five o'clock in the morning is a bit excessive, don't you think?

I roll my eyes. *I don't want to risk being late. Especially since we're dealing with railroad crossings. I'd be kicking myself if we got stuck behind a train.*

Fine. I can nearly hear the exasperation in his tone. *See you then.*

With that in mind, I briefly set a couple of alarms before placing my phone back on the nightstand. I've been curled up in bed almost all evening, reading through the book of runes in the hopes that it'll keep me from pacing or accidentally getting started on something that'll keep me up into the wee hours of the morning. By this point, I'm more than halfway through the book, and already feeling even more well-versed in the runes and their meanings. Since this is how the Sable Coven seems to communicate, I want to be as prepared as possible.

I turn over onto my side, closing the book as I recall what Madame Viessa had told me about getting permission from the Elders before going through their ritual. That book, the one I'd originally been searching for in the shop, would do me a world of good right now. I'm essentially walking into this blind. Although, if Madame Viessa is—*was*—their Elder, I shouldn't have much to worry about . . .

I hope.

I tuck the book under my pillow before throwing the covers off, suddenly feeling restless. I walk over to the lounge chair near my closet, double checking that I have everything I need for tomorrow. *Fuck, why am I so nervous?*

I go through my backpack, pulling out the concealed dagger to test its sharpness. Most people in this day and age carry guns—I say that that's the easy way out. Using a blade actually requires some skill. I don't intend to hurt anyone, but as a Noire walking into uncharted territory, I need to feel like I can protect myself. Especially since I don't know what to expect. I rummage around one of the pockets and grasp the Raidho rune. I've also packed the note, a pen, a bottle of water, a dried fruit bar, and a compass, just in case I happen to get lost or cell service is down. I researched the area around Birch

Crossing and it's mostly covered in thick woods which, if I had to guess, is where we'll be meeting tomorrow. *Just like in my dream,* I think, immediately having to shake off the image of Brant being buried alive.

I return to my bed and switch the light off, checking my phone one last time to make sure my alarms are set and that I don't have any unread messages from Brant. Much to my surprise, sleep finds me rather easily.

☠ ☠ ☠ ☠ ☠

At five 'til the hour, I'm standing outside my apartment with my car started, backpack thrown in the front seat, and directions pulled up on my GPS. The arrival time currently states an hour and a half which is perfect, seeing as I have everything I need . . . except for Brant.

I tap my foot impatiently, switching from the GPS screen to my text messages. *Almost here?*

I watch as the message sends and reads "delivered" after the string of texts I've already sent with zero response. I don't know why I expect this one to be any different, but I'm hopeful. I give it a few minutes, but nothing from Brant comes through. It's now exactly five o'clock in the morning.

I'm assuming he's just overslept—but he *does* have a car *and* he knows the address, so worse case, he can just meet me there whenever he wakes up. Would have been nice to have some backup, though. Especially since I have no idea what I'm walking into.

I multi-task as I open the door, my fingers typing a mile a minute. *I'm gonna head out. Meet me there when you're up, okay? And shoot me a text, too. You have the address, so you'll know where to find me.* I add a quick *Wish me luck!* before pressing send.

I slide into the driver's seat and strap in, loading the GPS onto my phone before setting it on the dash. With my backpack in the passenger seat and a full tank of gas, I'm ready to hit the road.

I cruise down the open thoroughfare, flicking cigarette ash out the cracked window, Lana Del Rey filling the car with just enough despondence to keep the numbness away. It's chilly outside, around forty degrees, but I couldn't care less as I roll all the windows down the minute I hit the back country roads. I've got an oversized sweater and a homemade coffee to keep me warm.

An hour into the drive and the day's first light is starting to peek over the horizon. Cobalt ebbs into a mixed canvas, the sky brightening with reds, oranges, and yellows. Birds begin to soar overhead in V-shaped patterns, circling and dipping before ascending again. Of all the things to experience in this existence, the sun rising has to be one of my favorites—those precious moments before anyone is awake, before the world can hassle you into its noisy distractions . . . *those* are the kinds of moments worth living for.

I turn the volume up and keep cruising, singing aloud as I flick my cigarette into my now-empty cup. I glance at the GPS. Seventeen minutes to go. I don't know when I'd gotten so close. Even though it's still at a distance, the first railroad crossing of many comes into view. At the sight of it, my heart speeds up. It's funny how something like confronting a group of strangers (powerful ones, at that) can evoke this kind of a response from me, yet facing murderers and the literal scum of the earth has the exact opposite effect—making me feel confident and empowered.

My thoughts carry me all the way to the first crossing without even realizing it, until I'm bouncing in my seat from driving over the railroad tracks. Worried that I may have missed the arrival announcement, I glance at my GPS, but it says I still have three minutes left of the journey. My heart sinks as the smooth pavement turns into a dirt pathway and leads straight to a fork in the road. The GPS indicates that I should turn left, so that's what I do. At least I still have service—I'm *way* in the heck out here.

I start down the narrow path, driving less than fifteen miles an hour as the area around me grows denser and more wooded. Through the trees, I can see abandoned railcars covered in rust that probably haven't been used in decades, but surprisingly haven't been graffitied—well, I suppose not all that surprising since it takes forever to get out here.

I'm about to continue driving when a calm British voice sounds from my phone, alerting me that I've arrived. At first, I'm certain there's a mistake because I don't see a damn thing, but then I notice another dirt path, except this one's lined with stones. It winds and curves, so I can't see exactly where it leads, but one thing's for certain: there's no way in hell I'm getting my car down this all-too-narrow footpath.

I put my car in reverse before turning it around and pulling off to the left in the tiny, cleared area that must be for guest parking. Granted, I don't know *who* in their right mind would journey all this way but, then again, *I'm* here, so I'm not really one to talk. It's one of those places you wouldn't expect to be on a map—a place where you *really* have to know where you're going.

I grab my backpack before stepping out of the car, tossing it onto the trunk before swiping my phone from the dash. I turn off the ignition and pocket the keys, suddenly immersed in complete silence. It's eerie enough to make me want to start the car again, just for some background noise, but I resist the urge. I shut the door and lock the car, then double check my text messages and call logs. Still nothing from Brant, which has me feeling a bit worried. *Made it safe,* I type. I'm relieved to see that I still have a signal after pressing send.

With how quickly dawn is breaking, I know I can't just sit around and hope that he'll suddenly show up. Had he sent a text while I was on my way to give me an update or let me know his ETA, that would have been a different story.

But I feel just as in the dark now as when I'd left.

I sling the backpack over my shoulders, slipping my phone into my other pocket, then start down the footpath that *hopefully* leads to 151 Birch Crossing. It crosses my mind to either sheathe my dagger in my pants or conceal it somehow underneath my sweater, but I don't think that'd start things off on the right foot, so in my backpack it shall stay.

I wind down the trail, feeling strangely claustrophobic as I get deeper and deeper into the woods, the trees closing in until so many branches and twigs litter the path, I almost feel like I've made a grave mistake, that perhaps this is a road that leads to nowhere . . . but a few more steps reveal a structure in the distance. Smoke billows into the treetops from what I assume is a chimney and, if my eyes aren't deceiving me, there's a small cottage made of grey stone just up ahead. I don't know why I'd had it in my head that we'd be meeting in a dank, musty place with only candlelight to guide us, like in a cavern or in a clearing marked with bones and skulls, but this is *much* preferred.

The dirt trail transforms into a path of large stepping stones that match the design of the cottage. The ivy growing up the front and sides, even over the wooden moss-colored shutters, gives it a charming and idyllic feel—which, again, is the opposite of what I'd expected. Bushes and shrubs of all types line the pathway, pockets of peonies and roses adding the perfect touch of pink to an otherwise green landscape. A small fountain trickles at the edge of the house, no doubt an attraction for the birds, and behind that are a variety of herb boxes on the window ledges.

I arrive at the front door, which also happens to be painted a mossy green, with wooden panels and bolts that give it a more modern feel, but somehow, it still manages to feel rather quaint. I take a steadying breath, preparing to use the little knocker designed in the shape of a crow, when the door begins to creak open. I take a step back, feeling so thrown off by this whole experience when a woman, no older than me, appears at the door.

The first thing I notice are her eyes because they're a color I've never seen before. They're purple, but not mauve, lilac, or even violet, but a deep plum color, which also matches her chest-length hair. Shorter tendrils frame her face, cascading in messy waves over her shoulders. Her features are sharp and angular—pointed, almost—between her eyebrows, her nose, and even her mouth. There's little color on her face, besides the onyx lipstick she wears, but honestly, she doesn't need any. She's absolutely stunning with full breasts, a curvy figure, and porcelain skin that looks like it's never seen the sun—the definition of *divine feminine*, if you ask me.

She returns my gaping with a sly smile before saying, "Maren Cordeau. I've been expecting you." She brushes a hand against the door before motioning for me to come inside. "Please, do come in."

I nod, too speechless to say anything even remotely intelligent.

"Allow me to properly introduce myself. My name is Astrid Sable. I'm the High Priestess of the Sable Coven."

I take the seat nearest me, unable to fully process my surroundings and what she's just said. Something about this place feels so familiar, so inviting . . . like I've been here before. But that's impossible, seeing as I had no idea where I was when I'd parked just moments ago.

"Forgive me," I say as I pull my backpack onto my lap, "but this is all a bit overwhelming. You seem . . ." I want to say *familiar*, but instead decide to go with, "welcoming. I honestly thought I'd be greeted with pitchforks and poison."

It must be the sheer absurdity of my statement that makes her chuckle. "No, not here," is her only response, which is definitely *less* comforting and welcoming than before. I want her to elaborate, but she doesn't.

"Seeing as I was one of the last people to speak with Madame Viessa, I thought your coven—"

"Would assume that you murdered her?" She lifts a brow. "They do."

I swallow the lump that's forming in my throat.

Astrid smiles. "But I don't."

Relief floods my body.

She turns to the hearth and pokes at the logs, breaking up the embers to stoke a greater fire. The flames roar in response, licking the sides of the chimney as if they're a living thing themselves. Astrid tosses a couple more logs on top, then brushes her hands against her obsidian skirts.

"It's a good thing my opinion holds some sway with our Elders," she continues, turning back to face me. "Otherwise, you'd be experiencing a very *different* kind of welcome party."

"But you're right," I say quickly, suddenly feeling the need to defend myself. "I *didn't* kill Madame Viessa. In fact, I was devastated when I heard the news. Before her passing, she even offered to help me get into contact with you so that I could travel through Mohra."

At this, Astrid stiffens, but it's so subtle, I wouldn't have caught it had I not been looking directly at her.

"I don't know how much you know about me," I continue, watching her closely, "but I'm a Noire. And I just recently discovered that Lilith has been visiting my Sigard to discuss his ovetyr sentence. I went to Madame Viessa for help after stumbling upon Mohra in the Sephiran." I take a breath, not realizing how fast I've been talking. "Long story short, I need to know *what* could cause my Sigard to claim an ovetyr sentence, what could be worth trading his soul for. Visiting past lifetimes seems like the place to start. Until then, I don't know how I can trust him, which affects both of our duties and the successful completion of any and all future assignments."

"I see." Astrid takes two slow steps forward, her brow creasing. "And when you find what you're looking for, what then?"

I blink. "Then . . . I'll be able to trust him and we can move forward as planned." As soon as I say it, I catch the flaw.

"Nothing is ever the same after traveling through Mohra. We incarnate without the knowledge of previous lifetimes because if we knew everything that had happened prior, we wouldn't be able to fully appreciate and experience everything that our current lifetime has to offer."

"So . . . why does it even exist, then?"

Her eyes twinkle in the firelight. "Because *all* things exist, Maren. If you can think it, it can manifest into form. Such are the laws of this reality."

It's the simplest, yet most profound answer I've ever received. "So, what happens after I finish my trip through Mohra?"

"Assuming you get admitted." She winks. "It's hard to say, really. You'll return with more knowledge, insight, and wisdom—but how you choose to view it and what you decide to do with it will ultimately be up to you—and you alone."

"Talk about pressure," I murmur, trying to fight the impending doom that's creeping in. "What do I have to do to gain admission?"

A shadow falls over the witch's face. "You'll have to convince the Elders, of which there are now three, seeing as they believe you killed our fourth."

I shake my head, eyes wide. "I already told you I didn't do it. Madame Viessa was helping me, she *wanted* me to find you—"

Astrid raises a hand to silence me. "Be that as it may, the Elders have their suspicions. And until they are proven wrong, they're a hard lot to sell."

"How do I do that? Prove them wrong?"

Astrid tracks to a kitchen table littered with herbs, spices, and corked jars of various sizes. "Unfortunately, you can't." She pauses. "But you *can* strike a bargain with them."

"What kind of a bargain?"

Astrid sighs. "That isn't for me to say. But I *can* tell you that it'll require collateral."

"I don't know that I have any collateral to give—"

"That won't be necessary," she interrupts.

"What do you mean?"

Her face falls. "It's already done."

I rise from my chair. "*What's* already done?"

But I already know the answer before she says it. Brant couldn't meet me here . . . because the Elders already have him.

21

ASTRID IS NOT one to waste time, which is something I appreciate even more now that I know Brant hadn't completely ghosted me. I've been here for less than an hour and she's already served me tea and biscuits with some fresh fruit from her garden, and now has me changing into what she refers to as "ritual garb".

I emerge from the tiny washroom in the back of the cottage, clad in a floor-length, pine-colored robe with intricate detailing along the edges by way of silver thread. The fabric is clasped together via an onyx brooch in the shape of a crow's head, which I can't help but notice is representative of their crest. My favorite part of the whole ensemble is the hood, which has beautiful lace detailing all over it, making the hood look nearly black instead of its deep jade hue.

Astrid stops what she's doing and looks at me. "Oh, don't you look just divine! Yes, this will please the Elders very much."

I notice that she's also wearing a robe, but hers is a different color than mine. She catches my ogling and immediately answers my question, even though I haven't spoken it aloud.

"It's to help distinguish among the members of our coven. These are specifically for the High Priestess," she clarifies, lifting the sides of her gold-threaded, eggplant-colored robes in a near-curtsy. "The Elders wear a different color as well— burgundy."

Much like Lilith, I think. I force the thought away, giving Astrid a gracious smile for taking the time to explain. "They're beautiful," I murmur. "And made so well, too."

"If there's one thing the Sable Coven *isn't*, it's cheap," the High Priestess quips as she finishes gathering the rest of her items before looping a black straw basket through one arm. "Shall we head out, then?"

I nod, grabbing my backpack, which honestly makes me feel a bit foolish given how sophisticated Astrid looks. I wait for her to walk to the door, but instead she leans against the circular kitchen table and pushes it to the edge of the room to reveal . . . a trap door.

Okay, this cottage just went from charming to badass.

Astrid shrugs at my stunned expression. "Poor choice of words on my part. I suppose we're not heading out, but heading *in* . . . or perhaps down?" She takes a large brass key from the basket and unlocks the door before pulling on the handle. It reminds me a lot of the cellar at *The Ivory Stallion.* She pulls two lanterns from the floor nearby and lights them. "I suppose you didn't bring a flashlight?"

"That would be a negative," I admit.

"Not a problem. Here." She hands me a lantern, which is much heavier than it looks. "I know how precious cell phone batteries are these days."

I smile in appreciation. She grabs the other lantern, but her expression goes from composed to flummoxed as her gaze settles on the ladder that leads to what I'm guessing is an underground passageway. "Seems I've outdone myself with both a lantern *and* a basket." She glances at my backpack with envy. "Would you mind handing this to me after I've made it to the bottom?"

"Sure thing." I take the lantern from her, bringing myself to the edge of the cellar door. I lower the flickering flame as she begins to descend into utter darkness, which honestly has my nerves fraying at the sight.

Thankfully, the ladder is a short distance from the ground because the High Priestess lands with a soft thud just seconds later. "Okay," she says, reaching a hand up, fingers wiggling. I secure the lantern in her grip, then get a tight hold on my own as I climb down the steps.

"You're a natural," she says as soon as I reach the ground. "Stay close, all right?"

I nod feverishly, not daring to ask or even think about what might live in this dank, musty tunnel. At first, it seems pretty straightforward because we've only moved in a single direction, but then the real challenge begins. Left, right, left. Another left. At times, I feel like we're almost making a circle, but Astrid forges ahead, ever the stoic leader. With each corner we turn, I notice rustling. If I had to guess, they're probably bats—quite honestly, if it's anything else, I don't want to know.

I can tell we're getting close because the High Priestess begins to slow her pace. The entire time I've been following her, all I can think about is how much I hope the rest of the coven is just like her. She's been so welcoming and helpful, not to mention direct. Even though I don't know what to expect from this ritual, I do know two things: that the Elders aren't exactly on my side, and that they have Brant.

We wind around the last corridor before Astrid comes to a stop. Even from here, I can see that we're about to enter what looks like a cavern. She turns to face me, lowering her voice before saying, "Whatever you do, just don't lie."

It's the last thing she says before her entire demeanor changes. With a grave face, she grabs my arm, pulls me forward, and tosses me into the ring.

22

I NEARLY DROP the lantern as I stumble into the open underground space—which is surprisingly spacious while also having the feeling of being slightly closed off. My eyes are still adjusting to the dim lighting when I hear it.

Chanting.

I take a few cautious steps forward until I'm standing in what I think is the center of the massive cavern. Light trickles toward me in narrow streams but doesn't hit the ground. It floats mostly near the top, unable to make its way through the jagged edges of the formation. My gaze travels down the rocky walls until I finally see them, the ones chanting. I realize I'm surrounded by hundreds of robed women, their hoods pulled taut over their heads, resembling nothing more than phantom cloaks in the vast space.

I turn to look at Astrid for guidance, but she's no longer behind me. Instead, she stands on the center dais before row after row of cloaked women. Three women in burgundy robes—which I quickly gather are the Elders—are seated just behind the dais, their hoods also covering their faces. The chanting continues, slowing to a low hum as lights begin to flicker intermittently amongst the group. It takes a moment for me to discern that they're all holding candles. Two conflicting emotions stir within me—terror and intrigue.

The Elders are the last among the coven to light their candles. I center myself in the middle of the ancient stone that's laid in a giant circle on the ground. The stone sprawls from north to south, east to west, nearly covering the length and width of the cavern. It also extends into the rows of cloaked women, each one just slightly raised above the last— much like a choir. Eventually, the humming dulls to a complete silence. I set the lantern at my feet and await further instruction.

Astrid turns to her coven, her arms raised as she says, "Welcome, Elders. Sisters. Merry meet."

"Merry meet," the coven echoes in unison.

"Our first order of business today is the untimely death of one of our dearest Elders, Madame Roisin Viessa, of which the woman standing before you is a suspect."

"The *prime* suspect," the Elder sitting in the middle seat chimes in.

I open my mouth to defend myself but decide that it's better to wait for the High Priestess's cue.

"However, I've summoned her for another reason, one that will likely not please the majority of you." Even though the coven begins murmuring amongst themselves, Astrid maintains her composure, waiting patiently for them to quiet back down. "In the days leading up to her untimely death, Madame Viessa sent word that a Noire by the name of Maren Imogen Cordeau would be permitted to approach us with her request."

"And what request is that?" the first Elder asks, her voice low and deep.

Astrid tosses a brief glance over her shoulder, her eyes solemn, before returning her attention to the coven. "To be granted access to Mohra."

Some of the coven members gasp as the murmuring starts up again. The Elders nearly spring to their feet. The first Elder removes her hood with a huff—to which the entire coven follows suit—revealing smooth caramel skin, deep-set onyx eyes, and flowing shoulder-length hair to match. She dons a crimson lip with thick lines of kohl rimming her eyes and her cheeks have just a hint of pink, likely flushed from the news she's just received.

"Permission denied," she says, cutting me a stern glare.

"Now, Madame Bhavna," Astrid says, approaching the woman with lethal calm, "is that any way to honor your sister's final request?"

"Proof," says the third Elder, a woman with short auburn hair that's angled at her chin. She purses her lips, narrowing her tawny eyes. "We need proof."

"Yes," the first Elder agrees. "Where is the proof?"

Even though Astrid has her back to me, I can feel both the annoyance and assuredness radiating from her. She sticks her left arm out to the side and whistles an impressive four-tone tune. Mere moments later, I hear the flapping of wings and a loud caw. I duck as a crow swoops overhead, wondering how in the hell a bird could get in here in the first place. Stunned, I watch as it lands on the High Priestess's outstretched arm, only noticing the tiny scroll in its mouth when Astrid retrieves it from its beak.

The second Elder, a lanky woman, takes a step forward, then snatches the scroll out of Astrid's hands without so much as a word. Bony fingers unravel it, her cobalt eyes darting wildly as she reads what's on the page. Like flies to honey, the other Elders attempt to gather around her, but she shoos them away in irritation. The tension is palpable. Finally, the second Elder lifts her gaze, meeting the High Priestess's cold stare. "She speaks the truth. Granting this woman access to Mohra was Madame Viessa's final request."

Astrid bows her head. "Thank you, Madame Caragh."

"Let me see that," the third Elder snaps, reaching for the paper to which Madame Caragh willingly hands over.

Madame Riona reads it, mutters something under her breath, then passes it along to the final Elder. More anxiety-ridden silence ensues.

Madame Bhavna scoffs, rolling the scroll back into its original position before crossing her arms over her chest. "I vote we submit it for analysis."

Astrid frowns. "You don't mean—"

"Handwriting?" the first Elder finishes. "Why, yes. That is precisely what I mean."

"If I may," I interject, having worked myself up to finally speak, "we're pressed for time. I'm already behind on my most recent Noire case. This is truly life or death we're talking about—" I stop talking the minute Astrid cuts me a menacing stare. *Spoke too soon.*

"Who's to say she'll even survive?" Madame Riona says with a sneer. "I'm inclined to agree with Madame Bhavna on this one. I think an analysis of the handwriting is more than appropriate, given the magnitude of the request."

"That could take weeks—possibly even *months*," Astrid counters. "And, although Maren spoke out of turn, she makes a fair point. Time is of the essence—at least, for the sake of *her* timeline . . . and all timelines connected to it. But I don't need to remind you of the consequences there, now do I, Riona?"

The sudden change in her tone and lack of formality tells me that the High Priestess and the third Elder definitely have a history—and it's one likely riddled with contempt.

Madame Riona scowls and returns to her seat.

If she didn't before, the High Priestess now has the coven's undivided attention. "Maren Imogen Cordeau," she says as she turns to face me, "do you swear before these wise women, your ancestors, and the Triple Goddess that you are not responsible for the death of Madame Elder Roisin Viessa?"

I can't say with certainty that I believe in anything she's just said, but I *do* know that I didn't kill their Elder. "I swear it." My voice is firm and unwavering, just as I'd intended.

Astrid keeps her face neutral, but before she turns away, I catch what I believe is meant to be a reassuring gleam in her eye. "The vote must be unanimous either way," she declares to the coven.

"Madame Riona." The third Elder rises from her seat. "What is your vote?"

"Nay," the woman says with a shake of her head.

"Madame Caragh?"

The second Elder looks over the High Priestess's shoulder, scrutinizing me, until I feel like I'm drowning in a sea of cobalt. "Aye," she says simply, returning her attention to the High Priestess.

"Madame Bhavna?"

The first Elder doesn't even hesitate. "Nay."

Madame Caragh takes a step forward, clasping her hands at her waist. "And you, High Priestess? What is your vote?"

Astrid clears her throat. "Aye."

It's a tie . . . but what does that mean? From the look on Astrid's face, it isn't good, but I'm not willing to give up so easily.

"Wait," I say, taking a liberty I probably don't have, "what if I can do something for you in return?"

Astrid shoots me a warning glare, mouthing the word *don't,* even as the Elders whisper amongst themselves.

It's Madame Bhavna who asks, "And what could *you* possibly offer *us*?"

"The proof you require. I—I can get that for you. From my understanding, as the Gatekeepers of Mohra, you are unable to travel through it. But, if you grant *me* access, I can revisit the day of Madame Viessa's death. I can bring you the name of the person responsible."

"And why would we believe you?" Madame Riona challenges.

"Because she can capture a recording of the events that day with an enchanted memory rune," Madame Caragh says boldly.

"It's an intriguing idea," the first Elder muses, scanning me up and down with that piercing gaze. "All right. If she'll agree to it, I'll change my vote."

The inflection in Astrid's tone tells me that the tables have turned for the better. "What say you, Madame Riona?"

The third Elder pins me with a threatening stare, her thin lips pressing into a firm line. I don't know why this woman seems to hate me so much—she's only just met me, for crying out loud—but I'm assuming she was closest in relationship to Madame Viessa. She lets out a long sigh, finally uncrossing her arms. "If it'll bring us closer to the truth, then my vote is *aye*."

"It's settled, then," Astrid declares, returning to the dais. "Maren Imogen Cordeau is granted conditional access to Mohra to fulfill her request and, in return, will provide proof of the person responsible for our Elder's untimely death. Now, if there is nothing further to discuss, this meeting is adjourned."

She grabs her lantern and yanks me by the arm, pulling me back toward the corridor that brought us here. I wait until we round the corner before whispering, "So, that's it then? I can go to Mohra now? And Brant will be released?"

The High Priestess's neutral temperament returns. "Not quite. I'm afraid it's not that simple. As I just stated to the coven, you have been granted *conditional* access."

"And what does that mean, exactly?"

"It means that, for now, Brant will stay under the watchful eye of the coven," Astrid says as she urges me forward. "It also means you must undergo the upcoming ritual . . . and survive."

23

ASTRID'S WORDS LINGER in my mind the entire way back to the cottage. She helps me through the cellar door, taking my lantern and propping it up on the table. I have so many questions about the ritual and what it entails, but I'm also hesitant to ask. I'm usually not one to ruminate but with something like this and how much is riding on it . . .

"Hungry?" the High Priestess asks as she closes the trap door and slides the kitchen table back over it. "It's nearly lunchtime."

"So it is." I remove my cloak and gently place it on the back of a velvet-lined armchair. I know I should take her up on the offer, but the thought of food is enough to make my stomach turn. Literally. Impending doom coupled with the great unknown can do that to a person. "Would it be too much trouble to ask for a glass of water?"

Astrid raises a brow. "You're being awfully polite—almost timid. I know we've only just met but, from what I've gathered so far, it doesn't seem like you." She angles her head toward the line of mason jars near the sink. "Help yourself."

Her astute observation catches me off guard, but I meander into the kitchen anyway and help myself to a very full glass.

"The fact that you're also a Noire—well, that alone tells me you're tough as nails." She doesn't bother to conceal the shiver that runs down her spine. "I just want you to know that you don't have to *pretend* around me. You don't have to put on a show like I know we just did for the Elders. You can be who you really are."

While it's a relief to hear, I'm still not entirely convinced that Astrid is someone I can trust—*especially* with how suddenly her demeanor had changed earlier, before we'd met up with the rest of the coven . . . I have every right to have my guard up. "Noted," is all I say.

"That's more like it," she says with a chuckle before heading into the kitchen and sifting through the frying pans hanging from the ceiling. She settles on a bronze one. After she's unhooked it, I expect her to take it to the stovetop but instead, she sets it down with a *bang* on the counter.

"Well?" she demands, fire in her eyes. "Aren't you going to ask me about the ritual? When it is? What to expect?"

I meet her stare head-on. "I . . . I didn't know I could."

"Bullshit." Astrid points a terrifyingly large kitchen knife at me. "That's complete and utter *bullshit* and you know it."

Her blunt tone makes me laugh because it reminds me so much of myself and my usual interactions with Brant . . . Astrid is laughing now, too, which puts me a bit more at ease. I relax into the chair. With Brant on my mind, I can't help but ask, "They won't hurt him, will they?"

"I take it you're referring to your friend." She gives me a sincere smile. "No, not while you're gone."

"Okay, good." I breathe a sigh of relief. "Since you brought it up, when *is* the ritual?"

"Tonight."

I suck in a sharp breath. "You Sables sure move quick. How long will it last?"

"That depends," she responds, grasping at some celery stalks and carrots from a nearby basket. She holds up a handful before asking, "Should I make a double batch?" Her gaze drifts to the colorful vegetables. "Who am I kidding? No need to answer that. Of course I should. You'll need sustenance."

I nod graciously, knowing that my denying or accepting her offer won't change her mind either way. She's a stubborn one. "You're a Taurus?"

She gives me a knowing smile. "And you're a Scorpio."

Dead on the money, that one.

"Complete opposites in so many ways, yet the fact that we're pitted against one another in the zodiac means we have a lot more in common than we might let on," I say.

"Like I said," Astrid says with a grin as she rapidly chops the vegetables, "I can just tell—when you're being real or not, that is."

It's then it dawns on me that she's just led her coven through a rather intense meeting, while also facing off with her Elders in a battle of wits and is now having to deal with me and my suspicious ass. "Is there anything I can help with?" I offer, immediately feeling like I don't deserve her kindness or her help.

"Actually, yes. If you could get the broth started, that would be great." She uses the knife to point to the cast iron pot that's already sitting on the stovetop. "The long-stick matches are in the drawer to the left."

I make my way over, careful not to bump into her in the exceedingly small space. We're nearly back-to-back as I open the drawer and pull out the matches. I turn the gas burner on, then strike a match and light the area underneath the pot.

"I hope you like tofu," she says as she removes a small packet from the icebox. "Our coven doesn't eat meat."

I'm about to tell her I've never cooked or eaten anything tofu-related but then think better of it. There's a first time for everything—meeting with a coven, cooking with a witch, saving my friend and colleague from certain death . . . yeah, we're covering a lot of firsts this week.

"Sounds great," I say, grabbing a wooden spoon to stir the pot with. "Old family recipe?"

"Old *coven* recipe is more like it. This one's been passed down for, oh, I don't even know how many generations. Vegetable broth, tofu, carrots, potatoes, celery, tomatoes . . . a dash of olive oil and a few cloves of garlic and you're all set. It lasts for *days,* and, if you happen to make enough of it"— she winks—"it can feed an entire coven."

I want to ask her if that's been a problem in the past— *hunger*—but feel that the question might be too personal.

"Once it starts to boil, let me know and we'll add the rest of the ingredients." She's moved on to the garlic now, and the reason I know that is because I can smell it.

"You grow all of this in your garden?"

"I do. Impressed?"

"I am, actually," I say with a laugh. "With a supply like this, you'd rarely need to go into town."

"A worthwhile endeavor, if you ask me. It's a bit of a drive, as you've just experienced firsthand." She smirks. "I only go into town once a month, on the eve of the Full Moon. Clearly, I have other plans this time around."

"Don't let my sudden appearance stop you," I urge, feeling guilty. "Why the Full Moon?"

"It's the best time to sneak contraband into the library. And by contraband, I mean books from my own personal library to beef up the occult section." She shakes her head. "For a town with such a storied history around witchcraft, it's a shame to see it so severely lacking."

"So it's *you* I should be thanking for what little research I'm able to do." I give her an appreciative nod. "Keep 'em comin'."

She grins. "I plan to."

I watch as she finishes wiping down the cutting knives before returning them to their proper place. "So, since you said that I could ask . . . what should I expect during the ritual tonight? And are we talking late, like 'the witching hour' or . . .?"

The High Priestess laughs. "No, it'll probably be closer to seven o'clock. There isn't an exact time just yet. We'll receive word from Magna once the Elders are ready for us."

I stop stirring the broth. "Magna?"

"Our messenger crow. That's her name—Magna."

An image of the black bird swooping into the cavern flashes across my mind. "That was pretty epic earlier today, what with you calling the crow and everything. You're like the Crow Whisperer."

"What can I say?" she says, nudging her arm against mine. "Animals love a Taurus. And vice versa."

Her response makes me guffaw, and I realize it's the first time I've openly expressed myself without hesitation since arriving here. Not surprisingly, it feels good.

"To answer the other half of your question, about the ritual . . . it's more of an *attunement*. At least, that's what I prefer to call it."

"It's boiling, by the way," I say, not meaning to interrupt.

"Perfect timing." She grabs hold of the cutting board and, with the edge of her knife, begins to guide the vegetables into the simmering broth. She dribbles a dash of olive oil in the mixture, adding the minced garlic afterward, and finally, the tofu. "Lid?"

It takes both hands and the majority of my upper arm strength to situate the heavy lid over the pot. Astrid turns the burner from high heat to medium-low, then grabs an adorable little pineapple-shaped timer and gives it a full twist. "Should be ready in about an hour."

"You were saying?"

"Ah, yes, the ritual." She walks me over to the sitting area, taking the seat across from me. "As I said, I consider it more of an attunement. And what I mean by that is making sure you're *fit*, more or less, to enter Mohra. On a number of levels."

I almost feel more confused now than when she first started talking, which is likely written all over my face because she quickly adds, "The ritual consists of elemental trials of air, water, fire, and earth. Unfortunately, I can't tell you exactly what each trial entails because it tends to change depending on the Elders' moods." Her face falls, but she doesn't elaborate further.

"Here's hoping Madame Riona has a change of heart before tonight," I scoff. "Seems she isn't exactly my biggest fan."

"She's a crotchety old bag." Astrid gives a flippant wave of her hand. "Pay her no mind."

"Kind of hard not to when she's one of three people deciding my fate."

"Point taken."

"So, if I understand this correctly, the ritual is a way to 'attune' me to Mohra's . . . *energy*?"

The High Priestess gives me an approving grin. "Precisely. You've just said it much better than I ever could have."

"I know you can't tell me the specifics of each trial, but is there anything I need to be forewarned about once I'm actually *in* Mohra?"

"Quite confident, you are."

"Blame it on my being a Scorpio."

Her smile grows even wider, but quickly fades as she answers, "Yes. There is something you should be aware of before entering Mohra."

I straighten in my seat, giving her my full attention before asking, "Which is?"

"Not everyone who goes into Mohra comes back out."
Superb.

"Does that happen often?"

Astrid bites the inside of her cheek, the first sign of insecurity I've seen from her thus far. "It . . . let's just say there's a 50/50 chance—"

"50/50?" I say in disbelief. "That's pretty high. Why is that?"

"To put it plainly, there's a time limit."

"Really?" I implore. "A time limit in a place where time doesn't actually exist and is happening all at once . . . and I thought I'd heard everything."

"I know. Quite the paradox." Astrid runs her hands down the side of the chair before folding them into her lap. "I wish it weren't so, but, seeing as that part of the ritual ensures your *physical* safety, I'm afraid there's no way around it."

"What happens to those who don't return? Where do they end up?"

"Limbo, for a time. We call it the Chasm."

"Like . . . purgatory?"

"Frankly, I haven't been there myself, but Lilith has confirmed it's more like that liminal space between life and death. She's the only one permitted to leave such a place and re-enter as she pleases."

At the mention of Lilith's name, a chill creeps down my spine. "So, their souls are just lost . . . forever?"

Astrid considers this. "I suppose that's one way to put it."

I can tell there's more by the way she presses her lips together after she says it. "What's another way to put it?"

Any trace of color there was drains from her face. "If I tell you, do you give me your word that you won't change your mind?" Her grip tightens around the tops of her legs. "I can't risk my current standing with the Elders. I'm already on thin ice as it were, especially after bringing you here *and* taking your side."

I give a firm nod. "I won't change my mind. You have my word."

She nods, inhaling deeply. "Those who travel to Mohra but end up in the Chasm are forced to meet with Lilith . . . and take an ovetyr sentence if they ever hope to 'get out'."

I can hardly even process what she's just said because all I can see is Brant . . . and Brant meeting with Lilith. Could *this* be the reason for his ovetyr sentence? Something so small and insignificant? . . . That *I'm* now risking my very livelihood for?

Astrid watches me closely. "Does that . . . change things?"

"Honestly, it does," I say, leaning back into my chair, "but there's no point in ruminating over my decision now. I chose this—"

The timer dings. "You stay put. I'll bring a bowl over to you."

I nod in thanks, then squeeze my eyes shut, hoping that I haven't just made an irreversible mistake—one that could cost me everything I've ever known.

24

I WAKE TO a gentle shaking of my shoulder and a quiet voice whispering in my ear. "Maren?"

Slowly, I begin to open my eyes, jolting awake when I don't recognize where I am. As Astrid's face comes into focus, a wave of relief washes over me—but that feeling is quickly replaced by a churning in my gut as I recall our conversation before I'd drifted off.

I sit up in the chair, wincing at the crick in my neck, before glancing out the window. The remaining sunlight is fading, filling the sky with cotton candy hues of pinks and blues. I stifle a yawn as I look to the High Priestess. "How long was I out for?"

"A few hours." She hands me a glass of water to which I hastily gulp down. She takes the empty glass and promptly refills it before bringing it back to me.

"Has the bird,"—I try to think of its name through my sleep-ridden haze—"I mean, *Magna*, shown up?"

The High Priestess tracks my gaze to the window. "Not yet, but I assume she'll arrive within the hour. That's why I wanted to wake you."

"Right," I say, "well, thank you. I can't say I got much sleep the night prior, what with our meeting at dawn and all."

"You're a night owl?"

"More than you would believe. Mostly because my work occurs during regular sleeping hours."

"Ah, yes. Invoking nightmares and such. I can't say the same, but my work does keep me up into the 'witching hour', as you so aptly described it. I, myself, have always been a morning person, so sleep is rare to come by."

"I bet being High Priestess has its perks."

"And its shortcomings," Astrid adds rather glumly.

"As a Noire, I can definitely say the same."

A long silence stretches between us, as I'm sure we're both contemplating how we got here and what the hell we were thinking when we each signed up for our respective incarnations.

She seems to shake the despondence away as she says, "There are fresh towels in the washroom, in case you'd like to freshen up before we leave."

"Do I look that bad?" The remark's meant to be in jest, but the witch seems to take it rather seriously.

"Not even in the slightest. It's just . . . a cold shower might help wake you up. And help with *other* things."

She doesn't clarify *what* other things, but it isn't hard to catch her drift. It's clear I need to be alert and focused for whatever's about to happen tonight. I'm in no position to turn down advice, no matter how cryptic it might be. At this point, I'll take whatever I can get.

Just as I'm pushing off the armchair, a light pecking noise sounds from the kitchen window. Astrid forces a smile. "That'll be Magna," she says, hurrying to the other side of the cottage. She pushes it open, holding out her arm for the crow to hop onto. The scroll in her beak is red, which seems to give the High Priestess pause, but she doesn't address why. As much as I want to ask, I wait for her to finish reading it.

"We have one hour," she says brusquely as she rolls the scroll back up. "Is that enough time for you to shower and get your affairs in order?"

"If by affairs you mean my backpack and my wits, then yes to the former. The latter . . . I'm not so sure about."

She smiles at my attempted humor. "Sorry. Whenever I read anything from the Elders, I immediately go into 'Priestess mode'. It's sort of become a habit."

"As it should," I say, giving her a mini curtsy as I pass by her.

"I'm happy to see you feel so comfortable around me."

I pause at the washroom door, rapping my fingers against it as I flash her a wide grin. "For once, I'm happy to say the same."

She rolls her eyes but her tone is light. "One hour, Noire."

She doesn't have to tell me twice. I salute her and shut the door to the washroom. I emerge twenty minutes later in nothing more than a bath towel. There's a small shelf to the left of the door and folded atop it is a slate gray bodysuit that's stitched from a material I've never seen before. It's thick and shiny like leather but has the flexibility of nylon.

"Is this for me?" I call out somewhat absentmindedly.

"It is!" Astrid answers from the front of the cottage. "Did I mention you should tie your hair back as well so that it's out of your face?"

I release a long sigh before turning back to the washroom and close the door. When I emerge for a second time, Astrid is waiting directly outside. She takes one look at my hair, which is a pathetic attempt at a fishtail braid, before grabbing my shoulders and pressing me down onto a nearby wooden stool. "Allow me."

Even though I can't physically see what she's doing, I can feel how fast her hands are working through my hair. She completes the braid in half the time it'd taken me and, when I steal a glance in the mirror, I'm pleasantly surprised at the outcome. I give her an appreciative nod. "Thank you."

"Don't mention it." She takes her cloak and throws it around her shoulders before tossing me the one I was wearing earlier. I glance at her in brief confusion, wondering why I've just gotten dressed if the end result is just to cover it all up, but she answers the question without my having to ask. "To stay warm. Although it *is* also tradition . . . but only for the initial stages of the ritual."

"Is that all you can tell me?" I tease, even though my tone indicates I'm more serious than I'm letting on.

"I'm afraid so." Astrid slides a few things into the inner pockets of her cloak, eyes shadowed as she asks, "Are you ready?"

"I am," I say, even though I feel anything but.

I expect her to move the kitchen table to reveal the trap door like the first time around, but instead, she walks to the front door and opens it. "Follow me."

25

DUSK CHASES US deeper into the forest, taking us farther and farther away from the railroad tracks, the cottage, from *civilization*. I make sure to stay close enough to Astrid so that I don't lose sight of her, but far enough behind so that I'm not on her heels. We're not exactly on a *clear path*, as it were, but more of a suggestive trail of overgrowth, leaves, and fallen trees. It leads me to wonder how Astrid could possibly know where we're headed, but then I hear the flapping of wings and realize that Magna is our guide.

Unbelievable.

We're playing *follow the leader* with a fucking bird.

With the temperature dropping as the sky darkens, I can only hope that we'll arrive soon because I don't think these cloaks are going to hold much heat. Perhaps my bodysuit will but, last I checked, Astrid wasn't wearing one.

The High Priestess turns over her shoulder, and it's only then I realize I've been so deep in thought that I've stopped walking. "It's just up ahead," she assures me, and, sure enough, I spot some flickering lights.

I jog to catch up with her, my backpack bouncing with the movement. "You know, I thought we'd be back underground, like we were earlier. Although, I will admit, I'm happy to be outdoors in the fresh air."

She shoots me a sidelong glance, her mauve eyes dancing in the encroaching firelight. "You assumed we'd be *inside* during a Full Moon?"

The heat that crawls up my cheeks is undeniable and pointless to try to hide. "Wow, that's probably the most inconsiderate thing I've ever said . . ."

"Really?" Astrid laughs. "Well, if that's the case, the rest of us should be worried."

"Why is that?"

"As a Noire, isn't it your *job* to be inconsiderate?"

"I suppose so . . . but when it comes to people I respect and admire, it's a completely different story."

"Respecting and admiring witches." She winks. "What a time to be alive."

Our banter's cut short as we approach a large clearing, about half the size of a football field. Torches line the circle, the flames casting an orange iridescent glow on the salt that's been spread around the perimeter, small wooden bowls filled with herbs, bones, and other offerings sitting just outside of it. I'm surprised to see that only the Elders are here and not the entire coven, but I simultaneously feel relieved knowing that there will be less eyes on me.

That relief is yanked away, however, when I spot Brant sitting just behind the Elders—in a wheelchair that appears to be crafted out of brass and bone.

My temper flares and, just when I'm certain I'm about to lose it, Astrid steps in front of me, blocking my view. "He's okay," she cautions, reading the obvious fury on my face. "He's just . . . asleep."

Trying not to be blinded by rage, I look past her, past the Elders, directly at Brant. Sure enough, his eyes are closed, his body slumped with his head leaning to one side; but the reprieve I feel is fleeting when I realize what they've done—what they're *doing.* "You're making him sleep . . . you're keeping him that way." I glare at the High Priestess, even though I know this isn't her doing. "You might very well be forcing him into a constant loop of his ovetyr sentence."

One of the Elders seems to have been eavesdropping because before Astrid can answer, Madame Riona, my least favorite of the three, decides to chime in. "Consider it an additional incentive to return from Mohra within the allotted time frame. No more, no less."

The smug look on her face is enough to make me want to strangle her, but I resist, fisting my hands at my sides instead. "Couldn't you start the clock once I'm actually *in* Mohra?" I seethe. "Why should he have to suffer now when my passage hasn't even been guaranteed?"

The smile that pulls at the Elder's face is unnervingly lupine. "Who says he's suffering?"

I know better than to respond to someone who's just trying to get a rise out of me. I turn my attention to the more level-headed Madame Bhavna instead. "What exactly do you need from me to get this ritual started?"

"Patience," she replies simply. "Some things cannot be rushed."

I can't help but glance at Brant again just as Astrid whispers in my ear, "I promise he's okay. What you need to do is focus on the task ahead."

I give a slight nod before taking a deep breath. My gaze travels skyward, at the giant supermoon that's illuminating not only the sky, but the entire forest as well, as if shining a spotlight on whatever insanity I'm about to embark on.

"Kneel," Madame Caragh says, gesturing to the center of the circle. "Put your arms out with your palms open, face up." She mimics her instructions before stepping aside to let me pass. I can feel the Madames' watchful eyes as I take my position, feeling dreadfully exposed, even though I'm fully clothed.

Although they remain standing, the Elders join me, forming a semi-circle in front of me. Centered behind them with her head bowed is Astrid, her expression shrouded by her cloak.

"The vial, High Priestess," Madame Caragh commands.

I watch as Astrid pulls an empty palm-sized hourglass from her pocket. One end is secured with a small cork.

Madame Caragh takes the vial rather hastily, then uncorks it with her mouth. I half expect her to spit it out, like we're in some old western movie, spittoon and all—but she simply releases the cork so that it drops into her free hand. She shoots a sideways glance at the third Elder. They exchange a nod just as Madame Riona steps forward, pulling a small dagger from inside her cloak.

I don't like where this is headed. Not one bit.

Almost instantaneously, I can picture this vile woman slitting my throat and laughing while I bleed out at her feet; but one look at Astrid assures me that I'm safe. As unnerving as it is, I meet the Elder's stare.

"Right or left?"

I have no idea to what she's referring, but seeing as I'm right-handed, I decide to answer left.

She scoffs. "You better believe that's the *only* choice you'll get this evening."

Before I can make a remark or even process what's about to happen, the blade comes down on my left palm, slicing a neat horizontal line. Crimson pools before my eyes, and I hardly have time to react as Madame Caragh rushes forward, vial at the ready, as Madame Riona tips my hand to direct the flow of blood into the hourglass.

"A little warning next time?" Madame Caragh murmurs, reaching for my wrist to steady my trembling hand.

Madame Riona cleans the dagger with the edge of her cloak. "One should assume that asking the question was warning enough." She slips the dagger back into the folds of her cloak, making it just as inconspicuous as before.

"Take this, will you?" Madame Caragh says as she nearly dumps the contents of the vial in the other Elder's hands. "That's more than enough blood."

Much to my surprise, she pulls some gauze and a small cloth from underneath the bangle on her wrist, dressing my wound with great dexterity. "Thank you," I say more shakily than I would like.

"Can I get you anything? Some water?"

"Ahem." Madame Riona clears her throat. "That won't be necessary—"

"Would you give it a rest already?" Madame Bhavna interjects, an amethyst glass filled with water already in her hand. "Here, dear. Drink up."

Determined not to let the presence of magick rattle me further, I graciously take the glass and gulp it down. I attempt to hide the fact that my hands are still shaking, which surprises even me, given my line of work—but it'd happened so swiftly, so suddenly.

I set the glass beside me, daring to look Madame Riona in the eye. She's playing with the hourglass, watching as my blood trickles from one end to the other.

"Give me that," Madame Bhavna orders, snatching it from the Elder's hand.

Madame Riona raises her hands in surrender, which is undoubtedly a rare sight. "All yours."

Astrid steps forward so that she's standing in line with the Elders. "With your blood willingly being given, the ritual has officially begun."

Not like I had much of a choice, is what I so desperately want to say—but I decide it's probably better to keep any hint of sarcasm to myself.

I'm still kneeling as the High Priestess says, "Initiate the elemental trial of air." She gestures for me to rise, which I do on unsteady feet.

I hadn't noticed when Madame Caragh and Madame Riona had left, but they return quietly with a foreign contraption rolling behind them. I realize there's no one pushing or pulling it, which has me perplexed for a moment, until I remind myself that they're witches and are obviously using magick to move the monstrosity. It towers over us, nearly reaching the height of the trees. Moonlight glints on the metal and I quickly gather, based on the two-pronged U-shape, that what I'm looking at are hundreds of tuning forks of various sizes.

Astrid looks at me, assessing my reaction as I take in what's about to happen next. I meet her gaze as she says, "As you've probably deduced, these are specialized tuning forks. For the air attunement, we must ensure that you can withstand the vibrations they emit for thirteen full minutes."

My gaze flicks from her to my first "test", my anxiety climbing as I assess the sheer number. "You're going to play every single one of those?"

"Yes. But not necessarily one at a time. Eventually, it'll be all at once."

I can feel my eyes widen at that.

"We'll start at the back," she continues, "with the deeper notes." She makes a forward sweeping motion with her hand to indicate the order. "We'll conclude at the front."

I gulp. One look at the tuning forks in the front tells me they'll be piercing. Shrill. Migraine-inducing. "For thirteen full minutes?" I confirm.

She gives a stern nod.

"May I ask why?"

"Stop delaying the inevitable and get on with it," Madame Riona snaps.

Thankfully, the High Priestess ignores the Elder. "That's the maximum length of time you're given to travel between timelines while traversing Mohra—although, unfortunately, it'll feel much longer. The structures you saw whilst at the dock—pillars, monoliths, pyramids—they emit the same vibrations as these tuning forks. To keep trespassers out."

Attunement. That's why Astrid had used that word.

"What happens after thirteen minutes?"

The High Priestess doesn't break eye contact as she says, "After thirteen minutes, you'll experience something akin to an intracranial aneurysm."

So, a brain rupture. Cool.

Before I can ask another question, Madame Riona removes her wand from inside her robes. She casts a shield around herself, the other Elders, and the High Priestess. I don't receive such a luxury. Cloaked in a veil of gold, she then flicks her wand toward the back row of the tuning forks. A low hum reverberates around us, building in strength as the forest floor starts to tremor. Pine needles, leaves, and pinecones topple over one another, unable to resist the vibrational pull.

Without giving me time to adjust to the sensation, Madame Riona aims her wand at the second row. The budding vibration strengthens in intensity, more so than I would have thought, and I nearly reach for a phantom tree limb to help stabilize my already unstable legs. Even though no one is speaking—not like I could hear them anyway—I can sense Astrid telling me to breathe and remain calm. To not let this first attunement get to me.

My nerves say otherwise.

Slowly, I widen my stance, hoping to regain some semblance of balance. I take a long inhale, and an even longer exhale. When I breathe in again, I tighten my core. As much as I want to ball my hands into fists, I keep them open at my sides. I lift my gaze to the trees that border the clearing, briefly imagining that I have the ability to grow roots—jutting from the base of my spine into the dense, dark soil.

Reaching, extending, intertwining.

Soaking up the very foundation I'm lacking.

I look to Madame Riona, realizing that we're somehow already through more than half of the rows of forks. My legs are beginning to numb, as is my core, and I can feel that same sensation creeping up my chest and across my shoulders.

Keep breathing.

I glance at Madame Riona again, sheer will blazing in her eyes. And that's when I see it. She *wants* to break me. She wants to watch me crumble, scream, shatter. To be the very cause of my demise. And, what's worse? She'll enjoy every second of it.

I grit my teeth as each new row's vibration is added to the forest's symphony, unnatural and unwelcome in every way. Birds vacate their nests. Field mice skitter to more stable ground. Rabbits leave the safety of their burrows. Even the moon itself seems to shrink into the shadows of the rolling clouds. And yet, I remain, withstanding it all.

I don't give Madame Riona the satisfaction of meeting her stare a third time. Instead, I shift my attention to Brant, knowing that what he must be going through—what he's having to relive over and over again—is probably a thousand times more painful than the numbness I'm experiencing. Pins and needles stab at my neck, rising with each new row that's played; but my focus remains steadfast on Brant.

Stay with me. Stay with me. Stay with me.

That mantra becomes my saving grace, my one and only guiding light. I hold onto it for as long as I can—until the chaos around me has no choice but to swallow my screams.

26

I DON'T KNOW how or when I ended up on the ground, but I'm not alone. Astrid kneels next to me, concern etched along her brow. As my vision sharpens, so does the monstrous contraption behind her. My hand immediately shoots to my temple as my body regains the feeling it'd lost during the first trial.

The words are muffled, but I can hear the High Priestess say to the others, "She's awake. She passed."

"Barely," Madame Riona scoffs.

Astrid helps me to my feet but doesn't pressure me to walk. I give her an appreciative nod. I've never had my entire body go numb before, and it definitely isn't something I'm hoping to experience again.

The feeling is just beginning to return to my feet when Madame Caragh says, "The water attunement is next. Come."

I glance at Astrid in a silent effort to request more time, but she's already guiding me forward by the arm. My knees buckle in protest. I stumble on the second step, dropping to the ground in an embarrassing heap of limbs. Heat crawls up my neck, flushing my cheeks.

"I just . . . need . . . a minute," I say as I struggle to push myself upright.

"Like I said," Madame Riona sneers, the bottom of her cloak whipping me in the face as she breezes by, "just *barely*."

"That's enough," Astrid snaps. "We'll meet you there."

The third Elder huffs but obliges, dragging Madame Caragh behind her.

Astrid reaches for me, but Madame Bhavna catches her arm before we even have a chance to make contact. "She must do it on her own."

Astrid stills, then slowly retracts her arm. The conflicted expression she wears tells me everything I need to know.

"I'm right behind you," I say, mustering a smile.

Even though Madame Bhavna is leading her away from me, Astrid turns over her shoulder, determined to maintain eye contact. The pins and needles in my legs have mostly subsided, but my arms are another story. I shift my legs so that they're bent in front of me and begin to rock back and forth, trying to gain the momentum I need to stand without using my arms. It takes me a few tries, but eventually I pick up enough speed to spring to my feet without falling backward. Now that my legs are fully functioning, I increase my pace to catch up with the Elders and High Priestess. Doing so proves to be a challenge because I can't move nearly as fast as I'd like—but, eventually, I'm moving from solid ground to damp terrain as we approach the edge of a small reservoir. I shiver as a cool gust of wind sweeps across the back of my neck, a subtle indication of what's to come.

Although I've stopped walking, the Elders continue onward until they've reached the other side of the reservoir. The distance between us isn't much, yet I notice Madame Bhavna pull out her wand, no doubt to amplify her voice.

"For the water attunement, the requirement is as follows: thirteen minutes submerged in freezing water."

This time, I don't even have to ask *why* thirteen— hypothermia is nothing to mess around with. I shudder at the thought, then reach down over the edge to feel the water. Much to my surprise, it isn't cold. It's actually rather warm. For a brief moment, I feel like I might get away with not having to do the water trial the way it was intended . . . until I notice the rest of the Elders and Astrid pulling out their wands. Collectively, they whisper in an ancient language I wish I could understand, but the meaning is clear as soon as I see the water in the reservoir begin to ice over.

Well, shit.

The crystallizing happens rapidly, crawling toward me like a bad dream. I haven't even fully caught my breath from the last trial and now they expect me to sit in what is essentially an ice bath? The Sable Coven takes no prisoners, that's for damn sure.

"Jump," Astrid says from my right.

I hesitate, taking the deepest inhale I can manage.

"Jump," she demands again, harsher this time.

I glance at her. "Here goes nothing," I mutter.

I bite down a shriek as icy water rushes over my skin. I'd hoped to land in such a way to keep my head from going underwater, but seeing as this is a depthless pit of subzero despair, there's no avoiding the inevitable. My head crashes through the surface of the water, teeth chattering almost instantaneously. My body freezes all at once. There is no subtle climb of cooling at my feet before moving to my legs, then my torso, then my arms—I'm just frozen all at once.

Like a block of ice.

I shiver as the water around me freezes over, leaving only a small circle of liquid around my neck so that I can still freely move my arms and kick my legs to stay afloat. The movement should help me maintain *some* heat in my body, but for thirteen whole minutes?

I'm a dead woman.

At least in the forest I could see Brant—could have a constant reminder as to why I'm suffering through all of this. But Brant isn't here and it's probably only been three minutes and I already feel like I'm freezing to death.

Okay, calm down.

Focus.

Thinking about how cold I am isn't going to make it any less cold. If I'm going to make it through this—and live to hold it over Brant's head—I need to focus on the one thing I *do* have control over. My mind.

These are mental trials more than they are physical.

In my mind, I can be anywhere other than here.

I can be somewhere warm, on a beach.

In the mountains, nestled by a fire.

On my couch with its many cashmere blankets.

In the cemetery, sharing a smoke with Brant . . .

Something about that last visual warms me, and there's little mystery as to why. Brant is suffering more than this.

He's suffering more more more

I try to hold on to the thought, my only motivation—but I can't feel my legs.

I'm numb. Completely numb.

My face feels puffy, swollen almost.

My lips are undoubtedly turning blue.

My heartbeat slows to an abnormal pace.

And my breathing . . . is shallow. So shallow.

I attempt to look at Astrid, but my eyesight is impaired.

I realize it then.

I'm on the verge of losing consciousness.

How long have I been in here?

How much longer do I have to go?

It's getting harder and harder to stay afloat. Seeing as they're numb, my legs are no longer kicking. My arms are currently flailing, but they'll be the next to go. And then I suppose I'll just sink to the depths of this glacial abyss, never to see the light of day again. Honestly, it doesn't sound half bad. At least I'll no longer be cold . . .

My teeth stop chattering, eyelids growing heavy.

Melting. Melting into the damp void surrounding me.

I exhale what should be a sigh but sounds more like shortness of breath.

Gasping. A dying woman's final breaths.

In the distance, I can hear shouting.

It's Astrid. Calling out numbers.

A countdown.

3 . . .

2 . . .

1 . . .

"Maren, get out!" The High Priestess's voice booms, shaking me from my near-unconscious state. "You have to get out!"

Slowly, the ice begins to dissipate around me, solid melting into liquid. It takes me a moment to register what's happening, where I am; but it's the next thing I hear that gets me moving.

"You did it. You passed!"

Albeit slow, the words finally sink in. *I did it.* I may not be able to feel my legs, but, thankfully, my arms are still functional. I begin to paddle toward the edge of the reservoir, panting as the motion sends heat barreling through my body. I've never swam without kicking my legs and the momentum is slow to build. Never again will I take for granted the privilege of having a fully functioning body.

After what feels like an eternity, I make it to the edge of the reservoir. Astrid is kneeling, frantically reaching for my arms to pull me up and out of the water. I do what I can to meet her halfway—which isn't much—before she heaves me onto dry land. I don't know when or how she'd managed to grab wool blankets, or if they've somehow been here all along, but I'm definitely not complaining as she wraps one after the other around me. It only takes a few seconds for the shivering to start again as my body begins heating up.

"You did great," she whispers, taking a seat next to me on the forest floor.

I can only imagine what I look like right now: hair sopping wet and laced with ice particles, blue-tinted lips, a swollen face, and ears the color of a clown's nose as the blood flow returns to my extremities. "Are you sure about that?" The words come out unevenly through chattering teeth.

Even so, Astrid manages to understand me. "Thirteen minutes in freezing cold water is a major feat. Most people can only withstand ten." She looks me up and down. "How are you feeling? Warmer, I hope?"

I force a smile. "Getting there, I think."

"Well, I caution you not to get too warm because your next attunement—"

"Let me guess? It's fire?"

Impressed, Astrid sits back on her heels. "You certainly catch on quick."

"That can't be healthy, though, right? To go from one physically demanding trial to another?"

"Unfortunately, Mohra doesn't care about what's 'healthy'. Now, could these attunements occur in a different order? Absolutely—and often I think they should." She pauses, biting her bottom lip. "But the way it's set up now guarantees safe passage through Mohra. Encountering all of this again won't be a shock to your system. It'll be, more or less, familiar."

The thought of having to endure any of this again nearly sends me into a tailspin, but I shake the nerves and put on a brave face. "Whatever it takes."

Before Astrid and I can talk further, Madame Riona appears before us, flanked by the other two Elders. "The next attunement awaits." Without warning, she rips the blankets away. It takes everything in me not to strangle her until she's blue in the face. "Come."

Seething—and still trembling from the cold—I clamber to my feet, shaking any remaining water from my hair and clothes. Madame Bhavna and Madame Caragh each give me an approving nod as they pass by. At least *they're* on my side—or seem to be, anyway.

"Only two attunements left," Astrid whispers as she gives my hand a quick squeeze.

I relish the warmth while it lasts, knowing it'll be pulled away too soon. And it is. Nevertheless, I follow the Elders and the High Priestess to the next location, mentally preparing myself for whatever round of hell they've decided I should endure next.

27

I SOMEHOW MANAGE to make it to the next location without stumbling, losing consciousness, or falling flat on my face. I can't say that I fully remember exactly how we got here or how long it took because I was focused on one thing and one thing only:

One foot in front of the other.

We arrive at the same clearing as before, although two things are different: Brant is no longer here, nor is the contraption from the first attunement. I give Astrid a panicked look to which she quickly reassures me that Brant is safe with the rest of the coven. I breathe a sigh of relief, but it's quickly extinguished as the ground beneath me begins to quake. I'm already unsteady as it is, so keeping myself balanced and upright proves challenging but, within seconds, everything stills. The Elders turn to look behind us. I track their gaze, realizing what's just emerged from the ground. Giant rings.

Rings that will no doubt be set on fire.

"If this is another thirteen-minute deal . . ."

"On the contrary," the High Priestess says, "traveling through the portals in Mohra is more unpredictable than anything else, but there is one common factor." She arches a brow. "Heat."

Madame Riona snickers, but I refuse to acknowledge it.

"However, thirteen *does* play a role in this trial." Astrid gestures to the rings and, after completing a quick count in my head, her meaning is clear.

"Thirteen rings. Of course." I pause, chewing on my next question. "Does that mean there are only thirteen timelines that can be accessed in Mohra?"

Astrid grins. "A fine question, but no. There are an infinite number of timelines; however, Mohra presents only thirteen at a time to each individual traveler. At least, it's our understanding that this is the maximum number that can be perceived by a traveler at any given point."

"And the heat?"

"Each portal is encoded with its own heat signature. When you enter a portal to another timeline, that heat signature is imprinted onto your skin. You won't be able to see it once it's imprinted, but in the event you get lost or are unable to find your way back to the gate, we can help you."

Madame Riona clears her throat. "Is there a reason you're telling her all of this now?"

"Because she asked."

"Well, it won't make a difference if she doesn't pass the attunement, now will it?"

Astrid glares at the Elder. Although her patience is wearing thin, she concedes. "Right. Let's begin."

Much to my surprise, the Elders don't pull out their wands to start the blaze. Instead, they move away from the rings to where both Astrid and I are standing. It only takes me a second to understand why. The rings are glowing orange, seemingly on their own, and I can feel the heat from where I'm standing. Everyone except me takes a few steps back.

"The attunement has begun," Madame Bhavna declares.

I choose the ring closest to me and slowly step into it. From where the Elders stand, the rings are transparent, showing either side of the forest depending on the viewpoint; but from my position, up close and personal, there is no forest on the other side of the ring.

Just a swirling vortex of color.

Like a wormhole.

At first, I'm so mesmerized by the colors and patterns shifting around me that I don't even notice the blatantly obvious: the heat. It sears into my skin, past the muscle and cartilage, straight to the bone. I bite back a scream as every inch of my body feels like it's ignited after being doused with gasoline. I try to switch my focus back to the colors and patterns floating around me, but it's no use—I'm fixated on the fiery ache that's scalding every square inch of my skin.

As if it's being etched into my pores, insignia appears along my arms, blazing like flames themselves. The designs look like something off the walls of Mohra, a combination of mythologies, alphabets, and hieroglyphs over the centuries. It remains visible on my arms for mere seconds before disappearing altogether. The heat from the portal dissipates as do the colors, patterns, and brightness from within.

I take a step back so that I'm no longer inside the ring and turn to face the Elders. The High Priestess gives me a nod of approval, but any sense of pride I feel is snatched away as Madame Riona barks, "Next ring."

I sigh, looking at what awaits.

Only twelve to go.

☠ ☠ ☠ ☠ ☠

As the attunement draws to a close, I hardly recognize the sensations running through my body. To go from ice cold to scorched skin is brutal, to say the least, and I can't help but wonder if my sensory receptors will be permanently fucked after this. If so, I'm holding the Sable Coven fully responsible.

The last ring had been the hardest as I'd dodged a pattern that somehow managed to shapeshift an infinite number of times. Talk about a headache. But I'd left that final ring feeling both confident and relieved, despite the inordinate amount of heat raking itself across my skin. Even my organs—*my eyeballs*—feel as though they've been set ablaze.

I suppress the urge to celebrate as Astrid approaches me, a coy smile tugging at her mouth. "And that's how it's done," she whispers so that the other Elders can't hear.

Not wanting to show my hand, I give her a solemn nod, as if she's just broken some devastating news. Our efforts may as well be wasted, however, seeing as it bypasses the Elders entirely. They hardly even notice the interaction.

Madame Bhavna approaches shortly after. "Well done," she says, moving to pat me on the shoulder before thinking better of it. "You're one attunement away from being granted access to Mohra."

I instantly perk up at the thought.

"You can follow me to the last one."

And here I'd thought *maybe*, given the strenuous, horrifying nature of the past three trials, that I'd be permitted a break—some time to recoup in between.

How foolish a thought.

I reluctantly follow Madame Bhavna back to the original location where the first trial had taken place. I'm eager to believe the feeling of relief that's rising within me because, at first glance, I don't spot anything out of the ordinary. No crazy contraptions. No bodies of water. No rings of fire. That isn't to say something hair-raising couldn't be summoned, but there's something about this return that feels safe, certain.

I catch Madame Bhavna's gaze as it drifts to the night sky right as the High Priestess and remaining two Elders join us. I'm tempted to follow her stare and see what, if anything, has caught her attention, but she quickly diverts her focus, eyes settling on me. There's something in her expression I can't quite read, but it causes doubt to flicker in my mind. The feeling is unnerving, having thought that at least two of the Elders were on my side, rooting for me. But that look . . .

Perhaps I'd been wrong.

Or perhaps I'm reading too far into things.

Instead of making a crass assumption, I wait for her to speak.

"Before we begin, I must caution you that the final attunement is the most challenging. While the other trials were physically demanding, the one you're about to embark on relies solely on . . . luck."

I blink. Slowly. I must have misheard her.

Witches believing in luck?

Fate, yes. Destiny, yes.

But luck?

To clarify, I say, "The final attunement is a test as to how *lucky* I am?"

Madame Bhavna shakes her head. "No. It's luck because it's 50/50. It is completely out of your hands."

I look to the High Priestess for further explanation, but she doesn't break her focus from the Elder.

"The final attunement involves summoning a familiar, which will not only be your guide through Mohra, but also our point of contact should anything go awry while you're away."

Astrid waits for a natural pause in the Elder's explanation before adding, "It should be noted that not everyone can summon a familiar, which is why it boils down to sheer luck. Either one will come, thereby agreeing to travel to Mohra with you, or one won't." She shrugs at the simplicity of her statement, even though it's anything but.

"So," I say, nearly grinding my teeth at the realization, "if I *don't* summon a familiar . . . then that's it? Everything I just went through is for nothing?"

"That's right," Madame Riona retorts happily.

And we couldn't have started the trials off with this?

"But I've never summoned anything like an animal before. How am I supposed to know how to do that?"

Madame Caragh steps forward with an ornately crafted conch. "Summoning is simple," she whispers, handing me the horn. "It's what happens afterward that you should be concerned about."

I take the shell from the Elder, turning it over in my hands, before slowly bringing it to my lips. *If this doesn't work . . .*

The bellow reverberates throughout the forest, a call to the wild unknown lurking within. I don't know what I'm hoping for, let alone expecting—it could be a damn field mouse for all I care—just please, *please* don't let all this be for nothing . . .

Thirty seconds pass.

A minute.

And another.

It's looking bleak.

I whirl around in a circle, tempted to sound the horn once more, but Madame Riona seizes it from my grasp.

"What a shame," she says, her tongue clicking against the roof of her mouth. "I knew my first instinct was right about you—"

The Elder is knocked off her high horse right then and there as the sound of wings flapping in the distance begins to grow closer.

Hope lights like a flame in my chest.

The sound continues to grow louder until I see a familiar black bird flying toward me, cawing incessantly as if to apologize for being late.

Magna.

I grin as the bird perches on my shoulder, unable to hide the smug look that I'm now directing straight at Madame Riona. "You were saying?"

The Elder's mouth drops. "This can't be . . . it shouldn't be possible!" the woman sputters. "Magna has *never* been summoned for Mohra—"

"Well, I suppose there's a first time for everything, now isn't there?" Astrid says, her grin matching my own.

Madame Caragh laughs, clapping at the sight before her. "Well done, Maren. Well done."

"Indeed," Madame Bhavna agrees, looking me up and down. "It seems we'll be out a messenger for some time."

Madame Riona gapes at her two sisters. "You're not seriously considering . . ."

"There's nothing to consider," Madame Bhavna barks, clearly fed up with the Elder's antics. "It's settled. Maren Cordeau will be granted access to Mohra with her familiar, Magna, at her side."

"Unbelievable," Madame Riona huffs before storming off in the opposite direction. "Just wait until The Morrighan gets an earful of this . . ." Her voice trails off into the distance and I can almost swear that, collectively, the entire coven's shoulders sag with relief at her departure.

"Congratulations," Astrid says with a wink.

I nod at her and the remaining Elders with pride, then nudge Magna's beak with the tip of my nose. "Thank you," I whisper, hoping the bird might somehow be able to understand me. The subtle twinkle in her eye tells me that she most certainly can.

28

SLEEP HAS NEVER come so easy.

Once we'd arrived back at the High Priestess's cottage, I'd collapsed onto the quaint sofa and slept well into the next morning. I'd awoken to a hint of freshly brewed coffee wafting by, and one glance through my pried-shut eyelids confirmed just that. I must have fallen back asleep, however, because when I stir again, the scent of coffee has been replaced by lemongrass, mint, and a hissing tea kettle.

I grunt as I bring myself upright, squinting at the afternoon light pouring through the windows. Astrid is sitting across from me, no doubt having kept close watch all morning.

"Good afternoon," she says, raising her mug of tea in the air. "You slept well, I take it?"

Groggily, I wipe the sleep from my eyes, then stifle a yawn. "Apparently not well enough."

Astrid smirks. "It's a quarter after two."

I look out the window to where she's motioning. "What time did we get back?"

"It's probably best if you didn't know."

No need to argue there. She's right.

"So . . . are you feeling rested enough to embark on your journey to Mohra?"

I gape at her. "Do you mean to tell me that I only get one evening—a few measly hours—to recoup? After *all that*?"

"First of all," she says, setting her mug down, "it was more than just a few measly hours. And second, your urgency to travel through Mohra hasn't gone unnoticed."

"That was before I realized the attunement would quite literally extinguish my soul from my fucking body."

She lifts a brow, amused. "Here, drink this. It ought to help."

I take the mug she's offering, catching a whiff of mint, lemon, and . . . hibiscus? I take a slow sip before sitting back into the sofa cushions, allowing the herbal concoction to seep into my veins. Its effect is almost instantaneous.

"I guarantee you'll be good as new in no time."

I don't second guess her. Inexplicably so, I'm already feeling ten times better than when I'd woken up. I down the rest of it, hoping she's brewed enough for a refill. Much to my dismay, she denies my request.

"That particular blend is extremely potent. No refills."

I frown, the now-empty mug drooping in my hands.

"But I suppose this means you're feeling better now?"

I sigh, hating the admission. "I suppose so."

Astrid claps, springing to her feet. "I'll gather the necessary provisions."

Just hearing her say that again reminds me of preparing for the attunement. I shiver at the thought, feeling thankful that that ordeal is over. "Can I help?"

"Yes, actually." A familiar conch comes hurtling toward my head. "You can summon Magna."

☠ ☠ ☠ ☠ ☠

A couple hours later, we're trekking back to my car. I'd requested to see Brant one last time, but Astrid wouldn't budge. Said it'd only distract me further from what I'm setting out to do. It's not like I could talk to him anyways, given his current state.

I open the passenger side door, Magna hopping off my shoulder, while Astrid fills the trunk with enough food to feed an entire town.

"When did you have the time to make all that?"

"During your marathon nap." She motions to the wand in her cloak pocket. "Trust me, it didn't take nearly as much time as you might think."

I smile at her before stepping in for a hug, unsure as to how to properly thank her. We've only just met, having been in each other's company for such a short time and yet . . . it feels like I'm saying good-bye to my best friend.

"You don't have to say anything," Astrid says, reading my mind. "And please know that you're welcome here anytime. I mean it."

"If I make it back from Mohra in one piece," I quip, trying to hide the fact that my emotions are getting the better of me.

"You'll make it back," the High Priestess says with certainty. "And, if it makes you feel any better, having Magna with you is essentially like having me there with you. She won't steer you wrong."

"Coming from you, that's high praise."

"You bet it is." She winks. "Now, remember, you can only bring one item with you into Mohra." She hands me the knapsack she'd packed a couple hours earlier. "This is the only caveat, but everything you take with you *must* fit in here. Understood?"

I take the bag from her and open it, noticing that the conch is already inside. "I can blow the conch inside any timeline to summon Magna?"

Astrid nods. "It's preferable you do it without the prying eyes of others watching."

I nod in understanding. The next thing I pull out of the bag is a sturdy leather bracelet with a rune woven into it. I study the inscription carefully—two parallel lines with an X between them, connecting them.

"Mannaz," Astrid confirms. "The memory rune."

I slide the bracelet over my left wrist and tighten it.

"It's already activated. As you access each timeline, it'll record the events that occur. We'll retrieve it from you once you're out of Mohra."

I swallow the knot that's forming in my throat. "And if I don't, you know . . . make it out?"

Astrid doesn't skip a beat. "In the unlikely event you end up in the Chasm, we ask that you give Lilith the rune, as she's the only one who can enter and leave as she pleases."

The mention of Lilith's name makes my stomach turn. "I suppose I can't summon Magna to retrieve the rune?"

"I'm afraid not. While animals are miraculous, highly adaptable creatures, they would not fare well in the Chasm."

"And how will I know if I'm approaching my time limit in Mohra?"

"Also through Magna. She'll appear with various colored ribbons knotted around her foot. A green ribbon indicates that you have 75% of your allotted time left. Yellow, 50%. Red, 25%. And if you see a white ribbon . . ."

I can tell by the drop in her tone that a white ribbon is not something I should be aiming for.

"A white ribbon indicates that there's less than 5% of your allotted time remaining and that you need to leave *immediately*."

"It's a warning that the Chasm is near?"

A grim nod.

I exhale shakily. "Anything else?"

"One last thing." She moves closer, lowering her voice, even though we're the only two out here. "It is imperative that you do not alter a single thing in *any* timeline. You are there to observe, to gather information, to merely be a bystander. Even if something you see angers you, even if it's unjust, even if you see one of your cases from your time as a Noire—"

Well, shit. I hadn't even thought about that.

"It's the Wheel of Life," Astrid continues. "And it's always turning. Know that karma *will* come around. Justice *will* be served. All in due time. You, of all people, should be aware of that, given your role."

I meet her gaze. "Are you sure sending a Scorpio into Mohra is a good idea?"

"Probably not," the High Priestess admits. "But you passed the attunement. Who are we to go against fate?"

I study her for a moment, waiting for her to elaborate. When she doesn't, I close the knapsack and set it in the front seat of the car. "I'll head to the Sephiran tonight, after I've decided exactly which timelines I need to visit."

"Make sure you include Magna in the process so she can be fully equipped to guide you. And please don't forget to visit the timeline where our late Elder . . ." Her voice trails off, eyes pained at the memory.

"I will," I assure her. "You have my word."

"Seriously, Maren," the High Priestess remarks as she produces the hourglass vial containing my blood, "do not fuck this up."

I watch with trepidation as Astrid pockets the vial. She takes my hands and gives them a quick squeeze before leaning in close, her lips brushing against my ear. "May the Great Mother, our Triple Goddess, be with you."

I open my mouth to thank her, to say good-bye, but she's already turned away, hurrying back into the woods toward the cottage. Shakily, I grip the bracelet that's secured around my wrist. *This is what I wanted,* I remind myself.

Magna caws from the front seat, startling me. I shut the passenger side door, then wind around the back of the car and plop into the driver's seat. I turn my head toward the familiar, who's staring at me rather expectantly.

"I suppose it's just the two of us, then."

Magna caws impatiently as if to say, *Drive.*

"As you wish."

Knowing that time isn't on our side, I shift the car into reverse and take off through the forest.

29

A FOURTH CUP of coffee probably isn't the best idea, per se, but I'm neck-deep into plotting my trip through Mohra. I try to ignore the way my hand trembles as I pour the last of the brew into my enormous mug, realizing I've likely had the equivalent of six cups and not four—but that doesn't stop me.

A glance at the clock signals that I only have one more hour until I need to leave for *The Ivory Stallion* with my knapsack, Magna, and my completed list of anticipated timelines. Feeling overwhelmed, I toss my pen to the side and sigh before rubbing my temples. The stack of manila folders on my kitchen counter grabs my attention. How different life had been just earlier this week. If not for my current situation, I'd undoubtedly be preparing for my next case with Brant . . .

but it's precisely *because* of Brant that I'm here, having to endure the unthinkable.

I reach for the pen in my periphery as I review the list I've drafted thus far:

The New Kingdom of Egypt, 1455 B.C.E.

The Greek Dark Ages, 1100 B.C.E.

The Iron Age, 564 B.C.E.

The Viking Age, 873 A.D.

I pause, realizing that I already have four timelines written down, nearly reaching my allotment. I scrawl the fifth and final location: *Madame Viessa's Parlour in Salem, MA, Present.*

I try to ignore the nagging feeling that the last trip will be a waste of both time and energy, but I'd made a promise to the Sable Coven, and there's no way I'd ever cross them.

Not with my literal livelihood on the line.

I'm about to blow the conch when I spot Magna on the windowsill, gazing at the streets below. Carefully, I walk over to where she's perched, then gently set myself down in the armchair adjacent to the window. She doesn't so much as blink an eye at the movement, and it's then I realize that she seems to be in a sort of trance.

"Magna?" I whisper, wondering what has her so enraptured.

But the bird still doesn't move.

"Magna?" I try again. I reach out to stroke the side of her head when, suddenly, she snaps to attention, caws, and flutters to the other side of the apartment. Mouth agape, I study her as she lowers her beak to groom her feathers, entirely oblivious to the events of the last minute or so.

I grip the sides of the armchair, slowly pushing myself upright, wondering what in the hell just happened. Is it possible that I'm already experiencing a glitch in the timelines? Because, if so, I need to get to the Sephiran—and fast.

I'm about to gather the rest of my things when the sound of glass cracking startles me. I turn my head toward the source of the noise to find Magna, talons clicking atop a picture frame—one I've certainly seen before. I draw closer to the bird and look at the frame's contents. Sure enough, it's the picture of Madame Viessa's granddaughter, the very one from her shop.

"How the fuck did that get here?" I murmur, wishing Magna could talk.

The bird just blinks its beady eyes at me.

"Move," I say, shooing her away from the shards of glass. "This is just what I need before I'm about to leave—evidence from a fucking crime scene in my apartment . . ."

Magna stares at me, as if waiting for a decision on whether I'm still going to Mohra or not. "Of course I'm going," I say out loud, trying to ignore the warning bells sounding in my head. I scoot the shattered frame underneath the armchair before setting a wooden crate over it.

"There. Now no one will be the wiser."

With the clock ticking, I grab my knapsack and hastily rummage through what very little food I have in my cabinets, grabbing only those items that are non-perishable and quick to eat—snacks like granola bars, pretzels, crackers, raisins . . .

The dryer dings, indicating that the outfit I'd worn during the attunement is dry. I pull it out of the machine and throw it on, even attempting to braid my hair as Astrid had done the eve of the full moon. The end result is somewhat disappointing and looks nothing like the masterpiece the High Priestess had managed to create, but I don't have the patience—nor the time—to try again.

Hitting the kitchen once more, I grab some water bottles and sports drinks, wishing I'd asked for a bit more information on the requirements for basic human needs while in Mohra. I scoff as I zip the bag up, like I'm packing for a god damn road trip and not a dangerously complex journey through time itself.

The stack of manila folders continues to taunt me as I pass by the counter to the door. With the key turned in the lock, I pause, hating the questions that begin to tumble through my mind. *How many offenders of the very sanctity of the human experience am I letting off the hook? How many more-than-deserving lowlifes are getting to "take it easy" because of me? Moreover, due to this selfish decision, how many innocent victims won't know justice?* All because of this trip through Mohra.

All because of Brant . . .

All *for* Brant.

Racked with guilt, I shake my head, muttering to myself that this better be worth it. I better find what I'm looking for. I pull the door to my apartment open, whistle for Magna to follow, and begin the first leg of the journey.

To *The Ivory Stallion.*

☠ ☠ ☠ ☠ ☠

It must be either my demeanor or the concerned expression I'm wearing because Charlie immediately asks, "Is there something I need to know about this trip in particular?"

I take the hooded cloak from him, realizing that it *may* have been my outfit that's tipped him off. Or the fucking bird perched on my shoulder. "Why do you ask?"

He sighs, rubbing the stubble that's peppered across his jawline. "Why is it never a straight answer from you?"

I force a smile, hoping it'll mask my brimming nerves. "For the sake of transparency, I suppose there *is* one thing you should know."

"I'm listening."

Making my voice as even as I can, I say, "There's no need to leave the door open." I fight the urge to chew on my lip. "This is . . . well, it'll be a longer trip than usual." I offer no further explanation as I throw the cloak around my shoulders and secure it in place. But when I look up, I'm met with the opposite reaction I'd hoped for: Charlie's complete and utter attention.

"How long will you be gone?"

"It's hard to say."

"More than a day?"

"It's likely."

"More than a week?"

I swallow. "Always a possibility."

The disapproving look in his eyes tells me he doesn't like that answer. *Too bad.*

"Maren . . . are you in some sort of trouble?"

"No." I shake my head adamantly. "But my current assignment is rather complicated, to put it lightly. It'll take longer than usual."

"And your friend?" He motions to my side, at the emptiness there, and it's obvious he means Brant. "Where is he?"

I want to say that *my friend* is the whole reason I'm embarking on this insanity in the first place, but I know better. I need to be discreet. That's what this situation calls for. In many ways, I've already said too much.

"It's a solo assignment," I say before starting the descent into the basement. "And that's all I'm going to say about it."

A familiar glow crawls up the sides of my cloak, illuminating my hands in a vibrant shade of orange. Any minute now . . .

"Just—be careful, Maren," Charlie warns, his voice growing fainter. "If you need me, you know where to find me."

If I make it out of Mohra alive. I force yet another smile, giving him a quick nod before plunging into the depths of the Sephiran with Magna as my only company.

3 0

IT'S QUIETER THAN usual in the Sephiran, which is actually much preferred over the usual clamor and chaos. Less to grate against my nerves.

With my head down, I grip the straps of my knapsack, tugging on them as I walk through the barren streets. More than a few times, I'm tempted to turn down the alleys leading to the shops I've come to know so well, but I already have everything I need. At least, that's what I keep telling myself.

I make it to the winding pathway unbothered, passing by familiar leafless plants and husks of trees until I reach the park I'd stumbled across last time. I continue onward, welcoming the encroaching darkness as the mausoleum begins to come into view. Surprisingly, I feel less paranoid this time around, and I wonder if it's because I have the support of the Sable Coven. Now that I've come face to face with Lilith, I'm not nearly as intimidated by her. If we happen to cross paths, then so be it.

I grab my lighter from the inner pocket of my cloak and flick it on before venturing into the massive crypt. As captivating as they are, I do my best not to get distracted by the symbology etched into the walls. Moments later, I'm breathing a sigh of relief as I step onto the pier. The cavern looks exactly the same, as does the water, the canoe, and the monuments in the distance . . . The very monuments I will be entering any second now.

The silence unnerving, I shakily retrieve the small piece of paper I'd written my destinations on. May as well go in order. First up: *New Kingdom of Egypt, 1455 B.C.E.* From her perch on my shoulder, Magna glances at the script before cawing and flying to the edge of the canoe. She looks at me expectantly and I have no choice but to oblige. One glance at the water has me shuddering involuntarily as I relive the attunement I'd undergone beneath the full moon. *I don't have to get in the water,* I remind myself as I carefully step into the boat. But the searing heat of the portal? I suppose I shouldn't get too far ahead of myself.

Suddenly, a reflection of blue and indigo emerges along the surface. I glance over the side of the canoe to witness the impressive collection of hieroglyphs glowing in the darkness. If memory serves, the next step is . . . Oh. Fuck.

The chant.

The Sable Coven hadn't prepared me for the chant!

How can I expect the damn boat to move if—

A melody so eloquent sounds from across the canoe, echoing throughout the cavern, and when I turn to look at Magna, toward the source of the song, there's no longer a bird perched there, but a woman with waist-length midnight hair, donning a black leather corset and matching pants. A tiara of crow's beaks adorns her head, and around her upper arm is an obsidian-encrusted Celtic pentacle. Dried blood coats her hairline, the black kohl rimming her eyes and shading her cheeks reminiscent of war paint. Even so, she is arguably the most beautiful woman I have ever seen.

And I know exactly who she is.

"The Morrighan," I whisper, bowing my head in reverence. Otherwise known as The Triple Goddess—deity of death, battle, bloodshed, and destruction. The shape-shifter she's renowned to be, the crow should have given her away.

The Morrighan doesn't smile, doesn't so much as acknowledge me, as she continues with the chant. The canoe jolts forward as we make our way toward the monuments. I watch her in awe, wishing I could ask her the hundreds of questions that now swarm my mind, to at least tell her the impact she's had on me, my life, my work as a Noire.

But all I say is, "As above, so below, Goddess."

This seems to catch her attention, but she doesn't respond. We make brief eye contact and something in her gaze warms me, but as quickly as it's there, she's turned away to face forward again.

We travel in silence—sans The Morrighan's song—back, back, back into Mohra. I'm beginning to wonder if there's an order to the monuments when the canoe finally slows, bumping up against a shore made entirely of crystallized glass—something that certainly isn't visible from the pier.

The Morrighan shifts her gaze to me and bows her head before saying, "Fortune be with you." But before I can open my mouth to thank her, she's swept up and away in a black mist, fading into nothing. I wait a few moments, wondering if Magna will return in her place. The water laps against the canoe, the crystallized glass nearly humming from the impact once it reaches the shore.

When it's clear that Magna will not be returning for this portion of the journey, I slowly swing one leg over the side to find stable footing on the uneven surface. I have never been more thankful for the leather combat-esque boots I'm wearing—any other footwear wouldn't survive a single step across this shoreline.

I'm so distracted by the glassy shards and *not* falling to a painful death that, as I make my way over to the monument, I'm nearly blindsided by the blazing heat. How I'd almost forgotten. At least this time it won't be thirteen portals of searing heat I'll have to withstand. Just five.

I take a shaky breath, stepping closer to the monument as it begins to do exactly what I'd seen in the forest during my attunement—morphing into a wormhole of various lights, colors, and patterns. One more step has me entering the cosmic gate, Egyptian hieroglyphs appearing on my arm.

At least The Morrighan had led me to the right place.

The monument's heat signature scorches my skin. I bite down on my lower lip, stifling a scream, knowing that it'll be over with soon. One extreme is suddenly replaced by another as I fall from the sky, landing face first into what feels like an enormous sandbox. But when I lift my head, I'm no longer in a vortex of swirling color . . . I'm on sandy terrain that leads to an Egyptian temple.

I'm here. I made it.

A knotted whip hits my lower back, causing me to arch in pain, the sun overhead blinding.

"Yalla!" a gruff voice shouts.

I can't explain how I know that *yalla* is Arabic for *let's go*, but I do. I obey the command, quickly coming to the realization of what this past life entails for me: enslavement. I don't dare look behind me—not at the man who's just whipped me nor at the hundreds of others I can feel staring at my back, hands bound just like mine.

"Damn it," I mutter, realizing that I'm speaking Arabic, possibly Coptic, but hearing English in my head.

"Speak again and I'll cut out your tongue."

On the bright side, at least I'm able to translate.

I'm ushered forward into the temple, wishing that there was another person in front of me to lead the way, but at least I'm getting a front row seat to the complete and utter inhumanity of my past life.

We don't walk for long, eventually reaching a chamber that is clearly unfinished. My guess? This is where I'll be working for as long as I'm here. The man who'd yelled at me earlier approaches, unbinding my hands with the precision of someone who's done this a thousand times. I don't dare look him in the eye, in case that's somehow a crime, too. He moves to the person beside me and begins to hastily untie the sturdy cloth binding his wrists. From my periphery, I sense it's a young man, around my age. Again, I don't dare look.

Ten minutes pass until the last person is unbound, our captor . . . *master?* . . . leaving us to work. In front of my workstation is a copper chisel and a mallet. I glance at the station beside me, noticing a couple of brushes and an array of bowls containing charcoal, gypsum, copper salts, yellow and red ochre, and copper wollastonite. The hieroglyph-filled wall to my right is indicative of what my task is for the blank slate that sits before me.

I hesitate before retrieving the chisel and mallet, feeling utterly underprepared and incompetent. To my left, the young man is busy mixing the ingredients from the different bowls to make an array of colors: black, white, blue, yellow, red, green. He picks up one of the brushes and dips it into the bowl of red, using careful strokes to paint what's already been etched into the wall.

Why couldn't I have had that job?

I watch the slight flick of his wrist as he coats the symbols in red, wondering if my back will carry the same fate if I don't get to chiseling soon.

"Testing the limits today, are we?"

I gape at him, not expecting his voice to sound so familiar, to sound just like . . .

Brant.

He turns his head. Tears prick my eyes at the boyish smile he gives me. He looks so different with his bronzed skin, dark eyes, dark hair, and rags for clothes, mere skin and bones . . . but it's him. I can feel it.

He tosses a quick glance over his right shoulder before removing a slip of papyrus from underneath one of the stones at my workstation. He points to the first hieroglyph.

"Hatshepsut, Foremost of Noble Ladies."

Of course. Hatshepsut, one of the few ancient female Egyptian pharaohs and the fifth pharaoh of the Eighteenth

Dynasty. And the year I'd traveled to . . . 1455 B.C. She'd passed around 1458 B.C., so here we are, approximately three years later, finishing her tomb, telling her story.

"Thank you," I say, giving him an appreciative nod. As much as I want to continue speaking with him, I know better than to get us both chastised. I look at the piece of papyrus, my literal saving grace, and study the first symbol of many. I bring the chisel to the wall, the mallet mere inches behind it, and begin my work for the day.

☠ ☠ ☠ ☠ ☠

Later that evening, as I'm escorted to my sleeping quarters, I'm relieved to find that my knapsack is in the corner of the small room. After the events of the day, I hadn't been concerned about it. In fact, I'd nearly forgotten about it altogether. Feeling famished and not knowing when my next meal will be, I grab a granola bar and scarf it down. While it isn't much, it'll have to do. I've never had to ration food before, but, seeing as this is only my first stop, now's as good a time as any to start.

As I'm digging around the bag, my hand brushes against the conch. I remove it halfway, wondering if today was all I was meant to see: the fact that Brant and I were ancient Egyptian slaves, tasked with finishing the chamber just outside Hatshepsut's tomb. But knowing Brant and I, that isn't even close to the end of the story . . .

I must have drifted, either from food deprivation or exhaustion or both, because when I wake, Brant is standing near the doorway with an impatient look on his face.

Startled, I jump to my feet, noticing that he's no longer wearing the ratty linens from earlier, but russet silk trousers and a matching tunic. He tosses me a similar set before asking, "What gives?"

I have no idea what he's talking about so I shrug, then motion for him to turn around. I quickly remove the dusty, torn clothes I've been wearing all day and replace them with the silk outfit. There's only one word for how it feels against my skin: *divine.* Just give me a hot bath, a cup of coffee, and my bed, versus whatever this straw mat is, and we're in business.

"We leave. Now."

His tone tells me that there's no time for questions, so I grab my knapsack before following him out of the shabby stone-and-mud shack, slinking across the sand underneath the moonlight. We're quick to arrive at the entrance since the slaves' quarters are mere steps away from the temple—I have to hand it to the ancient Egyptians when it comes to matters of efficiency. Brant steps behind a stone pillar, pulling out two shovels before tossing one to me. I catch it, wondering if this is part of the task we've been assigned, but we don't stop at our workstations.

No, we keep going . . .

Into Hatshepsut's tomb.

And that's when I realize this particular past life is about to take a grim turn.

We're fucking tomb robbers.

He directs me to the other side of the sarcophagus as I rack my brain for everything I know about tomb robbing.

What's the likelihood we get caught?

How severe is the punishment?

Was this his idea or mine?

Why are we robbing the tomb of ancient royalty?

Oh, the karma this will undoubtedly bring.

Astrid's earlier warning plays in my mind: *Do not change anything about the timeline, no matter how tempting.*

This certainly counts as one of those moments.

I bring my shovel to the side of the tomb, looking Brant square in the eye.

"Dig," he orders.

Much to my chagrin, I do as he says.

31

I'D READ ABOUT the riches ancient Egyptian royalty had allegedly been buried with, but nothing could have prepared me for the sheer *amount*. Not only was Hatshepsut's tomb filled with fine linens, cosmetics, and metals, but jewelry of the highest quality—gold and silver diadems, necklaces, pectorals, pendants, amulets, bracelets, earrings, and rings embedded with the finest gemstones known to humankind. In fact, the jewelry had been crafted with such a superior degree of refinement that I doubt it's been surpassed or even equaled in modern times.

I can see why tomb robbing was a beloved pastime of slaves, serfs, and peasants—well, maybe not so much a beloved pastime as it was a means of survival.

We'd managed to use the linens to create makeshift bags that could carry most, if not all, of the jewelry out of the tomb. Fortunately, with our living quarters being so close, it'd been rather easy to slip in and out undetected. We'd made sure to slide the cover of the sarcophagus back in place, giving the appearance of being undisturbed, as well as taken the shovels with us on our way out. The only way someone would know that it'd been robbed would be to take a look themselves, which, being a sign of disrespect, seems unlikely.

Having insisted on taking the loot back to his place, Brant and I are now in his room, carefully sorting through everything we'd pilfered—gold in one pile, silver in another—and from there, sorting into their respective categories. Much to my surprise, the number of amulets and diadems significantly outweigh the other categories. I'm tempted to ask what we're going to use it all for, but figure he'll tell me when the time is right. My guess is for food. Water. Clothes that aren't torn or ripped.

Damn is he about to prove me wrong.

The next day is almost an exact replica of the one before. Wake up, line up, enter the temple, and get to work. I'm groggy from our nighttime rendezvous, which I'd expect Brant to be, too, but he seems alert. On edge. He doesn't talk to me, look at me, or even *acknowledge* me.

It's off-putting.

I'm trying to ignore the dread curling in my stomach as I chisel the hieroglyphs into the wall, but the feeling is only amplified when a guard approaches me.

"Yalla," he says harshly. He doesn't even give me a chance to stand before yanking me from my seat on the dirt-ridden ground. I'm ushered out of the temple before I can say anything, but a glance back at Brant tells me I'm in trouble.

Head bowed, eyes darkened by shadows . . . *what has he done?*

When I'm brought before the pharaoh, it all becomes clear. Hatshepsut's jewels lay sprawled on a table for the entire court to see. The motherfucker framed me.

The pharaoh raises a brow as he looks me up and down. "Is this the perpetrator?"

The guard nods. "The jewels were discovered in her quarters early this morning, before her shift."

"And the sarcophagus?"

"Still intact."

The pharaoh considers the information, studying me with kohl-rimmed eyes. "All the jewels are accounted for?"

"Indeed. They are."

The pharaoh sighs, looking somewhat relieved. "Bring him in."

I don't even have to turn around to know they're talking about Brant. Hell, I can feel the guilt radiating off of him from all the way over here. Footsteps draw closer as the guards bring him in front of the pharaoh.

"Your testimony stands?"

Out of the corner of my eye, I see Brant nod.

Coward.

"Then you are no longer an indentured man."

Freedom. That was the price of his betrayal.

"As for you," the pharaoh says, his gaze shifting to me, "we'll see to it that you never rob another tomb again." He whistles and a man from behind him appears with a razor-sharp blade.

Fuck.

"Right or left?"

"Left." The pharaoh sighs. "We still have use for her—if not chiseling, then painting."

The man grabs me by my left wrist and pulls it onto the table. The blade sings overhead as it slices through the air, ready to meet flesh and bone. *My* flesh and bone.

I grit my teeth, not knowing if I should try and plead my case, but Astrid's warning sounds in my head yet again, clear as day: *Don't change anything.*

If this is how it played out, if Brant really is a traitorous snake . . .

The blade comes down, hot and heavy. One clean swipe and my left hand has been amputated. Looking at it will only cause the anger to swell inside me, so I keep my head turned, seething all the while. The smell of burnt flesh fills the room and I suppose I should be thankful that the wound's at least somewhat cauterized, but the next thing I feel are multiple hands tightly wrapping and pressing linens to my forearm to stanch the flow of blood.

"Remove her from my sight," the pharaoh orders.

The guards drag me away, passing Brant as we go.

"You piece of shit," I murmur, just loud enough for him to hear. But just like earlier at our workstations, he doesn't respond, doesn't look at me, doesn't acknowledge me; just keeps his gaze straight ahead, not a hint of remorse to be found. I may have been his way out in this lifetime, but luckily I have my own means to escape. The minute I get back to my quarters and the guards leave, I, quite literally, single-handedly rummage through my bag and blow the conch, desperate to forget that this entire ordeal ever happened in the first place.

32

ONE MINUTE I'M in Egypt and the next I'm back in Mohra, in the canoe, waking up from what can only be described as a nightmare. I must have passed out from the pain or blood loss or both because Magna's perched on the side of the boat, studying me.

I lift my hands, relieved to find that both are still attached and functional, completely unscathed. If I hadn't fallen unconscious, I'd still be reeling from the events that had transpired in Egypt. The way Brant had sold me out like that, with absolutely no remorse, no regret . . .

I now worry that it'll be the same story throughout time.

And, if that does happen to be the case, perhaps Brant's gotten what he deserves. But I don't want to give up hope.

Not yet.

Honestly, I could use some time to recoup and gather my thoughts after such a massive betrayal, but time is a luxury I don't have. The irony isn't lost on me.

Magna continues to stare straight into my soul with those beady eyes, urging me to choose my next destination.

As if she doesn't already know.

"The Greek Dark Ages," I say with a heavy sigh. "1100 B.C.E."

☠ ☠ ☠ ☠ ☠

The glow of the full moon is the only thing to illuminate the surrounding darkness. Solid rock greets me as I reach an arm out to my left, then to my right. I'm barefoot, in tattered clothes, covered in dirt and grime. I run my tongue over my teeth, shuddering at the grainy texture. Thirst overcomes me as I subconsciously lift my hands to my throat, feeling parched.

"Hello?" I croak into the void above.

There's no reply.

I wait for my eyes to adjust. When they do, I realize I'm in a stone pit. Either I'm being held captive as a prisoner against my will . . . or I've done something that warrants being down here. I'm not sure which is worse.

It's hard to say how much time passes when I happen to notice a dark figure looming overhead. From the stocky build of the shadow, I'm guessing it's a man.

"Quiet down," he barks, even though I've only said one word.

"Water," I plead, hoping this stranger is kind enough to show some mercy.

"Not for your kind," he says curtly.

256

My kind. How I wish I could ask for clarification.

"Please," I say again. "No one has to know."

His gaze hardens. "Just like no one had to know about our . . . relations?"

Maybe it's the dehydration, or maybe it's the fact that I've only just arrived with zero context as to how I ended up here, but something tells me I've taken the fall for this oaf.

For something I'm not guilty of.

Using the power of deduction, I take my chances. "You and I both know who really deserves to be down here."

He scoffs, hastily dropping to his knees before lowering his head into the pit. He glares at me. "Going back on your word, are you?"

I meet his stare head-on. "You tell me."

Pondering my response, he clicks his tongue against the roof of his mouth. Granted, I have no idea what the details of our little arrangement are, but I'm hoping he'll at least reveal *something.* Until then, I'll continue to improvise. So far, it seems to be working.

He runs a hand along his jaw, his complexion golden, even in the waning moonlight. "I can't help you escape. At least, not yet."

I grit my teeth. "Then the least you can do is give me some water, lest I die of thirst."

He sighs, reaching for a flask that's belted along his toga. "It's pure," he says, as if that's supposed to mean something to me. He tosses it down and I snatch it greedily, guzzling down every last drop.

The clanging of metal grabs his attention. "The guards are coming," he says, motioning for me to toss the container back up. "If they catch me here, we're both as good as dead."

I arch a brow. "Says the one standing *above* the pit, free to do as he pleases."

"Without me, *you're* as good as dead," he snarls. "Now, toss it up."

I reluctantly do as he says, watching as he secures it back into his belt, then crouches to disappear into the night. Footsteps approach, and something tells me I should either be out of sight or, at the very least, feigning sleep. I go with the latter. Even behind closed eyes, I can sense the shadows of two men hovering. Waiting. Watching.

"Can you believe the audacity of this *hetaira*?" a voice scoffs before proceeding to spit into the gaping hole. I peek an eye open as a glob of saliva lands inches from my head.

"Courting a noble is one thing, but seeking a business partnership is just plain despicable."

The fragmented pieces of this lifetime are beginning to come together. The man who offered me the water must be the nobility these men are referring to and I the courtesan, who, clearly, should take no part in the dealings of Greek commerce or trade. *That's* why I've been thrown in here? Because I'm an educated woman with a keen intellect, sharp mind, and *other* less discreet talents? Please.

Long live the fucking patriarchy.

As it's rather likely I'm an accomplished courtesan, given what these two are insinuating, I can only surmise that I'd made a business proposal in confidence to the wrong person. Someone who, more likely than not, sold me out to the highest bidder *or* claimed the genius idea as his own. All signs point to the man who'd finally obliged my request for water.

Given one guess, I'd say the man is Brant.

It seems we've turned pleasure into business in this particular lifetime—and to think, I'd been worried about mixing the two in our current incarnation.

I crack an eye open as the footsteps above recede, only sitting upright when they've faded entirely. I squint in the darkness, using what little moonlight remains to search the corners of the pit for my knapsack. It doesn't take long to find it. Knowing I'll have to sleep down here has me seriously considering blowing the conch to summon Magna, but that'd defeat the purpose of what I'm trying to find out.

I sigh, situating the upper part of the bag so I can use it as a pillow. I place my arms behind my head for extra support, gazing up at the moon until it disappears from the night sky altogether.

☠ ☠ ☠ ☠ ☠

Flecks of dirt and rock hit my face, but that isn't what wakes me. It's the shouting of men, the lugging of stone as it scrapes across the ground. I blink one eye open, squinting in the blinding sunlight. It's such a stark contrast to the night prior.

Not wanting to draw attention to my knapsack, I scoot to the edge of the pit to hide it behind a decent-sized rock. I stifle a yawn, observing the commotion above me, wondering what form of punishment the Greeks will choose to dole out. My flippant attitude turns grim, however, when I notice the boulders up above that now line the perimeter of the pit. My blood runs cold.

They're going to stone me alive.

The realization has me dashing back over to my bag to retrieve the conch. I'll be damned if I'm forced to suffer through this. I blow into it as quietly as I can, hoping the sound will be muffled by the ruckus taking place above. I search what little I can see of the skies for Magna, but only clouds drift above me. My breathing grows shallow as panic begins to settle in. If I stay pressed against the edge of the pit, I can avoid being crushed by the incoming boulders. But, with enough of them, any and all open space in the pit will be completely filled, living little room to move, let alone breathe. My choices are bleak.

Either a swift, painful death or a slow, agonizing one.

I turn my gaze toward the sky again. *Where the fuck is that stupid bird?*

"If I'm to understand correctly, not only did she attempt to derail your business proposal to the court, but she also planned to poison its members?"

I strain to hear as a familiar voice says, "That is correct. A substantial amount of hemlock was found in her chambers before the meeting with the noble council."

"I see," the first voice says. "By carrying out her execution, you will not be granted a replacement courtesan."

"Understood," Brant says.

"Then I'll leave you to it."

My hands fist at my sides as I hear Brant shouting orders, the boulders above inching closer to the edge. My anger getting the better of me, I emerge from the shadows, wanting to get a good look at the man who has no qualms when it comes to betraying me, yet again.

"So, this is how it ends?" I say, realizing I'm speaking Greek. "You discard me with such ease." I spit at the ground, wishing it were his face. "Despicable bastard."

The insult strikes a chord, but not the one I'd hoped for. His face turns stone-cold. He opens his mouth, prepared to issue the command that will result in my death, when I interrupt him.

"To execute by brutal force or by lethal poison and you choose the former." I scoff. "Your choice speaks volumes."

Brant narrows his gaze. "As did yours."

I'm not sure to what he's referring, but the vengeance in his eyes is unmistakeable. While we both may have wronged the other, it shouldn't have amounted to something like this.

Something so extreme.

My anger dulls, replaced by overwhelming sadness.

Knowing my fate rests in his hands and that I can't change it no matter what I say or do, I yield. "Carry on, then."

I stand there, completely and utterly exposed, waiting for a trace of empathy that never arrives. He turns a steely gaze away from me. "On my count," he commands.

He speaks the first number.

I shudder.

Then the second.

I bow my head.

And then the third.

I squeeze my eyes shut, wishing I could block out the sound of grunting as the boulders leave the precipice. Darkness encroaches as any remaining sunlight is snuffed out, much like my ability to breathe. But I remain standing, even through the downfall of crashing rock, in solemn defiance of such an undeserved fate.

33

I'M THRUST BACK into Mohra before I can feel the crushing weight of the stones—and thank goodness for that. The Morrighan sits across from me in the canoe, her face neutral.

"Thank you," I pant. "For a minute there, I thought you weren't coming."

Instead of acknowledging what I've said, she simply gazes across the water at the other monuments. "State your next location."

I struggle to collect my thoughts as I clutch the knapsack in my lap. "What if I've seen enough?"

She doesn't even hesitate before saying, "You haven't."

I'm taken aback by her answer, but still manage to defend myself and my decision. "It's my understanding that while I'm permitted to visit five timelines, I'm not *required* to do so."

"You took a blood oath. You have no choice but to see all five timelines through to the very end."

I glare at her. "Pull me out as indicated this time around, all right?"

The Morrighan smirks. "Only when you've seen all you need to see."

☠ ☠ ☠ ☠ ☠

Dinner by candlelight would normally be considered a romantic gesture, but with the man sitting across from me? It's anything but.

A casual glance at my lap indicates that I'm wearing a beige stola, my wrists adorned with precious metals. The man sitting across from me dons a toga, his expression harsh and unforgiving. The garb alone tells me that I am his wife.

"Erythia, are you listening?"

I snap back to, offering the brute a smile that doesn't reach my eyes. I nod, giving him my full attention. He continues rambling about some trade route or another, but I'm not so focused on the context of the words as I am the words themselves. *Greek. He's speaking Greek.*

Fortunately, he's interrupted by a small, young fellow who's carrying a tray with both hands, allowing me time to get my bearings. As per my request in Mohra, I'm in the Iron Age in Akragas, Sicily. 564. B.C. My name is Erythia. I'm a married woman. I speak Greek. But this man who is supposedly my husband . . . who *is* he? And why do I already dislike him?

"As you wish, sir," the young man says before taking his leave.

Damn. I was hoping to get a name.

"And what of Paurolas?"

The question is directed at me, but I have no idea what or who Paurolas is. I force another smile, reaching for the goblet in front of me, hoping to buy some time. It's then another gentleman appears, his gaze traveling first to me, then to my alleged husband. I can instantly tell by the way his eyes meet mine and linger that this man is Brant. Dressed in a military uniform, I'm guessing he's a commander. The decorated belt adorning his waist says as much.

In eavesdropping on their conversation, I finally catch a name. *Phalaris. My husband's name.* Which, I'm guessing, means the word he'd spoken earlier—Paurolas—is our son.

What I know of this time period is rather limited, so I take the opportunity to observe the room for additional clues as to what's going on. Ornate décor, paintings, and statues of gods and goddesses cover every inch of the room, but those aren't what catch my attention. Highlighted in the center of the farthest wall is a bronze statue of a bull, its actual size mimicked in every way.

The Brazen Bull. A torture and execution device built for the likes of criminals. Hollow and made entirely of bronze with a door on one side, the condemned are locked inside, a fire set just underneath to roast them to death. And I just so happen to be married to the man who ordered such a monstrosity be built.

My eyes flick to the Commander as I take another nervous drink from the goblet, but he doesn't meet my gaze.

"Perhaps it'd be best our conversation continue in private."

I raise a hand to interject my thoughts, but Phalaris gives me a stern look, one that says to keep my mouth shut.

"Follow me," he says, leading the Commander just out of earshot.

I'm not particularly keen on seeing where this is headed, knowing it'll likely end in my demise, so I begin to scan the room for any sign of my knapsack. I feel around underneath my chair, finally grabbing hold of it. I lean over as inconspicuously as possible to blow the conch, hoping that Magna won't leave me hanging like last time. Although the sound is quiet, I nearly jump out of my skin as Phalaris calls for me.

I stand, straightening my stola before approaching the two men. My heart thunders in my chest with each step I take toward the brazen bull.

"I've just been informed that Paurolas has declined his position in our military's service."

"Oh?" I'm not sure what he expects my response to be.

"And that you're to blame."

Confusion ripples through me, but I don't let so much as a flicker loose. "What mother, in her right mind, would knowingly choose to send her own son to his death?"

"Not many." The Commander pins me with a menacing stare. "Which begs the question . . . why send him to his death at our enemy's hands?"

I look between the two of them, at a loss for words.

"What proof do you have?" Phalaris demands.

"The correspondence." He hands over a stack of written letters. "Is that not evidence enough of your namesake?"

Phalaris sighs before running a thumb over the raised wax seal. "It is." He combs through the letters without another word. He doesn't even make it halfway before lifting his gaze. "What do you have to say for yourself, Erythia?"

"I have no knowledge of the sort."

Phalaris raises his voice as he says, "They're in your handwriting!"

"Undeniably so," the Commander quips.

"An imitation, then," I urge, trying to buy myself—and Magna—more time. "And a damn good one at that."

Phalaris shakes his head. "Our son deserves better than this. As his father, it's my duty to make sure of that."

Before I can protest further, they lunge for my wrists, tightening their grip as they pull me toward the brazen bull.

Where the fuck is Magna?

"If you put me in there, Paurolas will never forgive you," I seethe at my so-called husband. I turn my head toward the Commander; Brant in a fool's uniform. "And I'll never forgive you for betraying me, time and time again."

But my words carry little weight. He regards me with a soulless stare. "You brought this upon yourself. I'm only here to reveal the truth."

I can't get another word in edgewise. I'm no match for their brute strength as they heave me into the bronze pit of death and lock the door from the outside. The bastards waste absolutely no time lighting the fire that will bring me to my death. Remnants of the attunement flash across my mind, along with the searing pain from the scorching rings I had to endure. I shove down a scream as the heat beneath me begins to build.

That's what they want. For me to scream. To reduce my pain, agony, and suffering to the mere acoustics of a bull's bellow. I refuse to give them the satisfaction. I'll die with what little dignity I have left.

I squeeze my eyes shut as I'm engulfed in the scorching blaze. It threatens to strip me raw, to suffocate me. But I don't utter a sound, hoping that my silence speaks volumes to the men standing just outside what's about to become my bronze casket.

34

I WAKE UP on the edge of a ravine in the most beautiful place I've ever laid eyes on. Rocky cliffs surround me, further enhanced by lush overgrown pastures and crystal-clear waters. With the next timeline on my list being The Viking Age, it's safe to guess I'm in Scandinavia. How I wish I could be here under different circumstances.

It seems The Morrighan's had enough of my antics because I don't recall having a conversation with her before winding up here. Which is probably for the best, seeing as she most certainly did not answer the call of the conch in a timely manner, as I'd requested. Instead, I'd been left to suffer the agonizing torture of the brazen bull. I shiver, running my hands up and down my unmarred skin, my fingers catching on the plush fur wrapped around my wrists and draped over my shoulders.

My hands drift to my hair. Half of it is fastened in a messy updo with braids at the sides. I squint as I lift my gaze, flecks of maroon ochre and charcoal falling from the marks painted on my face. From where I stand, I can see a distant village, which appears to be the only one in sight. I hesitate, deciding whether to stay put or brave the trail ahead. It doesn't take a history scholar to know that the Norse are a proud, loyal people who don't take kindly to outsiders. If I happen to be from a rival clan, I'm as good as dead; but staying in this very spot won't reveal whatever it is I need to know about this lifetime. I sigh, packing up the area around me that must make up my solo encampment, before switching the conch and contents of my knapsack over to a less-modernized one.

The less questions I raise, the better.

I slink toward the village, using what little forestry surrounds me to conceal my presence. A puddle renders more insight about my appearance—the color and breadth of the fur, the placement of the war paint on my face, the feathers and cord woven into my braids. If I can just catch a glimpse of one of the residents, perhaps I can deduce whether I'll be welcomed or crossing enemy lines.

As I draw closer, I spot two brute men lugging timber from one area to another. The first thing I notice is in stark contrast to their tanned skin: the symbols decorating each of their faces. They match my own. I breathe a sigh of relief.

My confidence restored, I trek the rest of the way out in the open. A woman on the edge of town waves me over, her expression frantic. The ease I'd felt just moments prior begins to dissipate.

"Brana!" she calls out, as if I haven't already spotted her waving her arms. As soon as I approach, she pulls me to the side of a shed. "I've been searching for you all morning."

I pull on the straps of my pack, unsure how I should address this woman or what our relationship entails.

"It's Gorm." Tears well in her eyes. "He's offered himself up as tonight's sacrifice."

From context alone, I can only surmise that Gorm is either her husband, my husband, or one of our sons. "Where is he?"

She points across the dirt path to the stall where horses are kept. There's only one person in view and it's a teenage boy, no older than thirteen. I nod at the woman before saying, "I'll speak with him."

"Thank you," she says, her voice cracking. "Maybe he'll listen to you. You're like a second mother to him."

Well, that answers that question. I give her the most reassuring smile I can muster, then head over to the stables.

Gorm must have seen us chatting because the minute I approach he snarls, "Here to talk me out of my decision?"

I lean against a wooden beam, the picture of calm. "Would it be so bad if I was?"

He rolls his eyes. "I'll tell you what I told my mother. I'm not changing my mind. And that's final."

It's clear that Gorm's a stubborn one, so I'll have to try a different angle if I hope to get through to him. I purse my lips, drawing from my very limited knowledge of Norse mythology. "Do you really believe that Odin will be willing to accept someone of your age and stature?"

Gorm stops mid-stroke, brush in hand. "Why don't you ask your husband?"

His response gives me pause. "My husband?"

"Ivar says I'm the perfect candidate." The way he says it is so nonchalant, like he isn't facing a life or death sentence.

It looks like I'll need to have a word with this husband of mine. "Where did you last see him?"

Gorm doesn't seem to hear my question. "Did you know that my name means *he who worships*? If she'd hoped for a different outcome, perhaps my mother should have named me differently."

"Where is Ivar?" I repeat, more harshly this time.

"Where he always is this time of day." Gorm takes his time concluding his answer as he pats the mare's back before raising the brush to its mane. "He's with my father at the main longhouse. Discussing strategy."

I don't waste any time leaving the stables and marching toward the largest building in town. I push through the door, relieved to find that only two men are inside—the same two I'd seen earlier lugging timber. Not used to being interrupted, they look at me in genuine surprise. I don't have to wait for them to speak to know which one is Ivar because his demeanor is so much like Brant's, it's uncanny. Of course we'd be married in this lifetime. I knew there'd be at least one.

"Brana?" Ivar says, his voice rugged. "What's wrong?"

"You tell me," I start, keeping my tone even. "Or have you forgotten that you somehow managed to convince a teenage boy to offer himself up as a sacrifice to Odin?"

The other man pins me with a piercing stare. "That is no concern of yours. Even if it were, I'll have you know that my son made his decision of sound mind. Ivar, here, was only showing his support."

Ivar bows his head in gratitude. "Thank you, Gunnar, but I can speak on my own behalf."

I look back and forth between them. "He's a *boy*," I hiss.

"We've offered up younger sacrifices to Odin, all of which have been graciously accepted," Gunnar says with a shrug. "Gorm is just one in a line of many."

"Are you to tell me you do not care that your wife is in shambles?" I challenge.

"Sigrid?" he chortles. "An emotional wreck, that one."

"As she should be," I shoot back. "Seeing as it's her only son."

"We can always make another. It's not like I'm in short supply." And with that final infuriating statement, he waves a flippant hand in the air to dismiss me.

I nearly lunge for the joke of a man who claims to be a "father", but Ivar steps forward just in time, blocking my path. "We'll discuss this later, Brana."

"When?" I glare at him. "The ritual is tonight."

A muscle flexes in his jaw. "Later."

I flinch at the sheer dominance in his tone. Knowing I can't win this battle, at least not right now, I clamp my mouth shut before turning on my heel and storming out the door.

☠ ☠ ☠ ☠ ☠

Later never came. If I hadn't known any better, I would assume he'd just forgotten. But it's clear Ivar's been avoiding me. Even now, gathered around the stone steps that lead to the altar, Ivar won't even look at me. Sigrid clings to my arm, crying softly into my shoulder at the injustice that's about to take place. Lucky for her, I've had my fair share of idly standing by. Not this time, though.

The repercussions of altering the events of any timeline ring in my head. But, by my logic, I'm not changing *my* fate, I'm changing Gorm's.

"This isn't right," Sigrid says as another sob breaks free from her throat. "We have to do something!"

"I know," I whisper, patting her arm. "We will."

"Odin, save him!"

The outburst causes everyone to turn and look at us, which is the last thing I want. I lower my head, wishing I could be cast deep into the shadows. Their attention is finally drawn elsewhere as a horn sounds to indicate the beginning of the ritual. Ivar stands at the head of the sacrificial altar. Only now do I realize who he is to the clan: their leader. My throat goes dry at the thought of what I'm about to do.

Wearing nothing but a fur loin cloth, Gorm is escorted by his father to the dais. I distance myself from Sigrid as discreetly as possible, readying my knife at my side. Seeing as it's her kin and my husband, we're stationed at the top of the dais, mere steps away from the altar where the blood of countless Vikings has been spilled.

I count the steps as they're taken, waiting until the boy and his father reach the second to last one. *Here goes.* I grab Gorm's upper arm and fling him into the waiting arms of his mother. In one deft motion, I step onto the pathway and sling my arm around Gunnar's neck with the blade pressed against his skin.

A hush falls all around us. Paired with wide-eyed stares, it's enough to make me question what the fuck I'm doing, but I hold firm.

"If any blood shall be spilled in the name of the gods, let it be older, wiser blood. That of this boy's father." I don't dare take my eyes off my husband. "All in favor—"

"Silence," Ivar interrupts, anger blazing behind his usual cool exterior. "This breaks protocol."

I press the blade against Gunnar's neck with just enough pressure to draw a few drops of blood. "If saving an innocent teenage boy from certain death breaks your precious protocol, then perhaps it's something that needs to be revisited."

Ivar narrows his eyes. "Brana, why are you doing this?"

I scoff. "I just told you why."

"Your reaction is interesting," he ponders, his brows furrowing. For a fleeting moment, I can see Brant in his expression, but it's gone as soon as he says the one thing I'd never expect. "Where was this outrage for our daughter?"

I nearly drop the knife. If what he's insinuating is true, then that would mean . . .

"Perhaps you should join her. It would please Odin greatly."

There's no time to react as I'm disarmed and pulled away from Gunnar by two of the clan members. With my hands being held tightly behind my back, I'm forced to my knees. Ivar approaches me, carrying the very blade I'd wielded just moments ago.

"First your daughter, now your wife?" I snarl, spitting at his feet. "May Odin grant you everything you deserve."

There's a wistful look in his eyes, but it's brief. "I've already sacrificed my bloodline to the gods. It need not be done again." He looks to Gunnar. "Not with my brother."

I look between them in harsh understanding. "Blood runs thicker than water."

Ivar lifts the knife. "May Brana be received at the gates of Valhalla."

"Hear, hear!" the clan cheers.

I close my eyes as the blade slices across my neck.

3 5

I JUST WANT this to be over. I suppose it's a good thing I'm embarking on my last stop in Mohra because I don't have it in me to visit another timeline where Brant lies to me, betrays me, or murders me. I'd hoped that this little excursion would shed some light to ultimately help me trust him again, but it's done just the opposite. Having taken an oath as a Sigard to protect me, how can I possibly believe he'll follow through on that promise? Especially after what I now know: that he's had it out for me in every timeline I've visited.

Why would this one be any different?

The bell above the door jingles as I enter the shop. I lower my gaze, noticing how my stomach flips at the sight of Madame Viessa, who's very much *alive*, in her usual spot behind the register. She doesn't seem to notice my presence as I approach, which is rather unlike her. I toss a hand up in a small wave, even going so far as to clear my throat, but she doesn't so much as flinch at the sound. The clacking of keys continues, the framed picture of her granddaughter staring me in the face. Perhaps bringing Lisette up will get her attention. I clear my throat before saying, "Madame Viessa?"

Clack clack clack

Having had enough of whatever the fuck is going on, I march over to the register and slam a fist onto the counter. The picture and bowls of trinkets wobble from the impact, but Madame Viessa doesn't seem to notice.

I'm about to walk behind the counter and give her shoulders a shake when I hear the door to the shop open. It only takes a glance to completely set my nerves on edge as a hooded figure, with their head lowered so as to obscure their face, enters the establishment. I'm tempted to back into a shadowed corner when I realize something. If Madame Viessa can't see or hear me, will the same be true of this patron?

My question is answered as the hooded stranger breezes by me without a second thought. For some reason or another, I'm invisible. How I wish that'd been the case in the other lifetimes I'd just been forced to suffer through.

I take a step back, leaving enough space in front of me so that I can fully observe the interaction between Madame Viessa and her mystery customer. If it turns out to be Brant yet *again*, I may as well throw in the towel now.

"I warned you of the consequences, did I not?" I'm somewhat surprised to hear that the voice under the hood belongs to a woman. "And yet, here we are, at a crossroads."

Madame Viessa finally breaks away from the register, turning a pointed glare at the woman standing across from her. "Why ask questions you already know the answer to?"

I scoff, having had something similar said to me when I'd requested the book on the Sable Coven.

"It's gone too far," the woman says, keeping her head lowered. "I'm afraid you've left me no choice."

Madame Viessa sighs as she says, "There's always a choice. I made mine, just as you must make yours."

The woman stiffens. "Even against the counsel of your coven? Including the other Elders?"

Madame Viessa narrows her eyes, "Blood runs thicker than water."

My breath hitches. *Hadn't I just said the exact same thing?*

"That it does." The woman finally lifts her head, her features still shrouded by her hood. "It seems you already know what's coming."

Another sigh. "Painfully so." Madame Viessa tucks a corded necklace into the front of her blouse. "But if it means protecting those I love most, then so be it."

The woman leans an elbow on the counter, turning her body sideways as she whispers, "Give my best to Lisette."

The Madame blanches. "You wouldn't—"

"It's already done," she hisses.

Before I can fully process what's happening, the woman grabs Madame Viessa by the shoulders and slams her face straight into the counter. She shrieks as blood sprays from her nose and mouth. "And say hello to Lilith for me, while you're at it." She bashes the Madame's head against the surface with even more force this time.

I stand there in shock, unable to move as the Madame's head is beaten to a pulp. Of all the gruesome sentences I've carried out as a Noire, nothing could have prepared me for witnessing the brutal murder of someone I know.

Madame Viessa's body slumps over the counter, blood pooling around her head. I grimace, turning away as the stranger rips the corded jewelry from around the Madame's neck, leaving her collarbone horribly disfigured in the process. When she suddenly unsheathes a dagger and aims it directly at the Madame's eyes to begin carving, I can't help but gag.

"Stop!" I shout, bile rising in my throat. "Enough!"

I cover my mouth and, subsequently, muffle the sob that escapes my throat, moving my hands to cover my eyes at the sound of slicing and squelching. The metallic stench of blood hits me, nearly causing me to keel over in disgust.

"Stop!" I scream again. "*Enough!*"

Knowing my pleas are floating into dead air only makes this that much worse. I find the strength to step forward, to approach the counter, to stop this insane murderer from committing any more atrocities to this innocent shop owner I've come to care for—

I grab the stranger's upper arm, the dagger clattering to the floor. Crimson splatters, staining the worn carpet.

"Great," the woman mutters. "Make this harder for us, why don't you?"

I drop her arm, stunned. "You can see me?"

The woman sighs before stooping to pick up the dagger. She wipes the blade clean before sheathing it. "While I may be one to talk to myself more regularly than I care to admit, that isn't what I'm doing at the moment." Her gloved hand moves to her pocket where she removes the necklace she'd taken. "Here. Take it."

I hesitate, then shake my head. "If this is your idea of a peace offering, you're delusional."

She grunts, then grabs my wrist, forcing my hand open. "Are you always this difficult?"

"Are you always this ruthless?" I shoot back.

"Why don't you tell me?" She removes her hood, revealing the last person I expected to see.

Madame Viessa's murderer . . . is *me.*

36

I DON'T GET the chance to ask questions. Nor clarify what I've just witnessed or how it's even possible. I'm not given the opportunity to speak at all before being catapulted back through time into Mohra. I land with a thud just steps away from the monument—steps away from the portal that contains my heinous crime.

Except . . . it couldn't have been me. Not the me standing right here, right now, anyway. I did *not* kill Madame Viessa. How could I possibly commit murder with no recollection of doing so? The very nature of being a Noire involves meticulously planning every single step, every last detail so perfectly, that not even an illness of the mental variety could possibly make me forget.

Ergo, I would *remember* the murder.

Down to the last gruesome detail.

As I'm pushing myself to my feet, my gaze catches on my left wrist and the leather bracelet adorning it. My blood runs cold as I stare at the memory rune. The minute the Sable Coven gets their hands on this, they'll uncover what I've just witnessed: *me* murdering their beloved Elder. I swallow the bile working its way up my throat. I'm as good as fucking dead if that happens.

I attempt to quell the rising panic with a few deep breaths. What had Astrid said? That the rune would be activated as soon as I entered Mohra. And that Magna would be the one to retrieve it and bring it back to the Elders. An option to *not* return the rune hadn't been presented. However, she'd also said that if I didn't make it out in time, I'd end up in the Chasm, where not even my familiar could find me. But, in doing so, I'd also be forced to take an ovetyr sentence,

I cannot let the Sable Coven get their hands on this—not until I can make sense of it myself. Because, as of right now, *nothing* is adding up.

The last ribbon Magna had tied around her foot was red. Red, the color before white. Meaning I only have 25% of my allotted time left. Also meaning I'm dreadfully close to not only losing my life, but costing Brant's his as well.

Fuck. They have Brant. If I don't return the rune . . .

"It's admirable, really," a voice says from behind the monument as shadows slither around it, "that even after everything you've just seen and experienced, you still want to save him."

Although startled, I instinctually place my arms behind my back to hide the bracelet. *I know that voice.* I peer at the monument and the lanky figure coming into view.

"You are not at all what I expected," Lilith croons.

"Neither are you," I shoot back, wondering where this sudden surge of confidence is coming from.

Lilith tilts a crooked smile at me. "Not ominous enough for you?"

I bare my teeth at her. "You dole out ovetyr sentences as if they're just handfuls of candy to pass out on Halloween."

She actually has the nerve to laugh. "Quite the assumption you're making there, Maren."

Hearing her say my name sends a shiver racing down my spine, but I stand my ground. "When it's based on fact, it's no longer just an assumption, now is it, *Lilith?*"

Her mouth turns down in a scowl. "As a Noire, I thought you'd use your time more wisely than this." She clicks her tongue against the roof of her mouth in disappointment. "Tick-tock, Maren."

She turns on her heel to leave. Knowing Magna could show up at any minute with a white ribbon, I make a rash decision. "You know it wasn't me." I'm hoping the statement is vague enough to pique her interest.

She takes the bait. "Maybe not the *you* that's standing here before me, but a *version* of you did commit that crime."

Her response nearly sends my head spinning. "Do you mean to tell me that what I just witnessed was a version of me from another lifetime visiting my present-day timeline?"

Bored, Lilith glances at the painted talons she calls fingernails. She answers with a sigh. "Something like that, yes."

So that would mean . . . this isn't my first time traveling through Mohra.

"Why would I—that version of me, I mean—risk altering a timeline she's not even a part of?" As if this weren't already weird enough, let's throw in referring to myself in the third person.

Lilith folds her arms across her chest, her tone challenging. "Who says it was altered?"

"It has to be. Because *this* version of me, the one standing before you, has nothing to do with the murder of Madame Viessa."

Lilith narrows her eyes, smiling. "There's that sharp mind."

The praise comes as a surprise, but I don't return the compliment. "Still, my question remains. Why would this other version of me risk altering a timeline she isn't even a part of?"

"Isn't it obvious?" she presses.

It isn't until it is.

"Because it affects all the others," I whisper, more to myself than to her. "The enigma of time itself is the only constant across all lifetimes."

The flapping of wings in the distance should be cause for celebration—but not with all the unanswered questions that lay before me.

"I can't go back," I say, my eyes catching the glow of the rune. "If I do, the Sable Coven will kill me. They'll kill Brant." I look to her for answers, knowing she's probably the last person that would give them to me. "What do I do?"

"You swore a blood oath," Lilith says, her tone nonchalant. "Whether you like it or not, your fate is sealed."

A bird caws. Magna will be here any moment to retrieve the bracelet. To retrieve *me*.

I cannot accept this. I won't.

I drop the knapsack at my feet, the conch spilling from its contents as I race toward the monument I'd just been ejected from. I have to go back. I have to fix this. At the very least, I need answers. If Lilith won't give them to me, then I'll get them myself.

I lunge for the monument, Lilith's eyes growing wide as I do. Just as I hoped she would, she reaches for me, yanking me away from the entrance of one portal to that of another.

"Fucking Noires!" she screeches as we're pulled away from Mohra, down, down, down, faster and faster, until we arrive at the one place I'd never *ever* considered could be my saving grace.

The one place Magna can't reach me.

The one place the memory rune is safe . . . for now.

Lilith huffs as she straightens her cloak, lips curling in revulsion. "Welcome to the Chasm."

37

I KNOW WHAT this means, what I've willingly chosen, given my limited options. An ovetyr sentence awaits me. And Lilith will be the one to assign it.

The Chasm is nothing like I pictured it. I'd imagined a void, a yawning darkness that swallows its victims whole. A place so dismal that not even a streak of light could shine through the cracked exterior. But it's nothing of the sort.

The Chasm is more like a cavern—hidden from the outside world, welcoming only those brave enough to face the unknown and venture within. Now that I think about it, it makes perfect sense. A cavern represents the depths of the human experience, our inner and outer worlds. It's rather poetic, in the most unexpected of ways.

Lilith studies me, brows furrowed in annoyance. "If you're hoping for a tour, I regret to inform you that this is the extent of it." She motions to the vast expanse that lay before us.

"It's surprisingly . . . serene," I say, unsure that I've settled on the right word. "And not at all what I expected."

"The liminal space between worlds never is." She walks along the scattered patches of dirt. "As it turns out, I do my best thinking here."

"I can see why." I follow her, not wanting to trail too far behind. "Where does it lead?"

"Nowhere." She glances back at me. "Absolutely nowhere."

"So, it's a circle?"

She shrugs. "You could say that."

I look to my wrist, at the rune that's no longer glowing. "But I'm safe here, right? From the Sable Coven?"

She repeats her answer. "You could say that."

"Yes," I press, "but *would* you?"

She stops walking and turns to face me. "The word *safe* is subjective. If you're asking if the Sable Coven would dare enter the Chasm, then yes, you are safe. Magna can't reach you either, so, again, you can consider yourself safe." Her eyes drop to my wrist. "But, given that you've forced your way here, you are *not* safe from an ovetyr sentence."

I meet her stare head-on, determined not to show any sign of weakness, trepidation, or fear. "What will it be, then?"

Is this how it'd happened with Brant? Stuck between a rock and a hard place, had he been forced to choose the Chasm? After everything he's done—namely the betrayals in our past lifetimes—I shouldn't care in the slightest about what his ovetyr sentence entails. But try as I might to shut off that part of my heart, it will always beat for Brant. A soul tie that extends beyond the reaches of time and space isn't so easily discarded—nor should it be.

I wait with bated breath as Lilith assesses me. Her mouth quirks up at the side in amusement. "I sense a sliver of hope, even after all he's put you through." She frowns, pursing her lips. "Why?"

The terrifying precision with which she's just read my thoughts is unsettling, but I keep my tone neutral as I say, "I could ask you the same of Lucifer."

She flinches ever so slightly, indicating that my response has rattled her. "You know nothing of which you speak."

It's my turn to smile. "I know a lot more than you're willing to give me credit for."

She bristles at the remark. "You are well aware that I cannot disclose the details of Brant Colborn's ovetyr sentence to you. Especially since he's your Sigard."

I scowl at her futile attempt. It's a blanket statement to steer me in another direction. "Get on with it, then. Unless you prefer my company."

She scoffs. "Not in the slightest."

I'm about to respond when I notice a glimmer in her eyes. It's obvious enough to give me pause. The hope she'd spoken of earlier . . .

"You're stalling," I say. "This should be easy for you, seeing as you regularly dole out ovetyr sentences. Why am I still here?" I look around the cavern. "What are you waiting for?"

Her stare turns lupine. "How dare *you*, a lowly Noire, speak to me that way—"

"At least *I* do my job. Swiftly and precisely." I fold my arms across my chest, the portrait of defiance. "I don't hesitate to carry out my sentences and exact justice . . ."

My voice trails off as the realization dawns on me.

Lilith stiffens at the sudden shift in my demeanor. There's no need for her to confirm what I already know to be true. I can't help but grin. "Holy shit. You don't *have* an ovetyr sentence to give me."

<h1 style="text-align:center">38</h1>

HER STALLING MAKES sense now. But having this knowledge brings about an entirely new issue. Without the assignment of an ovetyr sentence, how the hell do I get out of here?

Lilith exhales a reluctant sigh. "Indeed, it would appear the actions in your current incarnation have resolved your karmic debts from past lifetimes." She pauses, pressing her mouth together in a firm line. "As a Noire, you carry out acts of justice for those who have committed heinous crimes, thereby an ovetyr sentence cannot be granted."

There's no point in trying to hide the grin that's plastered across my face. "Even though another version of me murdered Madame Viessa?"

Lilith nods. "That is correct."

I stand in silence for a moment, trying to wrap my head around this. "From my understanding, being granted an ovetyr sentence is the only way out of the Chasm."

Lilith is quick to answer. "By way of standard procedure, that is."

"So . . . there *is* another way out?"

She studies me closely, debating whether to reveal the truth. When it comes down to it, though, does she really have a choice?

"You can't expect to just keep me here."

Her shoulders drop in defeat. "No, I suppose not."

"Then enlighten me. How do I leave?"

"By taking an irreversible risk. One that will result in the amalgamation of your other selves." She releases another heavy sigh. "In order to leave the Chasm without an assigned ovetyr sentence, you must collapse timelines."

Surely I've misheard, but the grave look on her face indicates otherwise.

"When you say *collapse* timelines—"

"I mean that the other version of you—the one who committed the murder—cannot exist."

I stare at her, slack-jawed. "You want me to . . . *kill* myself?"

"In a word, yes."

The way she says it is so nonchalant, so simple, as if she hasn't just dropped a bomb on me. "Let me get this straight. By killing the version of me that murdered Madame Viessa, said murder becomes null and void? Like it never even happened?"

"Correct. Because that version of you will no longer exist to commit the crime."

One question remains that I don't dare ask. Because I know Lilith can't answer it. *Why would this other version of me kill Madame Viessa?*

I clear my throat, hoping that by asking vague questions, I'll arrive closer to the answer. "You said that collapsing timelines is risky. Why is that?"

"Because, in doing so, you're essentially erasing one of your incarnations. It's hard to say exactly how each incarnation affects the others, but one thing is certain: they are all delicately intertwined, however subtle the thread that binds them may be."

"So, my current incarnation could look completely different after doing this? After . . . collapsing the timelines?"

"It's possible."

"Would I still be a Noire? Would Brant still be my Sigard?"

"It's difficult to say."

I scoff. "That's a pretty gargantuan risk."

"There's another. And it involves the ovetyr sentence you would then take on after collapsing the timelines. As it were, you would become solely responsible for the actions of your other self leading up to the murder—the one that will no longer be committed—*as well as* the subsequent ovetyr sentence."

Feeling a headache coming on, I bring my hands to my temples. "As of right now, I'm free and clear of an ovetyr sentence—but by collapsing timelines, I'll be forced to take one on? *Hers?*" I say, performing a stabbing motion to indicate murderer-me.

"I'm afraid so. Otherwise, you will have no choice but to remain here. In the Chasm."

"So, there is zero chance of me going back to my current incarnation?"

"I'm afraid it isn't possible." She shakes her head. "Might I remind you that the Sable Coven warned you of this place. You chose not to return with the memory rune, given the consequences you assumed you'd face, thereby choosing this path instead. The one you find yourself on now."

I grunt, speechless. Well, this is completely and utterly *fucked.* What I need are answers from my other self . . . *time* to ask her questions so I can understand her reasoning—her logic—for going through with something as depraved as murder.

"I would be remiss if I didn't warn you that if you fail to collapse the timelines, your current incarnation—and *you*— will cease to exist. Seeing as you'll be the 'visitor' on *her* timeline, her existence will take precedence, should you fail or change your mind."

Maybe I should just give up now. Accept defeat and spend the rest of my days in the Chasm. How is it that I wind up dead in every scenario? If I had returned as originally planned with that memory rune in hand, it would have resulted in my demise. If I collapse timelines, a version of me must die. And, if I fail in my endeavors, I also die.

"So, basically, I'm being forced to pick between the lesser of three evils."

"I don't see it that way." Lilith tilts her head. "The decision that must be made is obvious, is it not?"

I nearly guffaw at her choice of words. But, as much as I hate to admit it, she has a point. I'll be damned if I have to spend the rest of my days in the Chasm. That isn't a life at all. I'm here because of Brant, *for* Brant, even after everything that's transpired between us in other lifetimes. So, in a way, I guess the decision is an obvious one. The other version of me has to go.

"I'll collapse the other timeline," I tell her. "Even if that means ending one of my lives in order to save this one."

39

I LAND WITH a thud on a freshly manicured lawn. Adorned with a variety of neatly trimmed hedges, blooming wisteria, and vines of ivy, the cottage before me feels awfully familiar. Unlike Astrid's residence, I'm not in the middle of the forest, but in a suburb with sprawling yards. Although the next house can't be seen for at least a mile—in fact, it can hardly be seen at all with the massive willow trees lining the perimeter of the property.

I gingerly push myself to my feet, brushing my hands against my sides as I approach the residence. The grass gives way to an immaculate stone path, which winds and curves toward the jade-colored door. Gleaming amethyst eyes stare at me from the owl-shaped knocker, urging me to come closer.

I'm only a few steps away, nearly jumping out of my skin when I hear someone nearby clear their throat.

I whirl to my left, toward the source of the noise, only to come face to face with a woman I recognize instantly—Madame Viessa's murderer. She resembles me more than I care to admit save for the leather jacket around her shoulders, a triple stack of delicate necklaces adorning her neck, and electric blue hair that perfectly frames her face. Sitting with one leg crossed over the other in an ornate white chair, she leans back against the matching cushion and proceeds to take a long drag of her cigarette. "Come to kill me?" She glances at her silver wristwatch, as if she's been expecting me.

"I suppose I don't need an introduction." I grimace, suddenly feeling woefully unprepared.

"Maren Cordeau," she says, pronouncing my name with ease. "I'm Halcyon Nerine, High Priestess of The Aether Coven." There's a subtle glimmer in her eyes as she removes a cigarette from the metal tin sitting beside her and offers it to me. "Seems we have plenty to talk about."

☠ ☠ ☠ ☠ ☠

I'm going to call it like it is: I'm fucked. There's no way in hell I'm killing Halcyon. After two hours of being completely engrossed in our conversation, I'm enamored with the girl. I know that isn't saying much because she's basically me. Or maybe that's saying a lot if we're talking in terms of ego. But, either way, whatever her reason for killing Madame Viessa, I'm convinced it's a sound one—even if she hasn't told me what that reason is yet.

"So, you went through with it. Traveling through Mohra, that is," Halcyon says with a disappointed sigh. "It would appear my efforts to stop you were futile."

I flick the ash from my cigarette. "By *efforts*, I take it you mean murdering Madame Viessa?"

"Gruesome, I know, but I'd hoped my message would come across. That traveling through Mohra would result in irreversible damage to *all* of your—our—incarnations."

Well, this is certainly news to me. "The Sable Coven assured me it was safe, seeing as I passed the attunement. They said that as long as I didn't change anything—"

Halcyon holds up a hand to silence me. "They set you up, Maren." She exhales a cloud of smoke. "Madame Viessa wanted *you* dead."

Words elude me. All I can do is stare at her.

"Why do you think the woman was so stingy with her inventory?"

"I . . . well, it's no secret that the Madame was slightly erratic."

Halcyon shakes her head. "Madame Viessa has a granddaughter."

"I'm aware." My mind immediately goes to the framed picture I'd seen on the counter near the register—the one that had somehow ended up in my apartment. "Lisette, if memory serves." I furrow my brows, wondering what this has to do with anything.

"Yet another warning you failed to recognize."

"It was you?" I narrow my eyes. "*You* were the one who put the frame in my apartment? Why?"

Halcyon hesitates, tracing the lines of her coven's crest on the metal tin. A luna moth. "Maren, are you aware that Lisette is also a Noire?"

I nearly drop my cigarette into my lap. "No. I—I can't say that I was," I stutter.

"So, it goes without saying that you're also unaware that Lisette's Sigard defected?"

"I didn't even know that was possible."

"Well, it is," Halcyon scoffs. "Apparently, he was apprehended in the shopping district of the Sephiran. Thought he could do a better job as a Noire than Lisette."

I gulp as I recall what Conall had told me. The shackles he wore were due to selling to a Sigard—and being caught in the act. To think, I'd brought Brant along with me, putting us both at risk . . .

"Madame Viessa knew that, without a Sigard, her granddaughter was as good as dead," Halcyon continues. "So, she decided to take matters into her own hands to send *you* to your death, thereby freeing Brant of his Sigard obligation to you."

Unbelievable. I try to quell my rising anger. "I was under the impression that my—*our*—current incarnation is Brant's ovetyr sentence. So wouldn't he be stuck with me, no matter what?"

"Not necessarily. Madame Viessa knew what you'd uncover about Brant while traveling through Mohra and hoped that his perpetual habit of betrayal might sway you to extricate him from his duties."

I scoff in disbelief. "Well, she was sorely mistaken."

"Beyond that, she knew you'd be faced with the impossible choice of killing *me*, another version of yourself, after traveling through Mohra. Assuming you'd fail in that endeavor, your existence would be wiped from the current timeline, again freeing Brant up to being Lisette's Sigard."

"But Brant and I are cosmically paired, always existing together across space and time—"

"But if you never existed in that timeline to begin with, neither could his Sigard assignment . . . or his ovetyr sentence, for that matter."

That last part feels like a punch to the gut. It must be apparent on my face because Halcyon runs a hand through her hair, her tone glum as she continues, "I, unfortunately, played right into the Madame's hand. Using a scrying mirror of her own design, she knew her death was inevitable. And she correctly assumed that some version of us would be the one to do it. Seeing as the Sable Coven is a rival to my own, I should have known better. Seen this for what it was." She blows out a long breath. "I tried to warn you *not* to travel through Mohra by leaving the note behind in *our* handwriting with a damn X through Perthro, the rune of fate and destiny, hoping it'd be enough." She gives a disappointed shake of her head. "Instead, I acted exactly as Madame Viessa wanted. And now we're here."

I'd been right to question the back of the note we'd found in Madame Viessa's shop, but I'd been so focused on decoding the meaning of the message that I hadn't given it another thought. "I think it's worth mentioning that I didn't change anything while traveling through Mohra. I let each lifetime play itself out, regardless of how difficult it was or the pain I had to endure—"

"And I commend you for that, I really do." Halcyon pauses. "But you didn't have to change *anything* in Mohra for it to disrupt the cosmos. Your current incarnation as a Noire is, for lack of a better word, a sort of *repayment* of the karmic debts you've accumulated across all prior lifetimes. Without it, the karmic imbalance is too great. That's why I could travel through Mohra to your timeline with little to no repercussions."

"So you left the note in Madame Viessa's shop, stole the picture of her granddaughter, put said picture in my apartment . . . what, did you bury Brant, too?" I say, half-jokingly.

Halcyon lowers her gaze. "It was a last-ditch effort."

My mouth drops open. *It seems I owe Lilith an apology.* "He could have died!"

"After what he did to you—to *us*—time and time again?" Halcyon scoffs. "He's lucky I buried him with that protection rune."

"Holy shit. It was *you*." Hands trembling, I set my cigarette against the edge of the quartz-embedded ashtray, suddenly feeling nauseous. "You've been haunting my dreams, paralyzing me in my sleep. *You're* the woman in white."

"How else was I supposed to keep an eye on our most important incarnation?" She shoots me an apologetic look. "I *am* sorry about the sleep paralysis. That isn't something I can control. It's just a by-product of overlapping timelines. A way to protect your physical body as the separation of your astral body occurs. Speaking of which, do you still have the corded necklace I gave you?"

I nod, retrieving it from my pocket. "What is it?"

"It's a talisman to combat against sleep paralysis. They aren't easy to come by, seeing as they belong to the gatekeepers of Mohra."

"The Sable Coven," I affirm as I secure the talisman around my neck. "That's why Madame Viessa was wearing it."

"This way, I'll be able to keep watch over your incarnation without the nasty side effects."

"No more sleep paralysis?" I ask hopefully.

She grins. "Exactly."

A long silence passes between us as I allow everything we've just discussed to sink in. "So, I guess there's only one question left to ask. Is there any way we can, you know . . . *fix* this?"

Halcyon lifts a brow. "Just to be clear . . . you *don't* want to kill me?"

"Not after everything you've just told me."

"What if I lied?" Halcyon challenges.

"You didn't. It makes too much sense to not be the truth." I pause, considering. "And, if there was any reason you'd want me dead, you would have just killed me instead of Madame Viessa."

Halcyon grins. "I must admit, I'm glad to see we haven't lost our touch."

"Well, technically speaking, we are one in the same."

"Great minds," she muses.

"I'll ask again . . . is this something we can fix?"

"I fear it's past the point of fixing."

I nod glumly. I'm not the least bit surprised at her response.

"However," she continues, "that doesn't mean all is lost." Her mouth quirks to the side. "We may not be able to fix or reverse what's already occurred, but we *can* undo it."

I straighten in my seat. "Undo it? How?"

"By sending you back to the point in time *before* Madame Viessa was murdered. Before you agreed to meet with the Sable Coven—"

I hold up a hand. "Let me stop you right there. In case you haven't noticed, the only reason I'm here right now is because I *couldn't* go back to my original timeline. I had two choices: stay in the Chasm or come to your timeline to"—I make a slicing motion across my neck—"well, you know."

"You didn't let me finish." She smirks. "I never said anything about going back through Mohra. If we were to use your Sigard, however—"

"Brant?" I shake my head. "He's incapacitated at the moment."

A hint of a smile. "In a perma-state of sleep?"

Holy shit. She's not seriously suggesting . . .

"You can invoke a nightmare for Brant, even across timelines, because we just so happen to have these." She pulls a small black pouch from inside her bralette, then shakes its contents onto the table. Encased in glass, as if they were marbles, are Madame Viessa's eyes. As a Noire, I've seen and dismembered my fair share of body parts but those eyes . . . I can't help but shudder.

"Regardless of where you are in the cosmos, as your Sigard, Brant is bound to you and your well-being, first and foremost."

I reach for one of the marbles, then think better of it. "I have to ask . . . why the eyes?"

"Represented by the Triple Goddess, our craft honors the divine trinity. As states the Law of Creation, for anything to be created or for an event to materialize into form, three forces must be present. One must be active, one must be passive, and one must be neutral.”

“Clearly, I’m the active force, which makes Brant passive. And Madame Viessa’s eyes are . . . neutral?”

“Similar to a gateway, she is the bridge between our two timelines. Organic matter has the greatest chance of producing the desired outcome.”

“And this bridge—it’ll somehow take me back to my timeline? Before Madame Viessa was murdered?”

Halcyon nods. “However, there’s only one question that needs answering before embarking on your travels.”

I angle my head. “Which is?”

“After everything you now know about your Sigard, can you trust him to bring you back home?”

Of course, it’s the one question I don’t have the answer to.

40

I LAY UNDER a canvas of stars in Halcyon's backyard, soaking in these final few moments of peace before embarking on what could be the end of Maren Imogen Cordeau, Noire.

"Stop thinking like that," Halcyon urges, reading my thoughts. "If anyone should understand how powerful the mind is, it's a Noire."

A sharp inhale is my only reply.

"You're worried." She shoots a sidelong glance my way as she plucks mugwort from her garden.

"You wouldn't be?" I raise myself onto my elbows, the peace I'd felt just moments ago fading. "He's betrayed me over and over again. In every lifetime I was able to visit."

"Which was how many?"

"Four." As soon as I say it, I realize it isn't a lot.

"Has he betrayed you in your current incarnation?"

"That I'm aware of?" I scoff. "No."

Halcyon sighs, joining me in the patch of grass in the center of her backyard. She gently sets the woven basket filled with mugwort at my feet. "Give the guy some credit, Maren. As your Sigard, it sounds like Brant's followed through. You haven't been lost in a nightmare. Or left to fend for yourself. For all intents and purposes, he's been doing his job. Why would that suddenly change now?"

Even though she's right, it does little to calm my fraying nerves. "Let's get this over with, then."

"That's the spirit," Halcyon teases. "Remember, when you reach him, you cannot tell him about anything that's transpired since traveling through Mohra. For Brant to possess that knowledge will only tip the scales of balance even further in the wrong direction."

"Understood," I say before quickly adding, "although, knowing Brant, he'll ask what's happened and why I'm approaching him in this way."

"Assure him that the details aren't important. That it's a Noire case gone wrong and reaching him through a nightmare is your only way out."

I nod, laying back down on the plush grass. I cross my arms over my stomach, fidgeting with the bracelet that still adorns my wrist. "And if he doesn't believe me?"

Halcyon secures the pouch containing Madame Viessa's eyes with a gold ribbon, then sets it atop my hands. "Make him. Or an eternal time loop awaits you both."

I clutch my interlaced fingers, feeling the weight of the pouch on my skin. "Thank you for helping me."

"I'm helping *us*." She smiles, but it doesn't reach her eyes. "Safe travels, Maren."

Before I can say anything else, the astral realm pulls me under.

☠ ☠ ☠ ☠ ☠

The nightmare I've invoked is a scene straight from a horror film we've watched countless times, one that Brant claims is his favorite. My hope is that it'll be recognizable enough to draw his attention away from whatever the Sable Coven's conjured up.

The setting of the film takes place at an abandoned asylum, so that's where I'll wait for his arrival. Patience has never been my strong suit, so I decide to pass the time by rehearsing exactly what I want to say and how I want to say it. Halcyon's reminder lingers. Brant cannot know about *any* of this.

A black and silver mist appears at the end of the cement pathway, signaling that my handiwork is about to pay off. Looking disheveled and slightly taken aback, Brant appears. His confusion only grows more apparent as his eyes lock with mine.

"Maren?" He glances behind him as the mist fades, the portal along with it. "What is this?"

"You don't recognize it?" My heart is thundering in my chest, but I know in order for this to work, I need to act like my normal self. Without our usual banter, he'll know something's up.

Brant studies me for a moment before taking in his surroundings. "Of course I recognize it. What kind of fan would I be if I didn't?" There isn't an ounce of lightness in his tone. "The more important question is . . . why are we here?" He quickly follows up with, "Why are you invoking a nightmare for me?"

"To make sure I got your attention."

"Well, it worked," he says, scratching his head. "But that doesn't really answer my question."

"The case I was working on . . . it fell through. I need you to pull me out."

"Through a nightmare?" He looks around again. "I have to say, this is a first. We've never done this before. Not to mention, it doesn't follow protocol."

"I know," I say, feigning exasperation. "But this was the only way I was sure I could reach you. I didn't want to risk it."

"Through a nightmare?" he repeats. "This isn't even real—"

"It's real to me," I interrupt, trying not to sound desperate. "As my Sigard, it's your job to help me, to pull me back to reality when I find myself in a bind."

He presses his mouth into a firm line. "And as a Sigard, I'm required to do my due diligence. This is an odd circumstance, one we haven't yet come across."

"And while I appreciate your wanting to be thorough, time is a luxury we can't afford. I need you to pull me out, unless you'd rather explain to Lilith—"

He lifts a hand at the mention of her name. "Say no more. What's a Sigard-Noire relationship without trust?"

As if I needed the knife to twist even more. I force a smile, resenting every lie that leaves my lips. I reach my hand out, waiting for him to take it. His hesitation causes my heart to plummet. When his fingers finally interlace with mine, I breathe a sigh of relief.

"Home?"

"Home," I say with a nod.

The agreement ripples between us, a silent echo of our loyalty to one another as the nightmare tears itself in half. All around us, tethers shoot down from every direction, joining together to form a bridge. I pull Brant along, eager to get to the portal. It's almost fully formed by the time we arrive. We stand before it. Waiting, waiting, *waiting.* For a brief moment, I allow myself to close my eyes, to bask in the triumph of what originally felt like an impossible feat.

It's this moment that changes everything.

Amidst my basking, I don't notice the hand that brushes against my side. The hand that removes the pouch from my pocket. The hand that now holds the evidence of a journey through time. One that desperately needed to remain undiscovered.

"Maren?" The animosity lining Brant's expression is undeniable. "Why the fuck do you have Madame Viessa's *eyes?*"

The portal flashes to indicate its readiness.

I look from Brant to the glass eyes to the portal, then grip his hand—*hard.* He grunts, trying to shake me off, but the shock of his discovery has him struggling to find any semblance of balance. Knowing what I have to do, I seize the opportunity and yank us both through the portal that'll end this nightmare once and for all.

41

THE RINGING IN my ears is so loud, it almost brings me to my knees. I squeeze my palms against the sides of my head, willing it to stop.

"Maren?" The voice is muffled. "*Maren?*"

My eyes fly open as if a jolt of electricity's just been sent through my body. I quickly realize that I'm outside, in front of Madame Viessa's shop. Brant's standing directly in front of me with his hands on my shoulders, concern etched along his brow. I raise my hands so that they're resting on his outstretched arms, instantly noticing what's managed to travel with me. The rune bracelet. I drop my arms and step backward so that I'm out of Brant's reach before scanning the rest of my body. Other than the bracelet, I'm wearing the same outfit I wore the day I purchased mugwort . . . the same visit where I'd noticed the book that would introduce me to the Sable Coven.

"You look like you've seen a ghost or something."

I lift my gaze back to Brant, recalling this exact moment when it'd first occurred. So *that's* what I'd felt. A ripple in time as my soul had bounced from one timeline to another. *It worked. It actually worked.*

I run to Brant and wrap him in a tight hug. He laughs and squeezes me right back. "What has gotten into you?"

"What? I can't show my appreciation for having a kickass Sigard?"

Color blooms on his cheeks. "Don't thank me just yet. This case sounds like one of the more intense ones."

If only he knew that what I've just been through is infinitely more intense than dealing with Nathan fucking Sharpe.

"Come on," he says, motioning for me to follow him to the shop's door. "Clock's ticking."

Right. The mugwort. "I'm just now remembering that I've actually already got an entire canister of mugwort in my . . . tea cabinet."

Brant backtracks to where I'm standing. "*You* have a tea cabinet? With the amount of coffee you drink?"

I force a smile, thinking on my feet. "That's why I forgot it was there. Because I hardly ever use it." I shrug nonchalantly, hoping it's enough to hide the fact that I'm flat-out lying to his face. "Meet me back at my place later tonight?"

Brant gives me a dubious look. "You're absolutely sure you have enough?"

"Positive," I say, quickly turning in the direction of my apartment. "And don't be late!"

I take off down the sidewalk before he has a chance to respond, only glancing back once I've rounded the corner. If I were him, I'd be scratching my head, too.

🕱 🕱 🕱 🕱 🕱

If I don't get my hands on more mugwort, tonight is bound to be rife with disaster. The risk of going into Madame Viessa's store is too great, but it's the only metaphysical shop that I know of that carries pure, unrefined herbs. And so, I find myself at the library, hoping I can dig around and find another place to source the necessary provisions from. If I happen to fail in *that* endeavor, then I'll have to research alternatives to mugwort. Come to think of it, perhaps that's worth doing now.

Under mounting pressure, I hurry past the rows of shelves toward the occult section. My last visit here was disappointing and yielded very little on the subject matter, but I can't lose hope yet. There's too much on the line.

I find the aisle labeled *Religion/Spirituality/Occult* and round the corner, stopping dead in my tracks as I take in the person standing just steps away from me. There's no way I wouldn't recognize her, but that's just the problem. I'm not *supposed* to recognize her because I'm not supposed to even know her . . . at least, not yet.

The High Priestess of the Sable Coven turns in my direction. In her hands are two books that most certainly are not in circulation within the library system. It's in that moment I recall one of our conversations . . .

I only go into town once a month, on the eve of the Full Moon. It's the best time to sneak contraband into the library. And by contraband, I mean books from my own personal collection to beef up the occult section. For a town with such a storied history around witchcraft, it's a shame to see it so severely lacking.

I smile at the memory, but it quickly fades as Astrid clears her throat.

"You don't work here, do you?"

I shake my head. "Nope."

Astrid relaxes, dropping her shoulders. "That's a relief."

If anyone's going to know where I can find more mugwort, it's her. "It's nice to see *someone* cares about Salem's history." I walk toward her, running my hand along the shelves. "I've always been disappointed in the selection. For a city with such a storied history around witchcraft, it's a shame to see it so severely lacking."

She looks at me in surprise, as if I've just spoken the exact words she was thinking. I suppose I have. "Right? I couldn't have said it better myself." She grins as she returns to shelving the soon-to-be-confiscated books.

"This might be a long shot, but do you know where I can find some mugwort?"

She raises a brow, momentarily giving me a heart attack. "What coven?"

"I'm sorry?"

She folds her arms across her chest. "What coven do you belong to?"

Shit. The only other one I know of is . . . "The Aether Coven." I regret saying it as soon as I remember that the two are rival covens, at least in Halcyon's timeline.

Her eyes grow wide with recognition. I prepare myself to book it out of here, if need be, but Astrid throws her hands up in excitement. "That's our sister coven!"

Thank the fucking cosmos.

"I love the way you've set up your apothecary. The one west off of Kernwood Bridge? I frequent it often." She throws a hand over her mouth and chuckles. "Don't tell my Elders, though. Madame Viessa will have my head."

I nod, wishing, more than anything, that I could tell her who I am. That we know each other. That I wouldn't be standing here now if it weren't for her faith in me and her unrelenting kindness. "Your secret is safe with me."

"Thanks," she says, straightening the contraband books one last time. "Now, I better get out of here before the librarian catches me. I haven't been banned yet. But I hope I'll see you around, . . .?"

The prompt for my name nearly sends me into a tailspin. "Halcyon," I choke out, the lie acidic on my tongue.

"Beautiful name," she says before gesturing to introduce herself. "I'm Astrid."

"Likewise," I say. "Beautiful name."

"I hope to see you around." She gives me a small wave before disappearing into the main aisle.

"Thank you," I whisper, lowering my head as I feel for the memory rune that's pressing against the fabric of my pocket. I blink back a tear, knowing that this will have to be both our first *and* last encounter, at least in this lifetime.

42

THE DRIVE TO the apothecary proves to be the perfect length, allowing me time to clear my head. I'm surprised I hadn't come across this place in my previous searches for mugwort. I parallel park just outside the door, digging in my console for quarters to pay the meter. The effort is futile, however, because when I go to insert them, I realize the meter isn't even working. "Typical outdated crap," I murmur to myself before pocketing the change and heading for the door.

Just like Madame Viessa's shop, a little bell dings above my head as I enter. There isn't a soul in sight, but I do notice rustling behind a black curtain near the back.

"Hello?" I call out. "Is anyone there?"

The store is dimly lit. Instead of glaring overhead lighting, taper candles line the perimeter, casting an ambient, yet eerie glow. I step forward, squinting at the cabinets full of corked glass bottles and metal tins. Upon further inspection, I realize the cabinets are alphabetized, which is about to make this shopping trip a whole lot easier. I meander the store until I find the bottles that are labeled with the letter M. I trace each row with my index finger, trailing to the bottom where the bottle of mugwort is . . . empty.

Shit.

I pick it up, just to be sure, but my initial observation was correct. Of course, they'd be out of the *one thing* I drove out here for . . .

"Looking for this?"

I freeze in place at the familiar voice, although I can't put my finger on how I know it or where I've heard it.

"That was a clever stunt you pulled. Astrid would be impressed."

At the mention of the High Priestess, I whirl around, coming face to face with . . . The Morrighan. I instinctively pull my sleeve down to cover the rune bracelet, but I'm not even wearing it. It's still safely concealed in my pocket. Even so, panic begins to set in.

The Morrighan places a large canister of mugwort on the counter before propping her elbows on it. "Don't bother. I may have been tasked with retrieving the bracelet from you, but, seeing as Madame Viessa is still alive, there's no point." She arches a brow. "She *is* still alive, correct?"

"Yes," I answer, feeling flummoxed by the whole ordeal. "That's why I'm here. I didn't even want to risk going *into* her shop knowing it could initiate the very chain of events I'm trying to avoid." I'm talking as rapidly as my heart is beating.

I take a breath before asking, "So, how is it possible you're aware of what hasn't yet transpired?"

"You mean *you* murdering Madame Viessa?"

I grimace. "Not me. A version of me. But yes."

"The laws of time and space work differently for familiars. I may not see all, but Magna does."

"So . . . you and I are the only ones who know about the potential catastrophe I could have caused?"

"Yes."

"Not even Lilith knows?"

"No. This isn't her jurisdiction." She narrows her eyes at me. "And it must stay that way. Understood?"

I nod, even though my understanding of what's going on is rather limited. "What about the bracelet the Sable Coven gave me?"

"I trust you'll figure out what to do with it." She begins to ring up the canister of mugwort as if this is a perfectly normal business transaction.

"Forgive my confusion, but I thought your loyalty lay with the Sable Coven?"

"It does." The Morrighan plops the canister into a brown paper bag and pushes it toward me. "As well as its sister coven."

I hand her my payment, but she declines it. "It's on the house. Courtesy of Halcyon."

My eyes grow wide at the mention of the name of my other self. "You know Halcyon?"

"My dear, I know *everyone*. And if that version of you knew I was charging this version of you something that grows in her own backyard, she'd wring my neck for it."

I can't help but smile. "Thank you."

As I turn to leave, she says, "You two are more alike than you might think."

At first, I assume she's talking about Halcyon, maybe even Astrid, but her meaning becomes crystal clear.

"Brant was never *assigned* to be your Sigard. He volunteered himself. And, in doing so, was cleared of his ovetyr sentence. As long as he follows through with his duty, his karmic debt will be paid in full." Her tone is soft, but serious. "So, let him protect you, Maren."

The relief and subsequent shock I feel must be written all over my face because all I can manage to get out is, "I'll try."

"Do more than try," she replies, her voice full of warning. "Your soul tie depends on it."

43

THE SUN IS setting, and I'm almost out of time. Brant will be arriving within the hour to Sigard over the Nathan Sharpe case. Of all my Noire cases, having to repeat his punishment is one I don't mind doing. The scumbag deserves to go through it twice, even if he doesn't remember the first go-around.

I pull the canister of mugwort out of the brown paper bag and set it on the counter. I'm about to toss the bag in the garbage when my fingers run across an embossing at the top. I trace the outline of a luna moth, recognizing its symbolism almost instantly. *Aether.* Given its philosophical association with air and the aetherial realm, the Aether Coven couldn't haven chosen a better depiction. I chuckle to myself, then toss the bag in the garbage.

I empty my pockets, almost forgetting that I'd stuffed the rune bracelet in one of them. I'm about to remove it when The Morrighan's warning sounds in my head. *I trust you'll figure out what to do with it.*

I didn't have the slightest clue what I'd do with it then, but I certainly do now. I glance at the clock, doing a quick calculation in my head. I debate whether to text Brant, but ultimately decide against it. I can make it back in time and no one would be the wiser.

More specifically, *he* can't be the wiser.

I rush out the door, choosing the path I've taken so many times before. Walking the blocks. Turning the corners. Crossing the streets. Passing the storefronts. Until I arrive at my destination. The cemetery.

It still carries its usual air of grandeur, even after my less than desirable experience digging up Brant. *But that didn't happen in this lifetime,* I remind myself. *Because neither Brant or I are even aware of the Sable Coven.*

I enter through the gates, taking the roundabout way until I find the perfect spot to discard the bracelet. To bury it so deep, not even an excavator could bring it to the surface. I cross the grounds to grab a shovel from the shed when I hear the door swing open from the other side.

Startled, I throw myself against the back of it. I wait a few moments, until the footsteps fade into the distance, before peering around the side. There may be little light, courtesy of the setting sun, but I'd know that walk, that build anywhere.

Why is Brant here?

I watch as he plunges the shovel into the ground, using the heel of his boot to break through the surface layer of grass and dirt. He digs and digs and digs, as if he's racing against an invisible clock. Dirt flies through the air, displaced by the brute force of the instrument. Finally, after what feels like hours, he stops digging. Drops to his knees. And pulls something the size of his palm out of his pocket. I'm too far away to see what it is, but he releases it into the decent-sized hole he's just created, then resumes with the shovel to undo the grueling work he's just completed.

As the finishing touch, he replaces the top layer of grass and pats it into the ground, then starts for the shed. I fade back into the shadows, pressing myself against the exterior wall. I close my eyes at the rattling of garden tools and clang of the shovel as it's returned to its hook. Refusing to give myself away, I hold my breath, waiting for him to leave.

For my apartment.

I hear the flick of a lighter and the tapping sounds of a text message being composed. I fumble for my phone, managing to put the damn thing on silent just as it vibrates with said message. I don't need to read it. I know he's headed to my apartment next.

Footsteps ensue and I'm forced to strain my ears, waiting impatiently for the click of the gate. When it finally comes, I inch along the side of the shed, only pulling the door open once he's rounded the corner.

As I'd suspected, his text indicates he's on his way over.

Grab a bite for us, will you? I text back. *I'm starving.*

I grab the shovel, racing to the very spot he'd just been standing over. My phone pings. *Chinese? Pizza?*

I grunt, hastily typing back, *Dealer's choice.*

Three dots appear to indicate that he's typing. I tap my foot impatiently as I wait for his reply. *Chinese it is.*

That should buy me an extra fifteen minutes or so. I toss my phone to the side, then remove the loose patch of grass and start digging. Seeing as the soil has already been displaced, it doesn't take me nearly as long to dig the same depth. I gulp as the item he'd abandoned comes into view. It looks like a woven band.

I drop to my knees, moving the rest of the dirt out of the way with my hands. I pull the item out of the hole, blowing on it to remove the excess dirt. Dread curls in my stomach at the symbol staring back at me. Two parallel lines with an X between them, connecting them. I pull the rune bracelet from my pocket to compare the two side by side.

They're exactly the same.

"Mannaz," I whisper. "The memory rune."

I turn each bracelet over, marking the only notable difference between them. The crest etched into the back. Mine's marked with an image of three crows, each carrying a different item in their beak—a key, a ring, and a serpent. The Sable Coven's crest. And Brant's . . . is a symbol I've seen just prior to coming here. The same one on the brown paper bag from the apothecary. And on Halcyon's metal tin of cigarettes.

A depiction of a luna moth.

The Aether Coven's crest.

My breath hitches. He came here to do exactly what I'd planned to do—bury his secrets so deep that not even the dead could be privy to them. I clutch the bracelets, weighing my options. I could take the rune back to the apothecary, back to The Morrighan, with a plea to view its contents. But it's her warning, echoing in my mind, that stops me.

You two are more alike than you think.
Let him protect you, Maren.
Your soul tie depends on it.

My hands drop to the tops of my knees, the bracelets splayed out in my palms like shining beacons that weren't meant to be seen. This is his way of protecting me, just as I'd planned to protect him. I'm not meant to know what's in that memory rune. Which presents yet another impossible choice.

I turn my head, willing my shaking hands to hover over the hole. I close my fists. Turn them face-down. Then open them. A joint tribute, to all we keep hidden—in this lifetime and the next.

I rein in my curiosity, my desperation, my need to *know*, as I grab the shovel and start piling the dirt back over the hole. Back over the answers that will never see the light of day, only the confines of Brant's mind.

But I know enough.

I've seen enough.

This is the only decision there is to make.

With the soil back in its place, I set the patch of grass back over top. I rise, glancing at my watch just as my phone pings. *Got the grub. See you soon.*

I smile at the timing. For once, it feels exactly right.

ACKNOWLEDGMENTS

To say this book has been over three years in the making is mind-boggling to me. What first started as merely the seed of an idea grew into something I never could have expected. It's a really neat thing when, as an author, you can weave your own personal experiences into your narrative and shape an entire story around one central theme. I've always wanted to write a story about witches and covens, and this one definitely fits the bill. Sprinkle in some spice, an unsolved murder, time travel, and elemental trials, and you have the makings of a perfect fall read, which is exactly what I was going for.

First and foremost, I'd like to thank the Triple Goddess for the many blessings bestowed upon me. I was pregnant when I wrote this book, postpartum when I began revising it, pregnant again while querying it, and now postpartum again as I prepare to publish it. It takes so much energy and effort to bring a book from idea to publication, and this one is certainly no exception.

To M.O.: my husband, my soulmate, my pea—Thank you for your unwavering support as I navigate postpartum, motherhood, and my career as an author. I wouldn't have been able to accomplish nearly as much without your willingness to help, no matter the task. You are a true partner in every sense of the word, and I am so grateful I get to call you mine. I love you always . . . to whatever end.

To my sweet Ivy and Violet—you've been my muse in more ways than I can count. You've taught me to slow down, be present, and fully embrace the moment that's in front of me. You are my greatest reminder that good things take time. I'm so lucky that of all the souls out there, you chose me to be your mom. I can't imagine life without you. I love you so, so much, my sweet girls.

To L&L—You're both getting so big I can hardly believe it. Before I know it,t you'll be in middle school! I'm so proud of who you are and who you're becoming. Thank you for reminding me of the importance of play and for keeping me on my toes. I love you both immensely.

To Anna Vera, for being the best friend, confidante, and soul sister I could have asked for. I love that I can speak whatever's on my mind and know it'll be met with zero judgment. I cherish each and every audio message you send my way, so keep 'em comin'! I love you, bb!

To my sister, Erin, for being my go-to reader companion. I love the little long-distance book club we've created (party of two), even if we don't always finish the books (haha) or fall into a bit of a reading slump. I can't wait for our future travels together. I love you!

To my Dad and Rachel, for being my creative (and spiritual) sounding board and for being such great grandparents. Thank you for indulging my creative whims, no matter the hour. I see many beach (and Italy, perhaps?) vacations in our future. I love you both!

To my Mom and Paul, for being such supportive grandparents! I can't tell you how much I appreciate your willingness to fly out at the drop of a hat. It's definitely made my transition into motherhood so much smoother and for that, I can't thank you enough. I love you!

To the incredibly talented designers at Damonza who continuously stun me with their artistry and professionalism. The cover for this book is certainly no exception. It is absolutely stunning. Thank you for always being such a pleasure to work with!

To my furbabies—Lacy, Denali, and Luna, you've been with me since the very beginning of my writing journey. I will never forget when it was just us. I know life looks different now and my attention is stretched thin more often than not, but I hope you know that you were the first to capture my heart. I love you so, so much!

And finally, to my YouTube fam, readers, and fans—Through the highs and lows, hiatuses and comebacks, thank you for continuing to support me, my books, and my many creative endeavors. I've always wanted my stories to reach people and to have meaning. My 7-year-old self would be so proud to know she's making that dream come true. Thank you so much. I'm so grateful for you!

Kristen Martin is the International Amazon Bestselling Indie Author of the YA science fiction trilogy, THE ALPHA DRIVE, the YA dark fantasy series, SHADOW CROWN, standalone novel BEYOND THE STARS AND SHADOWS, and personal development books, BE YOUR OWN #GOALS and SOULFLOW. A writing coach and creative entrepreneur, Kristen is also an avid YouTuber with hundreds of videos offering writing advice and inspiration for creatives and aspiring authors everywhere. She currently lives in Texas with her husband and their six kids.

STAY CONNECTED:
www.kristenmartinbooks.com
www.youtube.com/authorkristenmartinbooks
www.facebook.com/authorkristenmartin
Instagram @authorkristenmartin
TikTok @authorkristenmartin

www.ingramcontent.com/pod-product-compliance
Lightning Source LLC
Chambersburg PA
CBHW030530190726
48283CB00006B/1853